GNARLED PINES

A Novel

Edward Crosby Wells

Copyright © Edward Crosby Wells 2020.
All rights reserved.

This manuscript or any portion thereof may not be reproduced or used in any manner whatsoever without the express written permission of the author except for the use of brief quotations in a book review.

ALSO BY THE AUTHOR

NOVELS
Queen City
Gnarled Pines

PLAYS (Full Length)
3 Guys in Drag Selling Their Stuff
Desert Devils
Flowers Out Of Season
In The Venus Arms
Poet's Wake
Streets of Old New York (Musical)
Tales of Darkest Suburbia
The Moon Away
The Proctologist's Daughter
Thor's Day
Wait A Minute!
West Texas Massacre

PLAYS (30 to 60 minutes)
20th Century Sketches
Empire (40-minutes)
Slow Boat to China (30-minutes)
Tough Cookies (60-minutes)

PLAYS (under 30-minutes)
21 Today (monologue)
Civil Unionized
Cornered
Dick and Jane Meet Barry Manilow
Harry the Chair
Leaving Tampa
Missing Baggage
Next
Pedaling to Paradise
Pink Gin for the Blues (monologue)
Road Kill

Samson and Delilah
Sisters of Little Mercy
Slow Boat to China
Vampyre Holiday
Whiskers

COLLECTIONS
6 Full-Length Plays, Volume ONE
6 Full-Length Plays, Volume TWO
19 One-Acts, Monologs & Short Plays
A Baker's Dozen
Bananas
Lavender Ink

SCREENPLAY
Road Kill

For Ronald L. Perkins

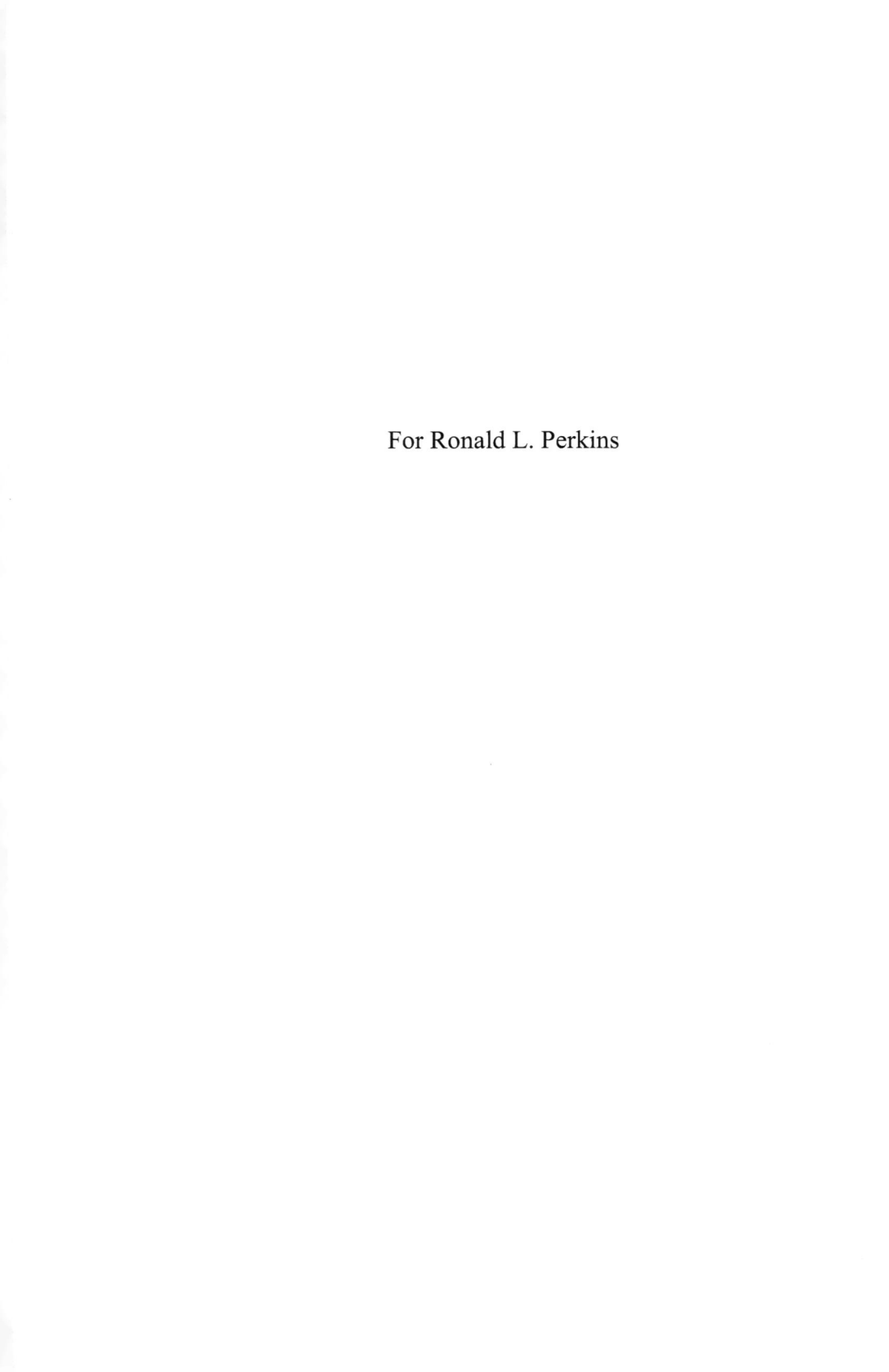

ONE

Adam John Goodblood was two years old when he snuck out onto a fourth story window's ledge, dove into the crowded street, circled the block, flew over the old sumac in the park, the benches along the Promenade, down the East River and over the bay to the tip of the Atlantic before his mother's agonizing screams—wails that sounded like she was already mourning the death of her son—were the sirens that guided him safely home and into her waiting arms; her sobbing could be heard on the street while she held her son for dear life. She told that story to young Adam often enough to challenge his suspension of disbelief until, eventually, he turned a deaf ear to it.

Thirty-nine years later, Adam had intended to leisurely travel across America on low-traffic roads before eventually reaching Gnarled Pines, a tiny island off the coast of Turtle Run, Maine. His attraction to Gnarled Pines was its macabre history, no doubt the reason it had been abandoned for nearly a century, and also the reason for one of America's most celebrated novelists of supernatural horror to lease it for the month of July. The brochure promised a supernatural adventure to those curious enough *"...to face your fear... to walk on cursed soil...to live with ghosts...where the darkest of dark spirits walk...where the unspeakable all began with a seance on the evening of the Fourth of July in 1929."* The brochure also promised, *"The Agency guarantees a full refund if the experience does not live up to its myth...satisfaction is assured."* This was certainly odd, since The Agency is at the whim of anyone claiming a refund simply from feeling unsatisfied. Until Adam's month-long lease begins, his plan had been to meander the backroads of the countryside in search of America; but plans change, and people die. The intentions of Adam John Goodblood, aka A. J. Goodblood, were unexpectedly interrupted by the need to take the highly traveled hi-ways directly from Denver, Colorado to Brooklyn Heights to attend his mother's funeral.

* * *

Adam watched as his mother's coffin slowly descended into the hard winter ground. As it was lowered, he shivered and remembered something he had told an eager audience at one of his book signings: *"There comes a time when 'death' is no longer just a word, no longer simply a concept—it is an inevitable event and there is nothing on Earth that can change that. 'Death' is the ultimate truth that ends the confusion of being. 'Death' is not a word nor a concept; it is the slash of a sword—at first it stings, then exquisite pain rips through the body until the gravity of the reality of it plunges you into an undeniable acceptance of the endless fall into nothingness. There is nothing to be done. That is your fate, and it is always just a breath away. But, it does not need to be all that dreary if you make friends with Mister Death. I don't imagine he has many, so he could use a few."* His audience chuckled.

Adam came back to his mother's funeral, back into himself standing in the bitter cold. *"Mother's not here. She's beyond the noise of mourning; beyond the false recollections and rehearsed condolences. The same words used at every funeral everywhere on Earth, I imagine. It all means nothing. An excuse to feel sorrow, and when it is analyzed, the sorrow you feel is sorrow for yourself. What does it matter? Why do I bother? Why does anybody bother?"* In the bitter bone-chilling cold Adam inhaled deeply and exhaled uneasily after getting a glimpse of truth: the truth of his inevitability. Mister Death himself came as a voice buried in the dark, deep within the heart of him, *"Adam, I am not done with you yet."* Adam could not reckon its tone, therefore he trembled.

After the burial, there was the traditional potluck attended by the tenants of the deceased—there were no living relatives other than Adam—along with a few neighbors with whom she had remained on good terms nearly all her life.

Rose Green in 2-A laid out an impressive deli which easily fed more than a dozen of the renters and neighbors who had gathered to mourn the passing of Ada Maria Goodblood, to celebrate her life, to wonder of their own tenuous futures.

"Life is for the living, Addy," consoled Missus Cohen from 4-B, "and the living have needs the dead don't know to need. Mister Cohen, bless his soul, he did what he could to provide. But a dollar don't stretch like it used to, does it? Or maybe it never did. I'm sure I don't know. You know from what I'm saying? Your poor blind father, a decorated war hero...the Purple Heart...and my Daniel, such a good man...my Daniel...they were partners in business over in Sheepshead Bay. Daniel was your father's eyes. Remember? He was, you know? That terrible accident...whose fault it was I could not say. They were more than partners, you know...your father and my Daniel...something more than partners, Addy. There was talk...true or not I don't know...I learned to live with it. I don't talk about it...to no one...I bet you didn't know that, did you? Well, now you know...you have a right to know. They were friends right up to the end when they died together in that terrible fire on that horrible old boat, the Ada Maria, named after your mother, of course...who else? Bless her soul. Poor Daniel... he provided. Your father gave your mother, may she rest in peace, the deed to this building for her birthday...not necessary...she'd get it anyway, but we had a little party and a year later...the fire. A decent landlady, your mother...you know, it's a struggle keeping up a building like this...what with the cleaning, the scrubbing, the painting...*maintaining*...such a struggle, Addy, *maintaining*. It's all about *maintaining*. The day-to-day things that can fall apart. By the way, that old boiler's not working like it used to. It needs to be replaced. I only mention. Don't get me wrong. You know from what I'm saying? Missus Huang in 5-B says foul odors are accumulating outside her door and they are suffocating her..so she says...but maybe she doesn't know what she's talking about...she kvetches. She's the only one not to smell that it's coming out of her own apartment. Missus Lieberman across from your mother's apartment hasn't come out of her apartment since she lost her daughter Sarah in 9/11. She gets everything left outside her door. Then she sneaks out when the coast is clear. Sad, *huh?* The Katz's in 5-A swear someone's been climbing up the fire escape and watching them while they sleep. Why? I don't know. I don't imagine there's much to see...if you know what I mean...or maybe too much of what shouldn't be seen. *Oy,* may God forgive. Your mother will be missed. Somebody urinates nightly in the vestibule. Filthy swine they are. Jehovah's Witnesses bang on our doors every other day. They get in the building because we're *still* waiting for the front door lock to get fixed. They don't fix themselves. And all that senseless graffiti. What does it all mean, Addy? Like dogs they leave their marks. Poor Ada, how she will be missed. And such a good son you are...a mensch...the famous A. J. Goodblood...*Me*...I don't like scary books...but that's just me...I guess you know what you're doing." Missus Cohen smiled through cream cheese and bits of chives, "We all loved your mother. So, Addy…you'll be moving back into our building…*yes?* So, how was Colorado?"

Exhausted from Missus Cohen's garrulous windiness, Adam wearily answered, "Colorado is good, Missus Cohen. You'll never know what you're missing. There's no place like Colorado, Missus Cohen. And…*no*…I'm selling the building."

Missus Cohen swallowed hard before speaking, "Selling the building? Selling the building?" She repeated with bitter shock and then she turned to a nearby mourner, "Addy's selling the building."

And quickly a nearby mourner parroted, "He's selling the building."

And then there was another, "Selling the building?"

And another, "Selling the building!"

"After I wrap things up here in Brooklyn…."

"Wrap things up? You mean wrap us up," Missus Cohen spat out bitterly.

"I wouldn't put it that way. I won't be staying in Brooklyn. I've leased an island for awhile off the coast of Maine. Starting in July. Then I'm going on another book-signing tour. After that I don't know. Europe, maybe. And then back to Denver."

"Europe maybe…you don't know…*hoity toity.…You don't know?*"

"I've no solid plans. I'll leave it to caprice."

"*Eh…caprice…*whatever that is I'm sure you can afford it…the famous A. J. Goodblood. I don't understand, Addy… Maine? A whole island?"

"Yes, Missus Cohen, a whole island, but it's just a tiny whole island."

"*Ahh*...just a tiny whole island."

"Yes, Missus Cohen."

So...*Addy*...what's on an island there's not here in Brooklyn? Brooklyn's an island too, you know."

"Well...it's *on* an island, Missus Cohen."

"An island...on an island...so what's the difference?"

"I need time alone, Missus Cohen...time to work on a new book."

"*Oy*...he wants to be alone. My nephew Benny...terrible teeth...he writes books, he's not alone...*and right here in Brooklyn he writes books!*" Missus Cohen snapped and disappeared into the congestion of hungry mourners, where slivers of most every food item from the deli and crumbs of every sort were ground into the old, frayed rugs under swollen feet, cautious walkers, unsteady canes, and the wheelchair of Mister Padilla-Bruno from 3-B. The news spread like a wildfire across the deli-littered surface, igniting contempt in the eyes of the mourners as, one by one, heads turned towards Adam, shaking their heads negatively before turning away to avoid having to look any longer upon the offending face of this stranger in their midst who, "*Should have stayed in Colorado where he belongs.*"

Someone whispered contemptuously, "*Goyim.*"

"So, where should we go?"

"On the street?"

"His mother will be missed."

"I'm sure."

The acerbic whisperings that will change nothing drifted and rolled through the parlor.

"I lived in The Montague all my life."

"What now?"

"You know from what I'm saying?"

Talk continued on with neither word nor thought to the late Ada Maria Goodblood.

Two months later, the building sold to a developer from Jersey City. A few weeks after that, the tenants of The Montague were informed that the building would be going cooperative and would they "be buying or leaving?"

* * *

It was in June of nineteen twenty-nine, after only a two-month run, *Manhattan Scandals, a Revue* closed, leaving Arthur Baumgarten, its Broadway producer, facing charges of embezzlement and sex trafficking if he didn't give-in to the torturous demands of Mona LaBaron, his leading lady and live-in lover. How could he be certain that paying her off would guarantee her silence? He could never be certain. It would require trust and that was no longer possible. She would always be there in shadows, around corners, in his sleep. His fear of what she could do to his life—*"destroy my life"*—would never abate. His heart would never pound more slowly. His sweat would never cease. Plainly, he needed her out of his life—permanently. He thought of ways to murder her and he seriously tried to work-up the initiative to do it, but a series of unfortunate consequences projected on the screen in the back of his mind, all with grave scenarios that outweighed his impulse for doing the mortal deed. All he needed was the right scenario; a scenario that left him scot-free, while giving him the pleasure of watching her suffer, but he didn't see one. However, he vowed to conjure one.

Arthur Baumgarten was the only child born to German immigrants who arrived on Ellis Island, then settled into the poverty of The Five Points neighborhood of Lower Manhattan. With only a sixth grade education, Arthur took to the streets where he received his real schooling in the ways of the affairs, the dealings, and the transactions of the world; at least, in his small part of it. He fell in with a gang that burgled apartments and stores, then sold their ill-gotten goods in the streets to the north of The Five Points. They rolled tourists and homosexuals in alleys for cash and jewelry. By the time Arthur reached his mid-twenties, he moved northward and walked the streets of Upper Manhattan where he developed an interest in theatre after meeting some theatre-types in a public house near the theatre district. They helped him get odd jobs in the neighborhood, building sets in Broadway theatres, painting them, and running errands. Young Arthur worked himself up to producing theatre after finding employment as a task boy for Florenz Ziegfeld. Arthur was a quick study. He carefully listened and watched. He learned the ropes and he knew what theatre-goers wanted; so he hustled for backers to mount his first production, which was a revue called *Lights Out!* featuring Mona LaBaron. It turned a profit and from that point on Arthur quickly rose to prominence.

Arthur Baumgarten became the *wunderkind* of Broadway. He had as many as a dozen productions up and running simultaneously—dramas, comedies, revues, musicals—and every one of them produced by other people's money. *"Of course! That's the way it's done, baby. Perish the thought of gambling with my own on such a fickle business. Look, here it is plain and simple, the producer's prerogative: If a show cost seventy-five cents to produce, raise three dollars and seventy-five cents; a fair and easily gotten amount. You don't want to scare away potential backers. First, there is the three bucks to pay your brokerage fee and seventy-five cents for the investors' percent, the expenses involved with the show itself, including the rent of the theater, the talent, the amateur writers—they'll work for nothing as long as you put their names in the program—and then of course there is the producer's percent—that's yours—add to that your portion of the box office receipts, also part of the producer's percent, and that's a pretty penny. I live on Park Avenue, baby."* From The Five Points to Park Avenue in less than ten years.

Baumgarten carefully picked investors who knew little to nothing about the financial workings of show business. It was the nineteen-twenties, monied New Yorkers were *"rolling in it,"* and gamblers were easy pickings. Investors should have made a decent return on their investment, though few ever did. If there were an unavoidable royalty to pay out, Baumgarten reluctantly paid it to avoid legal complications; or worse, out of concern for his health and longevity from dealing with "shady characters." The return to the investor was usually the least amount Arthur could get away with; the meager amount was little more than the interest anyone could have earned by putting their money into a bank savings account. It should not come as unexpected when a swindled backer never invested twice in anything with the name Arthur Baumgarten attached to it. And, having felt stung, many of them decided that investing in banking was their best bet.

More egregious than Baumgarten's greed—artful as it was—was the considerable amount taken out of the seventy-five cent production overhead that went to a flesh merchant in the Bronx whose business was procuring young women for older men; men who desired to reclaim the innocence of their youth. Baumgarten's taste was rarified and hard to come by: teenage girls. When the flesh merchant was able to provide him with a precious acquisition, it was Baumgarten's pleasure to pay the merchant a princely sum—a sum larger than the average annual income of a 42nd Street prostitute.

Mona LaBaron, who lived with Arthur Baumgarten for the past two years in his luxurious Park Avenue apartment, had him trapped between the proverbial rock and a hard place. Mona was a natural-born snoop, and being a natural-born snoop, it was her moral imperative to learn all she could, however she could, about the man with whom she was having a prolonged affair. A practical woman needs a cushion for that day she instinctively knows will come sooner or later—the end of a relationship—the day of reckoning. Today was that day. Her snooping had paid-off in spades. Arthur Baumgarten was an embezzler and a degenerate possessed by a cowardly demon with prurient desires. Mona made no moral judgment in that regard, nor was she intimidated by the machinations of his demon. She's dealt with stronger spirits than his. Mona's demon encouraged her to use the information she had unearthed. It was an invitation to a dance she could not decline; an invitation that left Mona's demon to determine how to make Arthur Baumgarten pay. *"Hmm…your silence must be worth something, dear one; so why should you keep quiet without fair compensation, my pet?"* Mona's demon advised with a question.

"You've got the goddamned deed to Gnarled Pines!"

"I need a place to conjure the dead. I want Charon, too."

"He comes with the island. He's all yours. I'd be careful with him, were I you."

"Well, I'm not, am I? I understand Charon more than you do, Arthur."

"I bet you do. You're both malevolent creatures," Arthur sniggered. "Look, I closed the show like you asked! All those people out of work. And why? *To conjure the dead?* You need to conjure an insane asylum, baby! That's what you need."

"You know what you need, Arty? You need to be punished."

Baumgarten scoffed. "*You pillaged my desk! Had me followed, for God's sake! Who are you?*"

"A mistake."

"*Jesus Christ!* You certainly are."

"You were a living breathing treasure hunt, Sweetie. You're the goddamned pot of gold at the end of the rainbow."

"I trusted you, Mona."

"Another mistake. Two sets of books. *Really, Arty?* You are so unimaginative. And that box of filthy photographs. *Photogenic you.* Weren't you afraid this day would come?"

"I hate you."

"Of course you do." *Oh,* by the way, the baby-pusher in the Bronx…I turned him in. That pig is headed for Sing Sing. Hope he doesn't squeal on you, Arty. That would be terrible for you, wouldn't it? But pigs usually squeal, don't they?"

"I let you have your precious little Hudson. You like them young, too."

"At least he's over twenty-one!"

"Mine were never under eighteen!"

"So you say."

"*Please,* don't do this, Mona."

"I must, Arty. I really must. You've been a very bad boy, Arty. *Oink, oink.* And you must be punished," Mona hissed. "I know you like it."

"*Stop it! You disgust me!*"

"*I disgust you?* How funny is that? I caught you doing bad things, Arty. So I figure I deserve something better and here's my ticket to Betterland—*you.*"

"*Enough!* Most men would have you snuffed."

"You're not 'most men,' Arty."

"You're right. I'm not! Go to Gnarled Pines! You'll see what kind of man I am. You'll see my horns, Girlie. You'll wish you never left Poughkeepsie, Toots. *You'll see!*"

* * *

Adam stood, shouldering a crammed-to-the-limit backpack and holding an overstuffed canvas carryall. A large blue and white plastic cooler rested next to him on the pier where he stood waiting to board the launch to Gnarled Pines.

A bank of fog descended when it should be rising over the early morning in Turtle Run, Maine. The lighthouse in the sound still burned bright, and sailors took warning. Clouds, filled with summer rain, began to gather and darken the sky. "We gotta go, dude," urged the young thin shirtless man in white shorts and no shoes. His pale freckled face was framed by rusty-red loose curls that blew in the strengthening wind. Again he urged Adam to board the boat that had begun to pitch on the churning Atlantic. The boat did not appear safe to Adam who hesitated before cautiously stepping down into the old boat that showed its scars from wicked winters, and which he silently dubbed the Pequod, although the faded decal on the bow read: FERRYMAN TAXI. The Pequod began its journey towards Gnarled Pines. Adam hoped the kid knew how to navigate the impending weather. *"How should I write this journey to Gnarled Pines? Should I open the book with it? Hmm,"* Adam mused.

From a distance, over the sputtering sound of the outboard motor, Captain Ahab spoke, "*Whales?* Do you know anything about whales, Mister?"

"No," said Adam. "I can't say I do."

"Vanishing breed, you know."

"I do. Yes, they are."

"All things...what have you...here to gone...nothing... Man ruined everything...one day Man will vanish...don't care what the preachers say...*do you?*"

"*Um*...That would depend on the preacher, I suspect."

"*Yeah,*" the Captain laughed.

Looking through the mist for the sun, uncertain if it'll show its face any time soon, Adam sighed as he created the countenance of Captain Ahab: Deep-set intense black eyes and a gray beard covering most of his sad and deeply wrinkled face, and the Captain said, "When something gets too big...Mister...like whales...or people...they ain't always necessarily whales...or people...you see...they get dangerous when they sense the coming of the end... all creatures...they kill and eat each other...whole civilizations disappear. Take where we're headed, Mister, what are your odds of survival? Mother Nature abandoned that place long ago...before me, man. I wouldn't step a foot on Gnarled Pines for nothin' you could pay me, Mister...I guess The Agency warned you. I mean... The Agency did warn you, didn't they?"

"They did. It said in the brochure they sent me that it would be *thrilling*. And from what I read, I trust it will."

"*Thrilling?*...in the brochure...and you trust The Agency? You don't know The Agency, do you? Ain't that a hoot?" The Captain mocked and tapped the tip of his nose as if he were giving a secret signal, but Adam hadn't a clue for what. "You know how the trees got gnarled, Mister?"

"I think I do," Adam answered. "The wind and the salty mist that blew across the island over the years caused the pines to bend...disfigure...and there is also the old wives' tale, of course."

"Wind. Old wives' tale. Of course." The Captain chuckled. "Then why ain't the trees on all the other islands gnarled?"

"Many are."

"Not like those on Gnarled Pines."

"I'm sure there must be a reason for that."

"You better believe there's a reason. The other islands aren't haunted. Where you're goin' they got gnarled from the flesh of human sacrifices seeping into the ground around the trees... gettin' sucked into their roots. There be demon spirits that grow inside those trees...they grow 'til they're evil as all hell...and then they are born and go out into the world."

"I don't think there's a whole lot of truth to that," Adam said, as he looked towards the island. From the water taxi, the island towered over its rocky shoreline.

"No problem. Go ahead and tell yourself that, Mister."

Adam had done his homework. He was keenly aware of the island's macabre history; its mythological narrative. It was the myth that attracted Adam to Gnarled Pines. He wanted to explore the setting for his new novel, to find the essence of his characters, especially Mona LaBaron—the actress whose Broadway credits included some of the most successful plays of her time. Now she's long since been forgotten, except for the superstitiously inclined who keep her legend alive; the legend that she lives in the netherworld and that she and Charon—a human-seeming creature—haunt the island to this day; the legend has it. Where better for A. J. Goodblood to gather atmosphere for his new novel about what had taken place on that flesh and blood-soaked island, than on that blood-soaked island itself?

Adam did not want to engage in a conversation with a kid who was probably still in his teens. He felt it was too private, too important, the stuff of a novel-in-progress, the structure, still germinating, too dangerous a time to talk about it, to *talk it out*. He's already heard everything the kid had to say and then some, so he was not going to have a conversation where anything either of them had to say would most likely fall upon deaf ears.

Adam muttered, "Nobody knows what happened...not what really happened."

"So you say...some say otherwise, you know. I'm a lot older than I look, Mister, and if I ever learned anything it's that there's always somethin' to it...everything has a bottom to it. Everything has some truth to it. There's somethin' wicked strange there to this day...maybe it's somethin' thrilling...like in the brochure. Who can say? *Ahh*...here we are, Mister. This is where you get off." Captain Ahab muffled a laugh.

After a gut-heaving crossing, Adam stepped up from out the Pequod and onto the pier. Tremors of anticipation began to overwhelm him, and though he did not know exactly why, or what, it was sure to be *"something thrilling,"* like the brochure said. Adam watched as the FERRYMAN TAXI went back out upon the ocean towards Turtle Run, sputtering over the choppy waters towards the mainland, to his wife perhaps. *"Did he have a wife?*

Nah, he was too young. Maybe no wife." Adam decided to give Ahab a wife, anyway; perhaps he would open the book with: *"Captain Ahab masterfully navigated over the violent waters towards the mainland back to his wife and to the daily grind of a life filled with fantasy and fiction, to the odor of fish frying in the greasy kitchen of his small gray clapboard house where his high school sweetheart stands bent against the doorway in her melancholy manner, waiting for her Captain to return. The pattering of rain drops on a tin roof, under the gloom of the darkening sky, leaves her vacant-minded as she tries to recall some vague and distant moments of happiness, just one moment, just one before the gathering clouds of one-too-many squalls overshadowed her memories. She no longer recalls another life, a different life, a prior life, one where hope still existed, something other, something elsewhere, something better than here, right now, where there are no expectations; only uncomprehending, uncompromising acceptance. The Captain's wife stood in her pink-flowered cotton housedress with a gravy-stained, blood-stained apron reeking of camphor, cigarettes, loneliness and resignation, as she worries for her Captain's return."* The crossing to the island of Gnarled Pines with Ahab, the Captain of the Pequod…that's it…the opening of A. J. Goodblood's new novel: *Gnarled Pines*.

From the dock, through the vagueness of the morning fog, Adam watched until the Pequod disappeared. He blinked and saw his former existence sink beneath a tide of morning gray; the looming fog that refuses to lift over this tiny island in the Atlantic; this island where you could take an early morning's walk around its circumference and be back in time for breakfast.

Next to the dock was the boathouse—a miniature replica of the lodge itself—moored in three feet of solid rock and concrete, with the Atlantic as its floor. In it, as promised by The Agency, was a motorboat tuned and ready to make those trips to the mainland for groceries, sometimes a movie, perhaps a dreadful mockery based on one of his novels, or an extra thumb drive—to satisfy his fear for losing his work in the machine—perchance to pick up a newspaper, though he always regretted the news which too often left him feeling both physically and mentally wounded, the entire world was going to shit, so reading about more of it in the news was something to be avoided—nothing changes for the good. His stay on the island of Gnarled Pines would give him permission to escape the anxiety created by world events; not to confront them. Adam wanted no intrigues to redirect his thoughts away from the work at hand. He had only thirty-one days to turn mythical lore into fantasy in his new supernatural novel—*Gnarled Pines*.

"When did I think to write this novel? What was it that started me thinking about it? It's gonna be—actually—it had to be more than just a little bit different—unlike my other stuff—hmm—from where in hell did the idea come? Yes! The emails—all those emails! Emails from something called The Agency arrived daily, I sent them to spam, but they kept on coming anyway. Usually right after I sent them to spam. Now how strange is that? After a week, or so, I gave up and actually read it. They came personally for me —they came specifically to me as the writer of—and listed all my books—freaky! The Agency suggested I write a book about an island called Gnarled Pines, off the coast of Maine. I responded and then they sent tons of information—not exactly tons—I tend to over-emphasize—hyperbolate—I know that's not a word, but it ought to be. My mind started racing. I thought it was a great idea. I had to do it. A month's rental—Jesus Aitch—that must be a mistake—but no, it wasn't—the total cost for the entire month was

so ridiculously low—no resistance—July was the only month available—I was free—they sent me the lease and I signed it—the rest is history." From an entry in Adam's *Gnarled Pines Journal*.

A. J. Goodblood, the author who came to be inspired by the island's infamous setting, climbed the rock and hewn pine steps up the towering cliff as briskly as he could; bouncing the heavy plastic cooler from step to step, as he climbed against the warm morning wind. It was the first of July; Adam's first day on Gnarled Pines. The ground beneath his feet was little more than solid rock without a hint of vegetation; only the pine woods that looked surreal, foreboding, and not alive.

There it was: The stone and timber lodge that he had leased sight-unseen, other than in photos over the internet. The Agency's brochure said there were *"...ghosts haunting, dark spirits tempting, and thrills beyond human imagination to be had."* He thought the brochure laid it on pretty thick. He walked towards the lodge. So far, nothing yet seemed out of place. No vibrations. Everything felt normal; dull, actually. He had hoped for something unusual. He had expected what the brochure promised, *"...from the moment you step onto the island be prepared for the thrill of your life."* But Adam's sixth sense hadn't yet kicked-in. He'd been lied to. However, if his sixth sense had kicked-in, if he actually had a sixth sense, he would have been aware that there were indeed disembodied souls watching him and they were wondering if he might be the one, their vessel—their host.

The lodge was constructed to blend with its surroundings, which it did and then some. Adam found it pleasing with its unvarnished splintered timber and rocks meticulously chosen from the shoreline; it did more than blend, it enhanced. He removed the skeleton key from the pocket of his khaki Bermuda shorts and unlocked the front door. When he opened the door he was struck with hot and humid air escaping. He entered the lodge and the first thing that caught him was its pungent, unventilated scent of mold and incense; the scent of an interminably-forsaken village church. The next characteristic to catch his attention was that the room was huge; not at all like his idea for what he expected a lodge to look like. This was a room for entertaining. Neither the online photos nor those in the brochure did it justice. The floor of the room was made of rough pine; uneven planks that had been painted brown were scuffed. Frayed, faded with wine and liquor stained rugs, with odd and angular patterns—perhaps Aztec—were scattered about. Most of the furnishings were made of pine with mahogany leather upholstery, worn, cracked, and here and there along the seams, threads had pulled apart allowing explosions of padding. Some accent tables of highly polished and lacquered pine were still in remarkably good condition. In front of an obviously well-used sofa, lopsided discolored leather cushions blotched with evidence of wine and sex, stood a coffee table topped with blue mirror. There was a long crack in the mirror and a ring-stain from the bottom of the glass of a careless drinker. The enchantment of the room comforted Adam in a nostalgically funky sort of way. The walls were made of timber and smooth ocean-sculpted stone, and was strikingly beautiful. Adam experienced a strong feeling of *déjà vu*.

  A huge propane tank stood against the outside wall under the kitchen window. There was a gasoline-fueled generator in the cellar; that was not exactly a cellar, but more of a crawl space. Gasoline was stored in two large tanks a couple dozen yards away from the back of the lodge, next to a pine so gnarled it twisted round from one direction to another before coming back to its source, and strangling itself.

Adam was prolific in his ability to write something every day, if only a single line, or a rewrite of a rewrite many times over; *"correct often and carefully"* was one of his many dictums. Adam came to Gnarled Pines expecting to write, to think, to ponder, to reexamine his life, and perhaps just a soupçon of reinvention. Adam was an introspective person whose life had become a metaphor for his work. *"I cease to exist when I write. I am the work,"* Adam told himself and may, in fact, believe it. Perhaps a month on a deserted island would bring A. J. Goodblood inspiration and, perhaps, a piece of self-knowledge, which often occurs with every novel he writes. Since he would be alone with his work, all day, every day, pouring a part of himself onto every page, something is bound to happen; something buried, or hidden within himself, fragments of history, pieces of a life that had been long-hidden, suppressed, or simply lost, are bound to surface and work their way into his consciousness, then into his writing. Every once in a while a rare blue moon brings Adam a miraculous moment—an epiphany.

Adam removed the contents of the largest blue and white plastic cooler Mariner's Mart had to offer—cold cuts, cheeses, condiments, bread, junk foods, a dozen boxes of Ding Dongs, candy bars, more junk foods—all purchased in a glaringly lit convenience store in Turtle Run which actually had a wooden barrel of pickles in homemade brine. *"My wife mixed that brine. Best pickles you ever tasted, yeah."* Adam arranged the items in the ice box. The Agency never mentioned an "ice box." He recalled seeing bags of ice in Mariner's Mart, but not blocks, which he most certainly would need. *"Fiddle dee dee,"* Adam feebly chuckled at the reference. Tomorrow will be another day, but in the meanwhile he had some exploring to do. First, there was the unpacking, putting things away and setting-up his workplace on the yellow oilcloth-covered pine dining table that could easily accommodate a dozen diners on two long wooden benches on either side, and two high-backed pine chairs on each end. There was no Wi-Fi, no access to the internet, no satellite dish on the island. The Agency informed him of that before he leased Gnarled Pines and he did not mind one bit, since he felt they would only be tempting distractions to interfere with his work. He deleted his facebook account—an addictive distraction—before beginning his last novel, but after the novel was finished, he did not reactivate it and he felt better for it. The last thing he stopped cold turkey was smoking and that was almost as difficult as quitting facebook. *"How could one not feel better about oneself after overcoming an addiction?"* Adam asked himself, rhetorically; he already knew the answer. To get online, he would need to weigh anchor and head off for Turtle Run, or get a satellite connection and hope that would do the job.

By mid-morning Adam hadn't done any exploring; instead, he was sitting in front of his computer hoping that something would come to mind. A throbbing headache came on and it felt like his brain was about to explode. He needed something more than the story of, *"The crossing to the island of Gnarled Pines with the Captain of the Pequod was...."* While he sat staring at the white screen, *"It was a dark and stormy morning on the ocean of...."* Nothing worth writing came to mind. He heaved a sigh of discouragement, yawned, slumped over the table with his head supported by his folded arms and fell asleep.

"He's asleep. I'm going in."
"Careful."

"We need to find out who he is."

"Find out if he's the one."

"What's your name?"

"Adam."

"Did you know this is a dangerous place for mortals, Adam?"

"So I've heard."

"What are you doing here, Adam?"

"I came to write…to write about the island…to write about all of you."

"Wait a minute! I know this guy. He's the writer."

"Ahh…yes! He's the guy."

"Of course. I remember him."

"I think I do, too."

"You know me? Have you read any of my books?"

"No, stupid!"

"He's dense."

"We met you during the seance."

"What seance?"

"It hasn't happened yet. It will, soon."

"And then we met you in Reggie's cabin."

"I don't remember any of this."

"It hasn't happened yet. It will."

"Soon."

"I know about the seance, of course. That's part of the reason I'm here."

"It's the same every year and it never gets boring."

"Some years it's more painful than others."

"I imagine."

"*My name was Reggie...Reggie Mooner. You might have heard of me.*"

"Indeed I have. I heard you were a funny, funny man—Reggie the Mooner, the funniest man on Broadway."

"*Thanks!*"

"*I was known as Annabelle Lovelace.*"

"*Ah, yes.* You were quite famous."

"*Was I?*"

"Yes, indeed. I read that you were the most employed actor on Broadway for ten years running."

"*And you read that about me?*"

"Indeed I did."

"*I guess I was. By the way, I'm an actress, not an actor.*"

"Sorry. Nowadays we call both men and women actors."

"*Hmm, about time.*

"*I was King...*"

"King Butcher. *Yes.* You're a hero in the gay community?"

"*Gay community? What's that?*"

"There's a worldwide community of men and women who love people of their own sex. They're free to marry. That's the LGBTQ community—Lesbian, Gay, Bisexual, Transgender and Queer. There's no need to hide anymore. There's surgery to change your sex now; that's Transgender. Nowadays, you could have surgery to become a man, King. And a man could have surgery to become a woman."

"*What's the difference between Gay and Queer?*"

"I don't really know, King. Degrees of belligerence, I guess. You're famous just for being who you are—were. In fact, your face is on a postage stamp."

"What? I don't remember what my face looked like."

"It's a good face, King."

"Thank you....When you read about me...was I referred to as he, she, or King?"

"You were, Mister Butcher. You were written about, in most every account, as he and as King. Those who knew you wrote: *'King Butcher was a better man than most, and he was the kindest gentleman there ever was.'* You are well remembered."

"That's overwhelming. Thank you."

"Is Mona LaBaron? Here?"

"Not exactly. She is and she isn't."

"We don't speak her name."

"You're beginning to wake...."

"Wait."

"Careful of Charon! He's...."

It was mid-afternoon when Adam awoke. He didn't remember his dream though he was certain that he had been dreaming, but like most dreams it dissolved by the time he was fully awake. The coming storm turned out to be a gentle summer shower, never gaining much strength as it passed over the island. The heat and the sun in the clear July sky evaporated all signs of there having been any rain. Adam was anxious to walk around and have a look at the island before sundown.

Adam spent the remainder of his first afternoon exploring. He saw where there had been guest cottages that were razed decades earlier, leaving only remnants of their foundations. Scattered about were some pine logs that appeared to have turned into weathered driftwood; gray, deformed and hollow, but not without a curious fascination. The brochure stated that there was no life on the island, and from what Adam could gather, the brochure was correct. He was struck by the idea of there being no life on this island—indigenous or otherwise—not a squirrel nor beetle, a tick nor worm. Nothing containing a breath of animated life lived on this sterile rocky ground scrubbed free from any trace of living—only the gnarled pines rooted in rock—otherwise, the island was dead. There was beauty in the deformity of the pines. There was an exquisite sadness in their disfigurement, like lepers left to rot untouched by as much as a finger of mercy. Wind and salty ocean mist did not do this; the pines were strangling themselves, embracing their neighbors, or alone apart from the others. Bewitching in their outlandish wonderland way; gnarled trees that had crawled and squirmed over the island froze into uniquely prepossessing convolutions—sculptures made of death.

At the northernmost end of the island, painted white with red trim, a lighthouse stood precariously close to the edge of the island's highest point above the rocky shoreline. Adam stepped back from its edge, steadied himself, and since he'd never been inside a lighthouse it seemed to him a fun thing to do, so he grabbed the handle on the door and pulled. The door flung open from the force of escaping wind that nearly blew him over with a stench so foul, he choked and retched. *"What in hell is that!?"*

Adam returned to the lodge at sundown. The three-hundred and sixty degree horizon, perfused with never ending stars, was a gorgeous sight unlike anything he had ever experienced—not even in the Rocky Mountains of Colorado. The lamp atop the lighthouse flashed-on, spreading its orbiting beams of warning over the lodge and over the ocean. When Adam entered the lodge he found all the lamps had been turned on. *"Hmm."* Adam was positive that they were not on when he left. Perhaps the lamp atop the lighthouse and the lamps in the lodge were on a timer. *"Yeah, of course. That's it."*

It had been a long day and Adam was exhausted. He had no idea who might have slept on bed in the bedroom, or when, or what condition the bedding was in. He decided to sleep on the couch and check out the cleanliness of the bedding in the morning. He switched the lamps off, still perplexed by their being on, then stretched out on the couch.

"On a timer. I betcha that's it," and he went to sleep, perchance to dream and talk with ghosts again.

TWO

The lobster supper Mona LaBaron served was prepared by the unsavory Charon, but Mona being Mona declared, "I made those big bugs with my own two little ol' hands, darlings."

"Sublime."

"Of course, Reggie. Did you expect anything less?"

"Not from you, Mona."

"Thank you, darling. Another, dearest?"

"I'm stuffed to the gills, Mona."

"Of course you are, Reggie. More champagne, anyone?"

"I wouldn't mind," Willy answered raising his glass to show it was empty.

"When have you ever minded, my dear?" Mona chided. There was a volley of chuckling before Mona shouted to the kitchen, *"Charon! We mustn't keep Willy waiting. Do bring us more bubbly."* Then to the table she inquired in a sly whisper, "Do you think he heard me?"

"They heard you in Poughkeepsie, *darling*." Willy may have sounded more sarcastic than was appropriate from a guest to his host, but he was in his cups and already teetering, so he probably did not know if he was giving himself away, or not; his honest thoughts and true feelings for Mona LaBaron. In any case, Willy's capacity to care about the sensitivities of others has never been his strong suit. And why should it be? Wilson—"the tyrant"—Woodhouse directed Mona in several of Broadway's most successful productions and he was, no doubt, one of the reasons for Mona's meteoric rise as a New York theatre fixture. As a director, Willy was tough, dictatorial, belittling, demanding, demeaning—

but his instincts were impeccable and actor's who survived his direction became better actors who received greater reviews. Wilson Woodhouse was a star maker. When Willy was not directing, he was usually mild-mannered and unassuming. Willy sighed and said to himself, *"Will that bitch never stop acting?"*

"There's nothing wrong with Poughkeepsie," Mona took Willy's remark as an affront. "Is there anyone on Broadway who's not from somewhere else?"

"Arthur. Arthur's from Manhattan," Annabelle almost raised her hand in the excitement of being the first to know the answer. Annabelle's enthusiasm for the theatre and for life in general, mixed with champagne, was pretty much her approach to everything. When in her company, people felt better about themselves—she knew how to listen.

Mona scoffed. "He doesn't count, Annabelle."

"Why?"

"Because."

"Where is he? He should be here. Here we are, celebrating on his very own island, and he's not here to enjoy it with us. Is Arthur alright, Mona? I hope everything's alright. He isn't sick, is he?"

"Arthur does not own this island anymore, Annabelle. I own this island."

"*Really?* How…?" Annabelle didn't believe her ears.

"*What?*" asked Willy, shocked. "You're joking?"

"No, Willy. I don't joke. He gave it to me for services rendered. I have the deed." After a bit of snickering made its way around the table, Mona continued, "Now, can we move on to something else?"

"'Services rendered,' *huh?*" Florence mumbled, her elbow on the table where she sat next to Mona, her fist under her chin, her mouth sideways with a crooked smirk, shrugged, and continued just loud enough to make herself heard, *"You'd get away with murder, Mona."*

"Maybe," Mona murmured.

"You just drop them in boiling water, right?" Hudson asked of no one in particular; poor Hudson Sky—so young, so pretty, so dumb. What a lovely combination, for some.

"Only if they're alive, dear boy," Reggie informed. "Isn't that right, Mona? When you dropped them in the scalding water, did they scream—*like the wail of a banshee?"*

Mona remained silent, in a loud dismissive way.

In an attempt to slacken what he perceived to be a tension too taut for this early in the evening, Ídolo offered, "The champagne's *magnifique.*"

"Of course it is. Just like you, my lovely." Mona contrived a smile.

"You're ingratiating."

"Willy, was that you?"

"It could have been," Willy smiled.

"Yes, I'm sure it could," Mona kept a straight, yet unhappy face.

"Must have been a good year," Hudson suggested.

"Beauty should be seen and not heard," Reggie informed Hudson.

"Do they put the year on champagne?" Willy asked.

"We shall have to look, shouldn't we?" Mona inspected a newly emptied bottle and announced, "Nope. But knowing Arthur, as we all do, it would need to have been a very good year."

"Speaking about Arthur...."

"We're not speaking about Arthur, Reggie," Mona hissed, firmly.

A general uneasy silence.

The wine and liquors stocking the shelves and racks in the kitchen closet had been the property of Arthur Baumgarten, so it would be reasonably safe to assume they were top notch. Charon entered from the kitchen carrying two silver buckets of chipped ice, each with a bottle of champagne plunged into it. Charon was a disquieting presence; a presence that each knew instinctively to avoid. So they gazed at the ice buckets, the flawlessly polished silver and the candles that reflected upon their surface, some caught themselves revealed in the silver's mirror-like quality; but, however they tried not to stare at Charon they could not help but take transient peeks into his dark gray eyes before quickly returning their attention to the buckets of champagne, feeling guilty for their avoidance. There was something about him that was not quite right, not quite human. There was something about him that caused them misgivings and chills that overcame each of them. Charon sat the champagne directing in front of Mona. "Shall I open them, Miss Mona?" Charon asked.

"Only if you feel it is your duty," Mona said with an air of self-importance. She was the Queen and Charon was her dutiful attendant; and by extension, all at the table were her royal subjects. That was Mona. That was her defining persona.

"It is my pleasure, Miss Mona," Charon said, monotonously, but not without precious little charm. He popped both bottles of champagne, set each of the buckets on either end of the table, removed the silver tray that had been held tightly under his arm all the while, and began to clear the table.

Charon, an inexplicable enigma, lived in the lighthouse. Once, there had been a small bungalow next to the lighthouse for the keeper, but that had been blown away more than a hundred years ago by a wicked nor'easter. Charon still remembers how it almost blew him away with it. He had been soundly asleep when a fist of wind punched the bungalow and threw it into the ocean, leaving him lying under the covers and still in his bed. So, Charon took his bed into the lighthouse. He sleeps amazingly little and spends most of his time in the caves beneath the lighthouse. Charon kept the lamp glowing and he doubled as the handyman for the lodge. He came with the lodge and had been on the island long before it was the property of Arthur Baumgarten. Arthur assumed that Charon represented The Agency, but he never knew nor did he question how and with what, and by whom was he paid for his services. Arthur decided that Charon came with the property and he left it at that.

Charon was tall and gaunt. He had thick black hair, huge hands and enormous feet, which Mona found stimulating. Whether by choice or from an unavoidably unpleasant nature, Charon was off-putting and seemed to have only one expression—deadpan. There was something menacing about him; one could sense it from across the room. What little Arthur knew about the man, was more than Arthur wanted to know. Charon was disturbingly dreadful to be around for any length of time; it was not his awkwardness, nor his aloofness that people found so repellent, it was his off-putting vibrations, the way he phrased his sentences, archaic and monotone—the embodiment of indifference—and then there was his wretched breath. His lips appeared to have never smiled, and if they did they might crack. The color of his eyes changed from steel-gray to the color reflected in a chunk of coal—intense and dispiriting. One could not read him, if indeed there was anything to read, but one senses something dark. One could not look at his severe demeanor for very long without feeling unnerved and wanting to run from him.

After all, Charon was never human, nor was he ever born. He was cobbled into being after the first human—the biblical Adam—died, leaving his soul lost in nothingness and desperately in need of help getting to somewhere beyond death. Charon came to Adam's rescue and escorted his spirit to its final destination: the place of the soul's strongest attraction. Thereafter, Charon became the ferryman to all abandoned souls in their final journey to the other side of the universe; until he was thrown aside when mankind began to take responsibility for their own destination, and then he was thrown aside. He was abandoned by a new reality that reasoned one must help oneself, rather than jeopardize their souls by putting them into the hands of a stranger.

After Charon was no longer needed, he awoke to find himself on the island of Gnarled Pines long before the island had a name, long before a single soul came upon it, long before white men crossed the ocean to steal the land they would call America, long before the trees had begun to gnarl. Charon had been cast aside and it left him angry and bitter. He questioned the universe, *"Why have I been forsaken?"* He cried to the stars, the sun and to the Earth, but he never got an answer. Charon's loneliness drew him farther and farther into himself, into darker places and deeper into evil. The spirits in those dark places, and there were many, could manipulate his thoughts and actions, but were unable to possess his soul; he hadn't one.

After Charon's arrival, Gnarled Pines soon became the birthplace of evil; the place where the souls of darkness were born.

Charon become an undying servant to the dark forces. His covenant required him to tend to the unborn spirits of the dark souls—in exchange for, *"Nothing I can think of."* He was grateful to be of use; indentured, once again. When a company of workers came to build the first lighthouse he joined them and helped to build it. When the first keeper of the lighthouse came, along with his disagreeable wife, Charon ate them. He has been the keeper of the lighthouse ever since.

The seeds of the unborn spirits were sown within the trees. To protect the unborn spirits, the island was purged of all living matter. As evil incubated within the pines, the pines bent, gnarled, and crawled upon the island's surface, their needles turned brown, fell to the ground and blew into the ocean, leaving bare branches that would never be green again. Charon's covenant with the dark spirits involved murder, feeding the trees with freshly killed human flesh, and other appalling acts that suited Charon just fine. Charon was a cannibal who recognized the depth of Mona's darkness and could not help but be attracted to her; not for his next meal, but for companionship. In Mona, Charon finally found amity to comfort his angst from unanswered questions.

Mona did not know Charon's surname; she didn't care and didn't ask; she supposed that he would let her know should it ever become necessary; she doubted it would ever become necessary.

"If all you thespians are ready, grab your drinks and let's go to the parlor, or the living room. Oh, dear ones, whatever shall we call it?" Queen LaBaron went into her act. Actually, the Queen was always acting; therefore, she went into overacting.

"The playroom."

"*Ohh.* I like that, Annabelle." Mona's arrangement with Arthur Baumgarten ended damnably, requiring him to share his surfeit of liquid assets—*and what fabulous assets they were!"* Drink up, kids. There's lots more where that came from." When Mona emptied her glass she raised it high over her head, threw her arm backward, posed in an unimaginative, affected, and derivative leading lady manner and roared with laughter as she threw her glass where it smashed against the wall. Her guests showed great restraint when it came to joviality. "Now let us all head for Annabelle's playroom, kids, and raise a little hell, and maybe a spirit or two."

Mona's guests, her handful of Broadway personalities, gathered every bottle on the table that hadn't been emptied and headed for the newly anointed "playroom" which wasn't a separate room at all, but merely an extension of the dinning area. The interior of the lodge was one enormous main room with a dining area, a large kitchen, a small bedroom and a large bathroom that was about the same size as the small bedroom.

Mona sat postured to watch the pantomime of guests from a leather love-seat, and to keep an eye on Hudson Sky—her latest investment in a lengthy string of paramours—while simultaneously remaining attentive to her guests by winking, waving, smiling, or simply nodding regal-like to any who glanced her way. Cigarettes were rolled and lit. Champagne, brandy and other distilled beverages, smuggled in from Canada, thanks to Mister Joseph Kennedy, were poured.

Reggie Mooner, the bumbling comedian known as Reggie the Mooner, who managed to show his ass at every party, who could make an audience laugh with only his rubber-faced expressions and nimble pratfalls—which earned him all the great character roles—who would do most anything to get a laugh, who was a shameless ham and he would be the first to tell you, who was more than a bit loud, un-comfortingly serious, and dangerously familiar when he drank, sat next to the director and his best friend, Wilson Woodhouse who, *"...did not rape that bitch,"* and shared a bottle of whiskey between them.

"Never thought you did, Willy."

"They're all alike."

"Indeed...all alike," Reggie confirmed.

"I gave her the lead in that snoozer by Eugene O'Neill, didn't I?"

"I never liked her, Willy. Trouble, I thought."

"Trouble indeed, Reggie."

"She's was the first to hop on the casting couch. She asked me, Reggie. She begged me. She thought I'd make her a star. One play and her career was over. *Yeah.* They're all alike. They would kill to be on Broadway, and then they will blame you for it. They're all alike. And that overrated Mona LaBaron is no different."

"Right you are, Willy. Right you are. They're all alike, Mona included. Just the same. Not different at all."

"Right...alike...the same. Threw herself at me. *Humiliating.* You know me, Reggie, it's...it's...oh, to hell with it... I could slit her throat!"

"*Ohh*...I wouldn't do that, Willy. *Hey!* This is your best friend talkin' here. Ya didn't...you can't say it enough...ya didn't do it, Willy. *Oh God!* Look what I did, Willy. Look what I went and did. I spilt it, Willy...I spilt it all over me and...*Oh God*...look at the rug...it oughta soak in...*eh*...you won't see a thing after awhile...what a waste of a glass of good Scotch, Willy."

"From Scotland."

"Pour another."

Reggie grabbed the half-empty bottle of bootlegged Scotch and poured Willy and himself another triple-shot on shattered ice.

"Here's to Mona for the invite, and nothing else."

"And nothing else." The sound of clinking glasses.

"Here's to Joseph Kennedy!" More clinking.

Hudson Sky, a stagehand with a stage name and an actor wannabe could, without saying a single word, seduce men and women alike; to bed him, to pamper him, to pay him for his expensive bad habits, simply by using his natural gift for making himself irresistible, for being a young bewitching Adonis from Nyack, New York. Sadly, he was flawed with a serious drug addiction, though some have found his poisonous vulnerability attractive. He can sparkle-on-demand and he also happens to be Mona's current inamorato. Hudson was busying himself on the surface of the blue-mirrored coffee table by carefully creating, with the help of a King Gillette double-edged razor blade, generous lines of cocaine—free to all. There's not all that much to say about Hudson, but *oh*...so much to see. He was young, recently turned twenty-one and hadn't yet done much to speak of. His father abused him sadistically and sexually. Hudson could have dealt with the sex, he loved sex, but the physical abuse was horrific. His mother knew but never said a thing. She would sigh from time to time, when she took the time to look up from her Bible reading. *"It's the mysterious Will of Jesus."* He hated the both of them.

Ídolo, *"just Ídolo,"* a single name of his own creation, danced solo in many of Arther Baumgarten's Broadway productions. Ídolo was every bit attractive as in his photographs—in fact, more so. His body was lithe, lean, and hard—the body of a trained dancer—an arresting face with a radiant smile, and beguiling brown, almost black eyes that had the uncanny ability to see through the masks of others. There was a balance of the masculine and the feminine about him. The natural scent of him was intoxicating. His was not mere beauty of the flesh, as it was with Hudson, but rather Ídolo was the concept of beauty—the essence of beauty itself—he was Michelangelo's David while Hudson's attraction was transitory. To enter Ídolo's life, his world, his soul, his reality, unique and separate, complete with unexplored ideas, images, alien thoughts with a language of their own, is to enter a sublime and omnipresent spirit. Ídolo, though only twenty-nine, was tiring of dancing. He felt too old for his years; not with acquired intellect—he looks forward to acquiring more of it—but as an old spirit, painfully intimidated by false sincerity, chosen ignorance, judgements of others, and not just those directed at himself; although, he hasn't escaped a number of those slings and arrows. An anger swelled within him from witnessing blatant uncaring and indifference committed every day by an endless parade of others. Ídolo was troubled by the thought that one day he might become uncontrollable and explode, but until he does he shows kindness to others even when he doesn't feel like it; and that's pretty much the overriding principle of show business—the show must always go on. Ídolo, while winding the Victor Victrola as Ruth Etting sang *"Button Up Your Overcoat,"* tapped his toes and mouthed the words.

  Annabelle Lovelace was what is known in the theatre as a triple-threat: she could sing, dance, and act. She was equally comfortable with comedy or drama. Her natural bearing and good looks could be seen from the back row. She possessed an innate talent, a skill that does not come from study. She had no expectations for being the star, the leading lady, the featured singer, or the one who taps down a flight of stairs. Although the latter was a secret desire of hers; each step lighting as her foot touched it, and the cleats on the soul of her shoes ringing out to the back row. *"Maybe if I spoke to Mister Ziegfeld."* Annabelle was sixteen when her father was killed in the Great War and when she left Albuquerque, New Mexico. She arrived in New York City penniless and, knowing she had to do something, she moved from man to man, from apartment to apartment; always for something to eat and a place to sleep; until, she landed her first job in the chorus of an Arthur Baumgarten revue, *Hot Night Out*. She hasn't stopped working since. Now, in her late twenties, still looks nineteen, strawberry blond hair, green eyes, a naturally wholesome appeal; all Annabelle wants to do is work, to pretend she is somebody else, to be anybody else, and she has always been grateful for each and every role in which she was cast. She made it to Broadway all on her own and that was her source of great pride.

Florence Mae Wallace, a retired leading lady who hadn't aged well, fidgeted with her dress, appearing to be dusting something off, *"...nothing fits right anymore; nothing is right anymore...nothing...."* sat within chatting distance from her friend-in-name-only, Mona LaBaron. Friendships, in a business where longevity for friendships is measured by the length of a production's run, dwindle easily. Florence mourned herself as if she were already dead. Florence was never a beauty, but she could act. She brought brilliance, clarity and insight to every character she played. Playwrights loved and wrote for her, directors and audiences loved her. She never married, nor ever took on a lover. Florence was never a beauty, nor was she unpleasant; she was dignified, arresting, engaging, and well respected. So, why should she think of herself as having fallen apart, as unsightly and destined to eternal loneliness? Yet that is exactly what she thought; hence, the sadness she carried within her. She managed to suppress those thoughts and feelings on every occasion, and unknown by none but herself. The elegance of Florence was in her acting—before the arthritis, the rheumatism, the trick knee that buckles without warning and could easily cause her to fall flat on her face while walking across the stage, and then there was her oncoming blindness from diabetes, and remembering lines became too difficult. *"...nothing fits right anymore; nothing is right anymore... nothing...."*

Missing from the group was King Butcher who was in his cabin recovering from ocean sickness. The twenty minute ride from the mainland turned him a ghostly shade of nauseous by the time he reached Gnarled Pines. *"If the ferry had gone a little faster I might not have gotten sick."* King was a set designer and one of the best. He worked on Broadway for many years keeping a decades long secret—he was a woman. Kate Butcher should have been a man and she cannot remember ever not knowing she should have been a man. It was a sadly painful burden that became unbearable by the time she was fifteen, when she ran away from home and made her way by foot and wagon from Kaneohe, West Virginia to Baltimore, Maryland. After a couple weeks of living on the street she met an older woman who gave her a home, showed her love and kindness like Kate had never known, and taught her to be a gentleman. A few years later, her partner died of consumption and, no longer Kate, King moved to New York City where he discovered his hidden talent for set design. It was Arthur Baumgarten who gave him his first break. There was not a person in the room who did not owe a debt of gratitude to Arthur Baumgarten.

It was after dark and a pyrotechnical display to celebrate the Fourth of July, which Hudson had volunteered to ignite, would soon begin. The festivities were planned to end at midnight with a seance—the conjuring of spirits by none other than Mona LaBaron who claims to have communicated with the *other side.* Nobody believed her, of course. Mona was re-imagining herself as Broadway royalty; however, whatever it was she was imagining herself to be, it only succeeded in making her appear as a clown.

The July ocean breeze that swept across the island at night was chilling. Soon after the delight from the fireworks display waned into a general shiver, the reluctant revelers dashed back into the lodge to warm by the fireplace, which was their only source of light since all the lamps had been switched off while they were out. King Butcher was standing and waving his hands over the fire.

"Cold, dearest one?"

"Frozen, Mona."

"Other than freezing, I hope you're feeling better."

"I am. Thank you."

"Well then," Mona announced, "let's go sit at the table, kids. C'mon, c'mon…it's almost midnight. Let's get this show on the road. *Chop, chop.* Willy! Stay awake."

Whether they were just plain drunk, or drunk with anticipation, the focus of the ritual was on Mona, as always. Mona herded her guests, as though they were wayward sheep, back to the dining table; all she was missing was a cattle prod. The table had been cleared in their absence. The sheep were instructed to, *"Sit. Chop, chop."* All eyes were on Mona who, with an ambiguous smile, turned from guest to guest, wordlessly making eye contact with each eager, or apprehensive face, then said, "Well, darlings, this is it! It's time for the big reveal. It's time to remove your clothes. Don't be shy. After all, every one of us is in the Theatre—with a capital T. We've all seen what the other's got. *Chop, chop, darlings.*"

"I haven't seen what any of you got and I don't care to." King was disgruntled and frowned.

"Did we all say welcome back to *Mister* Butcher?" Mona asked with a counterfeit smile.

There was a generous round of welcoming him back and concern for his health to which he responded, "Thank you," and "Much better."

"King, are you going to participate or what?" Mona was sharp and cruel.

"I'll *'or what,'* Mona. I won't do it," declared King Butcher. "I would not have come had I known this beforehand."

"Dearest King, do you honestly think I don't know who you are, what you have, or don't have?"

"I don't know what you mean, Mona." King was visibly taken aback. "I won't do it! I have no intention of exposing myself. I hope you can understand that."

"Stop it, Mona. Is this necessary?"

"Yes, it is, Reggie. I have been to the library and I had read many books on how to conduct a seance. Every one of them said that the best way to attract spirits from the other side is to lower the lights and get naked."

"*Donkey dust!* I'm keeping my clothes on, if you don't mind."

"But I do mind, Reggie."

"It must be confounding, minding what others do, but not minding the things you do yourself. I think that may be the definition of a hypocrite. What do you think?"

"Willy, I am surprised you can still talk using real words after drinking so much of my Scotch whiskey. Imported, you know. I hope you enjoyed it. Thank you."

"I'm still enjoying it, thank you. How else could I endure the winter of my discontent, your idle pleasures and your malefic plots, other than by drunken prophecies."

"*Jesus Christ, Willy!* If Shakespeare were alive, that would kill him. I won't strip either, Mona."

"Florence, out of deference to your age, you don't have to."

"Stop it, Mona! You stop it right now!" Florence shouted. Then, she looked at King who sat directly across the table and said kindly, "King, you don't need to take off your clothes. This is some stupid concoction of Mona's. Something to satisfy her deviance. I'm not going to take off my clothes off, Mona. *Period*"

"Thank you for sparing us that image, Florence. It's not a concoction. If we're to get in touch with the spirits our bodies must be free to receive visitations from beyond. We must let the spirits sink into our pores. Florence, I want you to think of yourself as an antenna that needs adjusting…or…*oh,* you know…that hollow reed thing."

"Horse shit."

"It's not horse shit, King," Mona barked. "Now take 'em off!"

The air in the room was alarming and wrought with anxiety.

"I'm with King, Mona." Florence snickered. *"Horse shit!"*

"Well, King? It's your turn. In or out, darling?" Mona quizzed.

"*Out…darling!*" King mocked, jumped up, and headed for the door. "I don't know why you persist, Mona. Now, if you will excuse me, *darling*, I'll say goodnight…*darling*."

"*Stop, stop, stop!* I was only joking. C'mon, can't you all take a joke?"

"I wasn't laughing," Willy said with a mean smirk.

"Me neither, *darling!*" King opened the door, went out and slammed it.

"*Okay.* We all heard that loud and clear, but the show must go on." Ídolo took the upper road.

"You're despicable, Mona."

"I've heard that before, Florence." Mona made an effort to maintain the semblance of dignity. "Everybody, hold hands and relax. Leave yourselves open to endless possibilities."

"What kind of possibilities?" Hudson asked.

"*Shh…! How would I know!*" Mona snapped.

"Services rendered, *humph.*"

GNARLED PINES

Edward Crosby Wells

THREE

Arthur Baumgarten roamed from room to room in his spacious Park Avenue apartment, carrying an un-capped bottle of bootleg gin, and every so often he'd gulp down a mouthful. The apartment was dark. Arthur was naked. A high-pitched shriek from the horn of an old Tin Lizzy rose from off the street and filled the emptiness of his plush digs. Arthur was on the far side of distraught; the dark side, the side where thought surrenders to raw and uncontrollable emotion, the side where comprehension and the power of Will deceases. He stumbled, moaned, cursed, took another swig of gin. Arthur could not think nor could he speak much that wasn't gibberish; however, his subconscious might have had some thoughts of its own: *"You ruined me, Mona LaBaron...after all I did for you...made you famous...you never deserved it. You may have been a star in a community theatre in Poughkeepsie, but I made you one on Broadway! You hurt everybody, don't you? You don't care...you seem to enjoy it. You don't care what you do to people. It's all about getting what you want, no matter how. Now look what you did. Take a goddamned look at what you did...all those men on his client list had families, Mona! Innocent families...wives... children...people who never did a goddamned thing to you. Jesus Christ! You're gonna pay for this, Miss LaBaron. Yes you will! You're gonna pay, baby. I'd sell my soul just to see how much this is gonna cost you, baby!"* And what about the flesh merchant from the Bronx? *"He'll sell me out. Sure of it...probably get off with a slap on the wrist...he'll turn his book of clients over to the cops... sure he will...for a reduced sentence...yeah, that's what he'll get, a goddamned reduced sentence! Not me, baby!"* Arthur took another swig of gin, staggered into the kitchen. *"What? Jesus! Jeez...us...."* Arthur had forgotten something. *"What, what, what?"* He surveyed the room, but saw nothing; only shadows in the dark, lacking definition. His hand came to rest on the wall where the light switch should have been. *"Who took it? Who got it?"* For a moment he came within an inch of the light switch, but he gave up too soon, he couldn't find it, someone had taken it and that was that. *"Not me, baby!"* Then, in his mind's eye, he saw the object of why he was in the kitchen.

In one last long guzzle Arthur drained the bottle of gin, then threw the bottle across the room. It just missed the window with a view on Park Avenue; it hit the wall below the window and bounced to the floor, never breaking. Arthur's mind had finally reached a safe distance from anything close to reality when he blindly grabbed a knife from out the drawer next to an ornate—possibly an antique—wine rack. Had he not been struggling in the dark and blindly drunk, and had his vision served him correctly, his choice of cutlery would certainly not have been the bread knife, but there it was. *"I'd sell my soul to watch you beg for mercy!"* And there it is.

"Would you really?" asked a disembodied voice.

"YES! In a heartbeat, baby."

Arthur Baumgarten staggered mindlessly into the bathroom, and he could not find the light switch. *"Who's stealing light things? Things should stay in their place! People should stay in their place, Miss LaBaron. Goddamn you. Ouch! What was that? Damn tub foot! Pour water. Okay, okay. Where's the...I need the plug...who took the plug? There ya go. Thank ya. Thank ya. The water...water, water everywhere...and not a drop to drink.*

Turn it on. There ya go. Fill, baby, fill." Arthur staggered around and, not waiting for the tub to fill, he crawled into it while it was filling up with cold water. *"Is this cold? I think it's cold. I hate cold...."* Arthur reached for the hot water handle and couldn't find it. *"Things oughta stay in their place...goddamnit!*

"You know what to do," the voice said.

"What to do...what to do?"

"The wrists. Remember?"

"Oh, that...I thought about it and changed my mind." Arthur's voice was slurred.

"Too late...look at what you're holding."

"What am I holding?"

"Look," the voice said. Arthur looked into the darkness and he couldn't see a thing. "In your fist, Arthur. Feel it."

"Ouch! What the hell? Don't tell me...don't...ahh...I remember. Well, dear sir, I changed my mind. Don't wanna do it. No! I wanna see her suffer. Suffer, Mona LaBaron!"

"Too late. Here. Let me help you. There you go. Use this hand first. Hold the blade to your wrist. Good boy. Now you need to saw it."

"Saw it?"

"Back and forth. Back and forth. There you go. That doesn't hurt a bit, does it?"

"No hurt. Charon? Is that you? I know that voice. What are you doing here, Charon?"

"No questions. Change hands. You know what to do. Go ahead. It doesn't hurt. There you go. Do not turn your wrist, Arthur. Saw. Saw...saw-w-w-w."

Despite Charon's voice guiding him to saw his wrists, Arthur drowned in the bloody water before his wrists drained enough blood to kill him—the irony would not have been wasted on him. It didn't take long for the tub to fill, overflow, and flood the bathroom floor.

Early morning, and Arthur Baumgarten's body was found by the building super after the tenant below complained that her bathroom ceiling was running with water and *"...about to come crashing down on my head, or other precious things!"* Arthur's body was taken to the morgue in the basement of Bellevue Hospital. It would not have been his morgue of choice, but there his body went and there it was and there was nothing Arthur could do about it. It lay, covered with a sheet on a slab next to the slab with the body of Fingers Costello—born with six fingers on his right hand, but, unfortunately, missing the pinky on his left hand—a man with a bullet lodged in his forehead, who had been a trigger man for Lucky Luciano. Soon after Arthur's body arrived at Bellevue, and somebody turned off the lights, Arthur felt himself awakening. When he became fully conscious, he tried to get off the slab, but could not move. His body was dead and he knew it. How? He just knew it. He was dead and his body was laying on a slab in the basement of Bellevue Hospital next to a known gangster, a celebrity stiff as a board.

As Arthur lay, he envisioned a world of injustices without mercy. He saw himself from a wholly new perspective. He was no longer mortal, or resilient in the ongoing flux of life. He was gone, absent, away, without humanity to soften a hardened heart with any sort of retrospection—he was a corpse tucked away in the basement of Bellevue, when his sense of self shattered into countless splinters of nonexistence and undecipherable projections upon a screen of nothingness. Then, sunrise awakened his spirit and widened the breadth of his vision, giving him something more to conjure than the fractured images of his own negation. The sun transported him from out himself, to beyond nothingness, into a new and unexplored perspective, a new sense of self; unshackled by his former impressions of reality.

Was there nothing tangible remaining of Arthur Baumgarten the Broadway producer? Nothing visible or touchable? A trifle of existence, perhaps. Maybe a document or two, a contract with an actor or a director bearing his signature and stored somewhere among the many mold and dust covered stacks; decayed and never seen. The public memories of the productions he had produced; those memories will quickly fade; so few give attention to who produced this, that, or what. *"There must be my signature hastily scrawled upon a letter of agreement, or some other, any other, long forgotten transaction. That's tangible. Somewhere my name may yet survive. If only for a time, my name may remain somewhere along with a few details of my life, along with all the memories I may have had, or only imagined. What does it matter now? In the journey through organic reality, all traces of existence transmutes and perishes. It shouldn't matter now. I am dead."*

In a new reality, if it could be called a "reality" at all, Arthur saw the black waters where memories surfaced only to wane and sink back into oblivion. Nothing to hold on to. Then, it came upon him like a thunderbolt, the flash of a bargain made, the sight of the betrayer, his spite for Mona LaBaron beckoned to him to give her her comeuppance. She was the reason he was alive in death. He gave his soul and now she had a debt to pay.

Morning exploded. A mystical and absolute inorganic universe merged into being—if "being" is the proper word for the dead. In those few brief moments, the new Arthur Baumgarten knew himself to be the center and the pivot upon which the planes of his new consciousness revolved and evolved. He perceived a serene and silent void as if in the eye of a phantom tornado. His body lay on a slab in a morgue, unmoving, in a heightened state of inertia, fearing the taking of unnecessary risks in his new reality. He was hurled into the centrifugal pull of the yet to be explored universe spinning around him. While being in the center of chaos, Arthur was in a safe haven from chaos. A great and inexplicable force seized him and guided him beyond all meaning of existence where everything is; just is. Arthur attempted to reconsider a moment that had passed not a nanosecond ago, but the connection between himself and the moment of his death, tore apart and took what was left of his former being into a world of annihilation. His point of view—the point of view that recognized itself—fell deeper and deeper into the consciousness of his death. There had been something on the other side of death, then there was nothing, then something again, death and life flickered on and off until he thought himself back to life—and he came to life on the island of Gnarled Pines, midway of the lighthouse and the lodge, in the middle of its distorted woods. He determined that he had a sense of vision. He sniffed the hot and still air and determined that he had a sense of smell. The air he smelled was scented with death and decay, but it was the scent of a rose to him. He saw blood on the branches and he heard the humming of the darkest of dark souls that lie within those limbs, waiting to enter the world. He determined that he had a sense of hearing. He thought about the return of his senses, and he determined that he had a sense for his own being. In death he was alive.

"When the dark spirits are born, I will watch Miss Mona LaBaron pay the piper. I will listen to her screams, I will see her

soul flung into nothingness...and then I will have peace before I take my place in the netherworld."

* * *

There was only King Butcher, and that was who he was; so, out of respect for our character's truth, he is *he,* and *he* only. He laid on the cot in his cabin, tearfully reliving the barbarity of others —those agonizing thoughts that seethe up from time to time— reliving the ugliness of the past to escape the cruelty of the present. This time, however, there was no escaping the heart-wrenching pain, viciously inflicted by Mona LaBaron. It was not exactly what she did, or what she said, but more importantly for King—*why* she did it? *"Absolutely no reason. Without provocation. Just to torture me. Make a mockery of me. It's not like I haven't faced hatred all my life. Was I invited here just for that...more of the same...for this...to persecute me...expose me...make fun of me...belittle me? What did I ever do to her, huh? Nothing!"* King had finally come to the end of his rope, as it were, tired of unending unease and the embarrassments of endless humiliations. *"For the love of God I should have been a man!"* He was supposed to be a man. As sure as air, water, and the ground beneath his feet, he was a man; a man incarcerated inside a woman's body.*"The evil trickery of a higher power. Once they know, they don't treat you with respect...they treat you like a thing...like a mistake! Enough! I've had enough, Jesus! Can you hear me? I've had enough! A freak of nature...a perversion...I could go on and on until the last line, and that will be, 'I have been here and I have done nothing to be forgiven for.'"*

King opened his suitcase and removed a straight razor. Had there been a bathroom in the cabin, he would have carefully placed it in plain sight, so it could not be missed by anyone. Beside it, he would have placed a shaving brush resting on a block of soap in a blue and white enameled tin cup; these were the outward symbols of manhood to help him maintain the charade; these were the bitter reminders of what should be and what is; these were enraging reminders of the indefensible actions of others; but, there was no bathroom in which to place the symbols to remind him that he was not a man.

"*Go ahead...use it...you know what you want to do.*" Whose voice it was, King did not know, nor did he know if the voice was within his head, his consciousness, or from inside the cabin, behind the door, or under the bed. He searched the small cabin and there was no one there. "*Slit your throat, Kate. Go ahead...you won't feel a thing.*"

"Stop it! Stop it! I'm not going to...don't call me Kate... wait a minute...I know that voice. You're the guy from the lighthouse, aren't you?" There was no answer. After a minute of standing absolutely frozen, his breathing slowed, somebody grabbed him from behind, he struggled to free himself, but whoever it was that was holding him with their arms wrapped tightly around him, was squeezing him tighter and tighter with each attempt to free himself. "I don't want to do this...please...." King Butcher kicked and screamed until his legs froze, he could no longer move a muscle, "Please...don't," he whimpered. He knew he was going to die.

Something took control. He could feel its fingers carefully opening the razor's blade from its ivory sleeve. "Why don't you slit my throat yourself!?"

"What fun would that be? I like to watch. I want to watch you gag. I want to hear you beg and scream. I want to see your eyes widen in disbelief...and then I want to see them bulge until they explode from out their sockets. The pain you feel is the pain of exquisite fear…and then…then, I cannot tell you how magnificent the sensation of that pain is as you lose your fight to survive…and as you die…I like to watch your life dim and cease. What a pleasure that is. It thrills me, dear Miss Kate Butcher…and then…*ahh,* then you are mine. Now lift the blade to your throat. Go ahead. You know you want to. You have been thinking about it for a long time. Here we go…." King lifted the blade, felt the cold steel on his neck, squinted, cursed Mona, and with one swift motion King Butcher slashed his throat, dropped the bloody razor, and he fell upon the pinewood floor. *"Good girl,"* Charon said.

* * *

Adam sat working on *Gnarled Pines* from early morning until late evening barely taking time out to eat; but when he did take the time, he stood, yawned, stretched, then hobbled off to grab a bite of something, which was usually short of wholesome and always bolted down. Today, for instance: Adam ate two chunky peanut butter sandwiches, a cereal bowl of leftover spaghetti drenched in olive oil and garlic, four packages of Hostess Ding Dongs, one 3 Musketeers candy bar, a handful of gummy bears, and a mug of instant coffee—that is pretty much the usual fare when he is working. When his jeans begin to tighten, as they always do, he swears he'll go on a diet as soon as his book is completed. He undertakes to do this with every book he writes, but it's usually halfhearted and it doesn't take long before,*"To hell with it!"* Then he buys larger jeans. When each of his novels is published, he goes on the road doing book signings, and then he generally eats well—at least better—since he is often a luncheon or a dinner guest of an admirer, and not wanting to be seen ill-mannered by wolfing down everything on his plate, making a hog of himself, he reluctantly endures self-control. He loses the weight he'd gained while writing—until the next time when the sorry cycle begins again. As he writes *Gnarled Pines* the cycle has begun.

For a millionaire, Adam had never reinvented himself into anything other than Adam. He may emphasize different aspects of himself, from time to time, but that isn't the same. He is the man he set out to be, while never losing sight of the child he was. Everyone has "sides," but they cannot express them all at once. Adam tells himself that he does not write for the money, but that he writes—for good or for bad—for himself, for his own amusement. And that's pretty much true; until it's time to merchandise the published book; when it's time to do the book signings, to mingle with his audience; then his vanity takes control and makes it all about himself; and then, of course, there is the money; each as important as the other; each true to Adam's sense of Self.

Adam, still a child at heart, never lost his love for pleasant diversions such as: street fairs, especially the Italian festival of San Gennero in Manhattan's Little Italy, the planetarium, the ferry to Staten Island, the Museum of Natural History, Coney Island, carnivals, board games and musical theatre.

Musical theatre remains one of Adam's topmost pleasant diversions. Every time the overture begins—sometimes when the musicians are only tuning their instruments—Adam bubbles up, raises his hands to his head and makes blinders with them to obscure his joyful tears from those in nearby seats. He's been going to the theatre since he was a thirteen year old young man from Brooklyn Heights. He would take the subway into Manhattan and the first thing he did was dash to the TKTS booth in Times Square for reduced seats to Wednesday matinees. He never knew in advance what shows would be available, but he certainly wasn't going back to Brooklyn without seeing something; and, as a result of that, Adam acquired not an insignificant degree of education in musical theatre, and also in "legitimate theatre"—a long-held term for serious drama—Albee, Miller, Williams, Shaffer, for examples. Adam wrote a few plays himself; disappointments that never reached the level of Broadway. *"Top notch, or forget about it!"* Adam thinks he may rewrite his plays with the benefit of acquired knowledge over the years; resuscitate them, *"They're certainly not bad. There's a couple I believe are brilliant, if you don't mind my saying it myself. I should give them the second chance they deserve; especially now, since the name A. J. Goodblood has a fare amount of cachet."*

Adam waited until after dark to celebrate Independence Day by maneuvering the steep rocky steps to the dock from where he would watch the fireworks that dotted the sky over the mainland. It seemed to him that every town along the shoreline had their own display. Adam could not hear the ear-popping booms as loud as he would have liked—the thunder from skyrockets overhead that gave him chills of delight as pounding waves of sound beat against him—but he could plainly see the explosions of bright colors and the incredible patterns they made; and he keenly felt a wistful sadness when they faded and fell. Afterward, Adam walked back to the lodge, pausing every so often to look behind to see if there were any more sparkling displays that he might be missing. Regrettably, there was nothing more, not anywhere was there something to miss.

It was midnight and Adam was bone-weary, so he stretched out on the couch—he still hadn't inspected the bed to see if it was sanitary, or not—and he immediately fell to sleep.

Adam was awoken by the sound of impatient knocking. *"The wind? No. They're definitely human knocks. I'm supposed to have this island completely to myself. Goddamn it!"* Adam rose, wearing the same khaki shorts that he had worn when he arrived on Gnarled Pines, a baggy yellow T-shirt, probably heavily scented with body odor—Adam's hygiene suffered for his art—then walked barefooted towards the door while rubbing his eyes. When he opened the door there was no one there. He went out on the porch to have a look around and saw no one. Adam turned back to the door, pulled on its handle and it would not open. He yanked with all the strength he could muster, and even kicked it, yet still it would not open. There was no getting back into the lodge; at least, not through the front door. He panicked. He felt compelled to knock, to hear the sound of his knock, to feel his knuckles sting each time they came in contact with the door. Oddly, he heard the sound and the rhythm of his knocking, and it sounded exactly like the knocks that had awakened him. He continued to knock enthusiastically, frantically, urgently, desperately; even though he knew there would be no one there on the other side of the door to let him in.

FOUR

When Mona LaBaron was seventeen she was given a full scholarship to Vassar, which was within walking distance from her finely appointed two-story home in Poughkeepsie, New York. Her mother was the professor of Pedagogy at Vassar. There may have been strings pulled concerning Mona's higher education. Mona decided to study drama, but she quit Vassar altogether after her first semester because, *"I simply do not have a penchant for the absurdity of Greek tragedy, nor the forbearance for spoiled, churlish girls."* She might very well have been born into a life of pretense. Mona LaBaron was on, and dangling from, the brink of fifty.

Mona was dramatically beautiful, she had aged well, not only naturally so, but by a meticulously orchestrated overture to herself. She was always seen carefully made-up to appear haute and sever. Her hair, an elegant shade of red, had at their roots shades drab brown mixed with dull gray. Her demeanor was generally aloof. She could have been admired, perhaps celebrated had her charm been less troubling. It was difficult to impossible to see behind her well-fortressed lamination, created by voguish design, perhaps to protect her from herself, which begs the question, *"Why?"* It never occurred to her to ask herself. The question itself was unimaginable, unfathomable, and far too difficult. Mona possessed the bullying certitude and the belligerent aggressiveness of an untrained canine. But, surely she had, at her core, a heart of gold. *Not a chance!* As an actress, Mona had a cursory encounter with greatness. She gave the impression of facing the world with *joie de vivre* and unbridled abandon, but it was all a carefully studied parody; and easily seen through—except by herself. Every movement down to her fingertips was carefully thought-out, rehearsed and irritatingly performed. Mona LaBaron had the arresting ability to mesmerize the unacquainted plebeian into seeing her as a compelling and likable human being. That is, until she doesn't get her way—*not even with the dead.*

"Is there anyone there?" Mona murmured in a ridiculous manner that grew in volume with each *"Is there anyone there?"*

"For Pete's sake, Mona. How long is this gonna take?"

"As long as it takes, Florence."

Florence scoffed, *"...past my bedtime."*

"Are there any spirits here? *Come out! Come out!* If you can hear me make yourself known. *Hello-o-o, hello-o-o? Oh,* for Pete's sake, we're not getting anywhere, are we? *Hello-o-o, hello-o-o,*" Mona pleaded. A pinch of doubt colored her thoughts as she began to regret making *"all that effort!"* and spending *"all that money!"* on a party for a group of ungrateful people she hardly knew; people she herded to the island to become fodder for Charon to feed the gnarled pines. They were not her friends, not really, and she certainly was not theirs. They were simply *"theatre people"* with whom she worked from time to time. They're *"all right,"* she supposed with malign indifference, but they were not in any sense of the word, *"friends."* The truth is she wanted a party to show off her very own extorted island—before her quests were murdered—and all she needed were partiers; so, for a price, she got some; analogous to hiring professional mourners to the funeral of a friendless corpse. Unfortunately, the *"theatre people"* were yet to know the demonic reason for why they were gathered.

Mona did not have any real friends other than Florence; although, even Florence was running low on tolerance and had begun to rebel, *"Ingratiating, artificial, and she'll never grow up. Oh, and treacherous!"* Mona simply did not know how to be a friend to anyone; she never cared enough for others; never took an interest in others; never took the time to listen to others; and she never understood, or perhaps she never heard of the word, "empathy." Florence had an epiphany months before her invitation to the island that had brought her to realize Mona was all and only about Mona; not much of an epiphany since it was old news and everybody already knew it. *"There's no relying on Mona. Friends should be reliable. They should be people you count on to be there for support."* However, Florence had taken a blind eye to what was plainly incontrovertible: she might as well have had a department store dummy for a friend; Mona LaBaron was no longer worth the bother. *"All the world may be a stage, but it's not all Mona LaBaron's!"*

Mona thought,*"What the hell! I wanted to give them something...a little party...make them happy before they're all dead...Charon will see to that. They'll wish they had been nice to me...Philistines! To Hell with them... I shall have the last laugh!"*

There was knocking on the lodge door.

"I feel your presence. Is that you knocking?" Mona asked.

"Who's that?"

"A spirit, Reggie. I don't don't know who. Just a spirit, Reggie, so keep quiet."

"It's just the door, Mona," Reggie smirked.

"Shouldn't someone answer it?" Florence asked of no one in particular.

"NO!" Mona shouted. *"Quiet! Don't break the circle."*

"It's not a circle," Florence whispered.

"Florence...."

"It's a rectangle."

"Florence!"

The knocking stopped and Mona closed her eyes before opening them again with wide-eyed bewilderment; and spoke in a masculine voice, *"Who are you people? I'm supposed to be alone on this island."*

"Who are you?" Annabelle asked.

"My name is Adam Goodblood, and how did all you people get here? I leased this island and you're not supposed to be here." Mona turned and looked about the room, allowing Adam to see from out her eyes that everything appeared new, although a bit out of kilter, a bit out of place. There was a chandelier above the dinning room table that hadn't been there before, the leather on the furniture was new and soft, the rugs were no longer faded and stained. The scent of mold was replaced by conflicting perfumes on the ladies and Ídolo. Mona loudly exclaimed, *"Oh, my God! I'm Mona LaBaron!"*

"You're certainly not up on your spirit voice, are you, Mona?"

"It's not me, Florence. *Honest.*"

"Then who is it, Mona?" Reggie didn't hide his hostility. "You're not funny, Mona, not even amusing."

"Neither are you most of the time—especially onstage." Mona blurted out in her own angry voice.

"For the love of God, Mona," Florence shamed.

Suddenly, Mona's body sat at attention and she once again spoke in her spirit voice, *"I'm here to write a book about all of you and what is about to…something is about to…I don't remember."* Mona turned so Adam could take in the faces of those sitting around the table, then Adam said, *"Wait! I know who all of you are. I mean, I know what I've read about you. Oh my God! This is the nineteen twenty-nine Fourth of July seance, isn't it? Holy shit! This is tremendous."*

"What in hell are you talking about, Mona?" Willy unkindly asked.

"How did I get here?" Adam asked. *"I live nearly a century in the future. How am I here? Maybe I'm here to warn you…I wish I knew what. The Agency promised me thrills, but this is something else altogether. I really think I should warn you."*

"Warn us about what?" Ídolo was keen to know.

"I don't remember, Ídolo." Once again Adam looked into the faces of everyone around the table. *"I know who all of you are."*

"This is fun," Hudson said, sincerely enjoying the "show."

"You're all going to…what?…every time I think of it, I forget it before I have the chance to say it. It's on the tip of my tongue and it stays there. Maybe for the best. I don't want to suffer the consequences of a chancy choice. I mean, I don't want to take any unnecessary chances by meddling with the future of the past. I mean, I don't want to mess with the future present…that's what I mean. I suppose the bottom line is I don't want to be responsible."

Florence piped up, "I hope you're happy, Mona. This isn't a seance!"

"It's your pathetic attempt to draw attention to yourself by trying to pull us into your warped world of fantasy," Reggie got down to the grist.

"What else is new?" Willy yawned.

"I don't know what's happening," Adam sighed. *"Something happens…during the nineteen twenty-nine seance…or maybe because of the seance. Jesus Aitch…I can't remember."*

"I don't know what's happening either!" Willy barked. "If you're not Mona, then you should know that this is a seance to raise the dead. Are you dead or lifeless in any way, Mister... um...?"

"Goodblood. My name is Goodblood."

"Are you dead, Mister Goodblood?"

"I hope not. But I am from the future...nearly a century from now. In this time, your time, I haven't been born yet. I don't know where I was before that...before I was born, I mean. Well, there is a time I was here, wasn't there? Was I not?"

Willy thought a bit, shrugged, then said, "You seem confused."

"I am."

"You are *supposed* to be dead."

"Well, I don't believe I am."

"It would be better if you were," Willy advised. "This is a seance...a seance is to *raise* the dead...not...not to conjure people from the future, Mister Goodblood."

"So what happens?" Reggie asked. "Try not to think about it, Mister Goodblood, and maybe you'll remember."

"Um...I think it has something to do with demon spirits...."

"Hey, Reggie. You should know a little something about demonic spirits," Annabelle jested.

"I should be insulted, my dear," Reggie giggled and Annabelle followed suit. "I don't drink to raise spirits... I drink spirits...something like that...who the hell knows? I say stupid things and fall. How funny is that? It's not funny when somebody stumbles and falls. It isn't my nature...nope...I'm a blind drunk... maybe I should have stayed in vaudeville. It suited me." Reggie said sweetly through a great big rubbery smile, "I loathe you, Mona LaBaron."

"I think I may be dreaming—"

Mona slowly inhaled deeply, then exhaled explosively. With a double dose of sarcasm, she announced. "It's over! My seance is over! You needn't thank me. *Ingrates!*"

All of a sudden, Willy shouted in a very different but a quite familiar voice, *"But I am dead, and alive, Miss LaBaron!"*

"You can't be dead and alive. Who the hell are you?" However, Mona was certain she knew that voice; it was unmistakable. She trembled.

"You know perfectly well who I am, Mona. You robbed me of everything. Everything I had in the world. You might as well have murdered me. I saved you the effort...I did it myself. Now, I am here and I am going to make what's left of your useless life, miserable! Miserable, Mona, miserable!"

Everyone at the table knew whose voice it was. It was Arthur Baumgarten, their benefactor. They all had their eyes fixed on Willy. They were frozen to their chairs. Not an animated body in the bunch.

"Does everyone here know why you are all unemployed? Huh? Mona, why don't you tell the good people at this table why they are out of work? You might also tell everyone why there won't be anymore Arthur Baumgarten productions. You've destroyed many careers, Mona. And now I'm dead. Well, I'm not actually dead. I could be right outside this lodge, for all you know...talking through my dear friend Willy."

"Bullshit."

"Are you happy, Mona? No, of course not. Nothing makes her happy, folks."

"*Stop it!*" Mona shrieked. "You are *not* Arthur! *Not Arthur.* You're Wilson Woodhouse the rapist and an amateur director at best!"

"*Jesus Christ, Mona,*" Annabelle said with disgust.

"You've gone too far," Reggie added.

Willy stood, pointed his finger at Mona and, while staring through meanly squinted eyes, slowly and deliberately said, *"I am coming for you, Mona LaBaron."*

"You're not coming for me," Mona replied.

"I am a spirit of the living dead, waiting to watch you punished...and when you are, I will be here to watch as you melt into insignificance. I will be here in the flesh to savor every moment...watching you as you melt into nothing more than a rotting soul, endlessly suffering, trapped within one of the gnarled pines, tortured by the most evil demons the world will ever know. You will want to scream in pain, but you'll have no voice. I will be here when you will wish you were dead, but the irony of it is you already are. You are a petty demon, and you never could act, Toots."

"Bullshit."

"Is that all you have to say for yourself, Mona?"

"I'll have you know, Arthur, Willy, whomever you are, I played Lady Macbeth and Medea to packed houses."

"*Type casting.*"

Mona stood and yelled, "Stop it! Stop it right now!"

"*Jesus Christ! It was a goddamned bread knife, Mona!*"

* * *

It was the knocking on the lodge door that awakened Adam from a deep sleep. The knocking stopped, but just as Adam was about chalk it up to a dream, turn over and go back to sleep, there was another knocking on the door, louder than the first. Adam rolled over on the sofa, stood and staggered towards the door, opened it and there stood Charon with a block of ice wrapped in burlap, hanging from a huge pair of ice block tongs in one hand, holding it up as though it weighed absolutely nothing. *"No man should be able to do that,"* Adam said to himself.

"Who are you?" Adam asked.

"Here to help."

"You do know you're on my property, don't you?"

"Indeed, I do, Mister Goodblood…for the next twenty-six days. I live in the lighthouse, always have. I illuminate the beacon every night to warn the sailors. I shut it down every morning. Did the Agency not tell you? The lighthouse doesn't keep itself."

"No, they assured me I would be alone on the island."

"I'm in the fine print, no doubt. I should have been here sooner. I had other matters needing my attention. I am also the handyman. Anything you need…*or want*…just ask. I am all yours, Mister Goodblood." Indicating the dripping block of ice, "May I bring this in? It should go in the icebox right away."

"Yes, of course. Thank you." Adam opened the door wider to accommodate Charon and the block of ice. "I should have thought of that…you know, about somebody needed to keep the lighthouse."

"Yes, you should have thought of that, Mister Goodblood," Charon said as he stomped across the aging pinewood, taking long, loud and decisive steps into the kitchen where he slipped the block of ice into the icebox and returned holding the scrap of burlap and the dripping ice tongs. "I know what you're thinking, Mister Goodblood. You're thinking you don't want me around. I understand. Okay, I will stay out of your way. You will not know

I'm here…if that is what you want. Like I said, I know what you're thinking, Mister Goodblood."

"What did you say your name was?" Adam quizzed.

"Is."

"Excuse me?"

"My name…it always was and it still *is*…Charon."

"You sound like a writer or, God forbid, a grammar nazi…bad word…nazi…I shouldn't have said it."

"But you did."

"I did. Sorry. Truly sorry."

"I'm just playing with you, Mister Goodblood."

"You don't appear to be playing with me. Sorry again. I'll be sure to remember your name, Mister Charon."

"*Charon.* Just Charon."

"Yes, of course, Charon just Charon. I had a sleepless night, Charon, so please forgive me if I'm not on my toes yet. I'm a slow thinker."

"I won't hold that against you, Mister Goodblood."

"Good to know. I'm thinking you look familiar. We've met before, haven't we, Charon?"

"I cannot say, Mister Goodblood," Charon thought a moment. "Anything to fix? Anything I can do for you?"

"No. Nothing. Thank you. Not a thing…except…you said that you live in the lighthouse."

"If you want me, Mister Goodblood, that is the place to go."

"I was up by the lighthouse the other day…."

"I know." While opening to the door, Charon said, "Just knock anytime you want something…*anything*. I'm here for you.

All you need to do is knock...next time." Charon went out, leaving Adam to close the door.

Adam stood nonplused, pinched his arm, *"ouch!"* and he felt certain this was not a dream.

* * *

No one went to their cabins, nor did anyone sleep that night. They all stayed in the lodge awake and in disbelief. Contempt for Mona was in the eyes of everyone. Tempers were quick to trigger.

Hudson leaned into Mona and asked, "Was that from a play?"

"Was what from a play?"

"The seance scene...was that from a play? It was terrific... scary...but terrific."

"My dearest Hudson, you are here for my pleasure, and while you are here, you are to be seen and not heard. *Shh.*"

"But...." Hudson whimpered.

"Shh!"

"I believe our ride back to civilization isn't coming until Monday, right?"

"That is what I told you, Annabelle."

"This was supposed to be fun...a vacation away from the city. Some vacation! Mona, I think you got us up here under false pretenses. You have done nothing but bully and humiliate us. *Why?* I don't know. What have you really brought us up here for, Mona? Certainly not for our pleasure. None of us are happy about how you are treating all of us."

"If you're not happy, Annabelle, you could swim to the mainland. That goes for every one of you."

"Go to Hell." Annabelle had nothing more to say.

"The typical response of a child," Mona scoffed. She then turned to Willy and said gleefully, "Willy, Willy, Willy. How brilliantly you performed those characters, especially Arthur," Mona gleefully condescended. "And that Goodblood fellow…what genius, Willy. What depth of character. You pulled them right out of a hat. Darling Willy, your acting forces me to say that you must give up directing immediately, and act, darling, act your little heart out. If only the critics were here to see that performance. They'd rave, Sweetie…they really would have raved. You were a living breathing *tour de force. Bravo you.*"

"Are you finished? We both know I wasn't acting."

"Don't be modest, Willy."

"Ya know, I could really kill you."

"Of course you think that, Willy. Anybody could kill most anybody, but they don't. Words, words, words. How silly you are, Willy.

"Mona?" Florence asked.

"What?"

"You haven't a sincere bone in your body. Can't you go one minute without acting like a spoiled two year old?"

Charon entered from the kitchen before Mona had a chance to conjure a riposte to Florence. The room went silent. Charon was wearing a black apron, carrying a silver tray with a carafe of coffee and one of tea which he placed on the dining table, removed the empty carafes, put them on the tray, turned to Mona and whispered, "Miss Mona, Mister King has left the island."

"Really?"

Charon continued to engage Mona's ear for a minute or so until she could be heard to say, "Thank you for taking care of it, Charon."

"Anything, Miss Mona. Anything for the host." Charon stood straight and marched back into the kitchen without making eye contact with anyone in the room.

Charon and Mona had been acquainted for several years. She and Arthur came to the island every chance they had to escape Manhattan's torturous and humid summer heat. They could always count on Charon being there to greet and to serve them. He anticipated their every need; as a good servant should.

Hudson broke the silence. "*Jeepers*...that man is creepy."

"Seen and not heard, Hudson...or you'll find yourself walking the streets...*again.*"

Hudson crossed his arms, cowered like a child, shrunk into his leather chair and pouted. *"Sorry."*

Mona made an announcement, "Listen up, dear ones. Our Charon tells us that King Butcher has left the island."

"What!?"

"About an hour ago."

"What are you talking about, Mona?"

"If he can get off the island, so can we."

"How...?"

"How did he do it?"

"What in hell is going on here?"

"You better be able to explain that one, Mona."

"*Listen!* Charon informed me that the weekly supply boat made a delivery and King...or whatever his or her name is...rode back to the mainland on it."

"You're despicable, Mona."

"That liberal bent of yours will be your undoing, Annabelle."

"Why didn't you know about that supply boat. After coming up here every summer with Arthur, you must have known about it."

"I must have forgotten, Annabelle."

"You're something else, Mona...*you really are.*"

"Well thank you, Sweetie." Mona was knee deep in sarcasm.

"See what you did, Mona, with your sick performance? He's on his way back to the city and we're stuck here on this God forsaken island."

"We might as well make the best of it, Ídolo. And you might show a bit of gratitude," Mona sneered. "Not to mention, *respect.*"

"Respect? What have you done to deserve respect, Mona... degrade and humiliate us?" Ídolo sneered at Mona and angrily asked, "So now what? What are we supposed to do for the duration?"

"You could put on a record and dance for us."

Ídolo took a deep breath, slowly exhaled, squinted with malice and said, "You could put a lid on it, LaBaron. You really are one heartless bitch!"

"And everybody knows exactly what you are, Mister Ídolo. So much for gratitude. You're a joke...*Missy.*" Mona accused.

"I warn you, Mona, don't push me!" Ídolo rose and headed for the door.

"Don't go, Ídolo. Stay, please." Annabelle was sympathetic.

"I need to take a walk, Annabelle. If I don't get out of here I'll kill that bitch." Ídolo stormed out, slamming the door behind him.

Mona screamed at the door, *"Nancy boy!"*

Ídolo re-entered and bolted towards Mona. "I'm going to strangle you, you worthless piece of shit!"

Florence managed to get in his way, grabbed him, held him, and said, "She's not worth it, Ídolo. You're a better man than that."

"*Man, huh?*" Mona flared.

Tightly holding Ídolo, Florence warned, "I'm going to come over there and knock the living daylights out of you myself!"

"Try it, sister."

Reggie recognized a dire need to change the subject. "Hey Mona, enough Scotch 'til Monday?"

"Cases, Reggie."

"Then the party's just begun!"

"It's too early."

"Not for this crowd. Certainly not for you…for what ails you," Reggie told Willy.

"You're right, Reggie…you're absolutely right. Bring on the bottle, MacDuff," Willy said. "It's the balm of Gilead."

"I need a drink and I'm not a drinker!" exclaimed Florence. "Mona ails me, too. In fact, she makes me sick! I'll join you two gentlemen if you don't mind."

"Why should we mind?" asked Reggie. "Its Arthur's hooch."

Mona didn't move. She was busy calculating what her next move would be, what she would do to make them sorry—every single one of them. Except, of course, her precious Hudson who had left her side and went to the couch and began making lines of cocaine on the blue mirrored table.

"Any takers?" Hudson asked as he was about to sniff up a line.

"It would be my pleasure to join you, Hudson."

"Well, why not?" Annabelle went over to the couch and sat next Hudson. Mona watched with a malevolent intensity.

"Here's to Arthur!"

"And Mister Joseph Kennedy!"

"And Herbert Hoover!"

"What about that Goodblood guy?"

"Here's to him, too!"

* * *

Charon removed the body and the belongings of King Butcher, washed the cabin floor free of blood, then set out for the lighthouse along a trail of jagged rock, through the forest of gnarled pines that Charon will tell you he has, *"heard them whisper…they tell me things…wonderful things…terrible things."* The energy emitting from the trees sterilized the island of any trace of animated organic life, *sans* Charon and potential food. For Charon, the energy that radiated from the slithering pines was the fuel of his existence—a precious gift from the demons for his being their caretaker. Soon, after nearly a century, waiting within the gnarled pines were the demons who have gained unimaginable powers while they waited to be born. The demons in the gnarled pines had no form of their own; they simply were nasty spirits—call them evil demons if you like—the difference is perspective. In either case, they are the embryos of evil spirits who are born fully adult. These spirits have the wherewithal to initiate a multi-cultural change into their own image—malignant cruelty. These spirits have the power to enter any human and take control of their thinking and of their actions. For the time being, the island is filled with live food, *"Theatre people!"* for Charon to prepare.

The lighthouse was little more than twenty minutes from King's cabin. Charon trudged the rocky trail dragging King's body by one ankle, toes down, face-down, causing the body to bounce from jagged rock to jagged rock, breaking teeth, ripping out the gullet—already partially severed by King himself—and cracking the skull leaving little shards of bone helter skelter along the way. By the time Charon reached the lighthouse King's face was unrecognizable; one eye had popped out and was left somewhere along the trail, the nose was down to pieces of cartilage and what was left of his face was raw, mangled, unrecognizable meat, the forehead of the skull was missing, exposing a bloody battered brain.

After reaching the lighthouse, Charon pulled King's body inside. The brick and plaster walls were painted dull gray, badly applied over Army green with visible angry brushstrokes. The staircase that led to the beacon was covered with rust that ate away at the same unpleasant drabness of gray and Army green and and it was smeared with dried blood and feces from the floor to the beacon. In front of the staircase was a trapdoor Charon never bothered disguising to hide its existence; he knew that no one would dare set foot inside his lighthouse. Under the trapdoor there were steep stone steps that led down into the cave where Charon dumped the body of King Butcher and grimaced with enjoyment as it landed on the damp stone floor of the cave. The floor was covered with a thick viscous sludge left by hundreds of dead bodies on their ill-fated journey to the bottom. Bodies were then moved to mulching beds, where Charon monitors the flesh as it decays into the perfect consistency to shovel into buckets for spreading its putrefaction around the trunks of the pines as foodstuff for the demon spirits within. The ambrosia was absorbed into the roots of the pines within an hour.

The cave's passage led onward and downward to where it opened out to the sea and where Charon kept the boat in which he sets sail, under the cover of night, to the mainland at least once a month—often more—to bring dead bodies back to the island to feed the demons. Although, his victims were not always dead on arrival, they were dead by the time Charon was finished dragging them through the cavern by their feet while their heads bounced upon each and every bloody stone; so that by the time they reached the dungeon their heads had been turned to pulp. Once there, the bodies needed to be disemboweled and the entrails spread out atop several makeshift tables to speed up the ripening process.

The night before Mona and her guests arrived on the island, Charon sailed to the mainland and brought back a three-hundred and eighty pound man he found stumbling out of Ye Olde Mariner's Tavern; a rendezvous for tourists, pimps, prostitutes and johns. After the man was bludgeoned, rolled down the embankment and onto the boat, he regained consciousness and refused to cooperate—he just would not die. The fat man kicked and screamed during the entire trip, nearly capsizing the boat. Charon was more than powerful enough to pull the body up into the mulching bed, but there were sections of the passageway that would not accommodate the corpulent body. Charon had to divide it into manageable sections; he sliced off a portion of the belly, removed the arms, the legs, then finally the head, before the unwilling man stopped writhing and screaming. King would be prepared to be the next ration for the pines. After Charon dumped King Butcher's body, he hurried back to the lodge to report to Mona: *"...For you, Miss Mona, it is never too much...and Mister King has left the island...."*

* * *

After Charon brought the block of ice, Adam tried working on his novel, but meeting Charon was such a disturbing experience he could think of nothing to write, his mind had gone blank. The face of Charon was stuck in his head; those fearsome steely eyes, penetrating and chilling; his unnatural aura, wretched and portentous; there was no forgetting such an unsettling presence. Adam felt certain that he had encountered Charon before; somewhere else. But where? *"Think Adam…think…where?"* Adam went back to an earlier chapter in his book—the dream he had of the seance. *"Yes!…there it is…I remember!…that's him…that's Charon…the same Charon…how could I forget an unholy thing like that?…something made in Hell…steer clear. How could it be that he was here and now, while yet being there and then? Impossible!"* Adam reread the seance chapter in *Gnarled Pines* only to discover that he had no memory of having written it, other than a few notes to himself to expand upon later. His heart throbbed in his throat, choking him, and he gasped for breath. *"Jesus Aitch! Who wrote this?…not me…I was at the seance…I saw it…I haven't written about it…these are not my words…how did I write three chapters in one day…absolutely impossible. I only made notes!"* Adam felt sure that someone else had written it, a stranger, his subconscious, or maybe he was possessed by one of the infamous spirits inhabiting Gnarled Pines. *"It doesn't even sound like me. I don't write like that. It's stiff and unnatural. Not me. Not me at all."*

Adam sat spellbound facing the computer; he could not get the noxious image of Charon out his head however hard he tried to change the subject within. *"One of the island spirits wrote it. That must be it. How many island spirits are there other than the theatre spirits? There are demon spirits that gestate in the pines, Adam…*

they're waiting to be born...how do I know this?...from a half-remembered dream...that must be it...The Agency's brochure...I should have read it more carefully...who, or what in hell was The Agency?...and how did The Agency find me? Their ad popped up on my computer...from nowhere...it read, 'come and visit the dark spirits that bred Vlad the Impaler, Charles Manson, and evil-doing tyrants and dictators the world over. Why did I sign that contract? Maybe it wasn't me...was it? Jesus Aitch!...I'm going crazy. The Agency did warn me about that...going crazy...and a heart attack...don't forget the heart attack...for God's sake...it had to be me...who else could have written it?...there are island spirits...yes, I can feel them...the spirits of Mona's dead guests...they're trying to communicate." Adam was five days on the island with only two days of actual work and already he had completed much more of the book than he anticipated, more of the book than he felt possible. "How is this possible?...it's not!...it wasn't me...I was drugged...by what?...the malodorous stench from the lighthouse... yes!...that's gotta be it...the gas that escaped from the lighthouse was a hallucinogenic. Yes! That's it...certainly not by Ding Dongs and instant coffee." Adam reread the brochure. "Okay...okay... thrills, hauntings, things that go bump in the night...it was right there in the brochure...and there was Charon the keeper of the lighthouse. How did I miss that? The Agency spelled it all out... and I signed that goddamn release...'THE AGENCY IS NOT RESPONSIBLE FOR HEART ATTACKS OR INSANITY'... specific..in an extra large font...beyond hyperbole...it was all part of the experience...the experience itself...it had to be...but now there were many remaining questions: Where is The Agency? What is The Agency? Did I choose to come here? Or did The Agency choose me? Everything was done online...there was no hand to *shake...no individual to deal with. Who has been writing Gnarled Pines? Charon said something about a muse...a spirit who would write...or did he say that...or did I just hear that...in my head? Here I go...gone crazy."* Adam closed the computer, pushed himself from the table, stood, stretched, picked up his empty mug and went to the kitchen to make himself more instant coffee, but first, he grabbed the last package of Ding Dongs, *"Oh, crap!...I can't think...what?...oh, yes...boil water...how could I forget a thing like this?...what's happening to me?...need more Ding Dongs...the boat...should've tried it earlier...before now...now I have to drive the damned thing...why didn't I tell The Agency I only drove a motorboat once?...once!...piloted...drove...whatever the term is...I had an experienced man sitting right next to me so it doesn't count...I suppose...other than that...just a rowboat...a kid in Catholic summer camp...blisters on my hands...gotta get to the mainland...Ding Dongs...top of the list...oh, Christ!...I'm losing my mind. So why not?...for the love of...I'm obsessing...better ask Charon...he can take me over...no!...no!...for the love of all that is good...no, no, no!..that creature is not human...I couldn't be more certain of that...he makes my skin crawl...and that disgusting stench that came from out of the lighthouse...what was that stink!?...the scent of Hell?...I don't think I want to know...so... what are my choices?...I only see one...I'll drive the friggin' boat myself!"*

Adam put the MacBook into his backpack, stepped outside the lodge and walked down the steps to the dock. After he arrived, he tugged on the heavy rope that was tied to the dock cleat, then pulled with all the strength he could muster until the motorboat came out of the boathouse, following the dock line to Adam. He then stepped down into the boat, reached up and untied the line. Taped to the steering wheel was a manilla envelope containing step by step instructions for manning the boat, where to dock it on the mainland, the rules of the road, so to speak—and don't forget to tip the docking attendant. There was more, but he would read it later. Right now he had to concentrate on, *"How in hell do I get this damn thing started?"* He did note that it was signed, "The Agency." He put the instructions on the seat next to him and began to pilot the boat. *"How did they know I was lying...that I was only behind the wheel once before...slowly... slowly...look at me...I'm on the ocean."* In the heat of a July afternoon without a hint of a breeze under the fierce and blinding sun Adam sweated profusely; not so much from the heat, but from the mounting fear of the journey ahead—his first solo on the ocean and he had no idea what he was doing. The ocean hiccuped and an unexpected wave sloshed against the pier. Emboldened by having steered himself free of the pier, Adam took the boat farther out on the ocean, faster and faster, until he felt an adrenalin rush; the boat was driving itself and Captain Ahab was sailing upon the Atlantic. *"Now I gotcha!... you're not getting away from me...you're my bitch now...yup...I gotcha now, bitch!"* As Adam came closer to the mainland he began drowning in a sweat of anxiety. He picked up the instruction sheet, read the final instructions, then looked for the pier where he was supposed to dock, he spotted it and slowly steered in its direction. *"Cut the power! We're gonna slide in, matey...all hands on deck...there are no other hands, we're going to do this, kiddo."* Sweat rolled into his eyes, stinging them and for a moment he went blind. *"God help me! I'm going to crash. You're not going to crash...pull yourself together!"* He wiped the sweat from his eyes and saw the docking attendant waving at him. *"What does he want?...what's he doing?...is he waving at me?...yup...Jesus Aitch...gliding...slowing...wait for it...there...just a little bump... made it!...easy peasy. Thank you, sir...I hope I didn't scratch the pier...or the boat...it's not mine....wow...that was exhilarating!"* He jumped out and tied the boat to the pier.

Without acknowledging the existence of the pier attendant, Adam walked to the mainland-end of the pier, then up the six wooden steps over the embankment to Water Street. Turtle Run Cafe was directly across the street between Mariner's Mart and Captain Billy's Clams & Lobsters. *"Hmm, I don't remember Captain Billy's. Oh well."* Up and down Water Street were all the typical shops for tourists: souvenirs, rocks and minerals, arts and crafts, ships in bottles, taffy, fudge and giant lollypops, rainbow-colored ices, crystals and books for witches, wizards and warlocks, a dozen flavors of Mary Duggan's homemade ice cream, ocean shells, dried starfish, snow globes, books, postcards, homemade masks and more.

Adam crossed Water Street and sauntered into the cafe: funky with a nautical theme, fish netting with old corks hung unevenly overhead. Adam repaired to the far corner table beneath a dusty shaft of sunlight. He opened his MacBook and found he had hundreds of emails and there must have been many more attempts after the mailbox had reached its limit. Before reading them, or at least some of them, Adam checked his bank account and was stunned by how much money his agent had deposited into it. Then he Googled himself to see if there were any new reviews of *The Thing in the Crypt,* but the first thing he happened upon was a review of *Gnarled Pines. "What the!..."* and then he read a nice, but misunderstood, review of it. The review went on to say that *Gnarled Pines* was published after A. J. Goodblood had gone missing and was presumed dead. *"Jesus Aitch!...what the?...I'm crazy I tell ya, I'm crazy."* He saw by the date of the piece that it was written five years earlier. *"What!? Is this a joke?...what's happening here?...I haven't finished Gnarled Pines...I just started it for God's sake...this has to be a joke...of course it is...but it's in a legitimate newspaper...who wrote this thing?...Samantha Flores...who the hell is Samantha Flores?"* Adam noted that she was a staff writer for the "Denver Post," a newspaper Adam knew well. He found a phone number for the newspaper and called it. After listening to silence, without canned music for fifteen minutes, he was finally connected to Samantha Flores. "I'm not dead! I'm not missing! What is this about, Ms. Flores?"

"Excuse me. Who is this?"

"A. J. Goodblood, the writer. The one you said was dead! I'm in Maine. A place called Turtle Run, which might be dead, but I'm not. I've been here five days and you write that I'm missing and presumed dead! What the fuck is this!?"

"Sir, there is no need for that kind of language."

"I'm sure you've heard it before. I want to know what is going on. I'm not dead and I have only been gone for five days. *Five days, Ms. Flores.*"

"Sir, please calm down. Can you prove you're A. J. Goodblood. *The* A. J. Goodblood, the author of *Gnarled Pines.*"

"What is going on here? I don't understand why you don't believe me."

"Calm down, sir. Just convince me that you are who you say you are, and then we'll talk."

"I don't know how to do that, Ms. Flores. How can I do that? I'm Adam John Goodblood. I'm in Maine, staying on an island called Gnarled Pines. I'm writing a book titled *Gnarled Pines* about the island, which is turning out to be a wretched place, but I am not dead!"

"Stop right there! I read *Gnarled Pines* four or five years ago. I gave it a nice review, by the way. I'm going to hang up now, sir."

"*No! Please.* Wait. Do you have Skype…or FaceTime?…or something like that? You can see who I am. We can talk. Please. *Please.* Did you say *'nice?'*"

"Okay. I don't suffer prank calls easily. So show me, or I'm gone."

And he showed Samantha Flores, an attractive woman who appeared to be in her mid-thirties. Adam was always totally inept when it came to guessing anybody's age—especially a woman's. The woman on his computer screen appeared to be wearing little or no make-up. She was a natural beauty, dark skin, sensuous; or, at least, that was how she appeared on the computer's screen.

"*She doesn't believe me! Those lips…oh, God…I want to feel those lips on mine…damn!…Angelina Jolie lips…straight black hair…shoulder length…wide brown eyes…Jesus Aitch! Nice? Just 'nice?' She said 'nice.'*"After nearly a half hour on FaceTime, Samantha Flores said, "I'll be there tomorrow. I can catch a flight out of DIA in the morning and rent a car. I'll call you when I get there."

"You can't call me. There's no phone service on the island. It's a dead zone. Besides, you can't come because it's dangerous and…and you'll step outside of mainland time."

"You're a funny man. Of course, I don't believe you."

"You should. I only came here five days ago and your review of *Gnarled Pines* was written five years ago."

"Well, I'm coming anyway. I want to meet you. I want to interview you in person. Your death has created quite a stir. An interview with the dead novelist, *blah, blah, blah*."

"Blah, blah, blah yourself. I'm not dead. Goddamnit! I'm not dead. You are not invited. Stay in Denver."

"I'll take the risk, Mister Goodblood."

"If you are hellbent on coming, then come at your own risk. I would pick you up in the motorboat that came with the island, but how would I know what time to meet you…besides, I don't really know how to properly drive it yet. I've only driven it once. Don't come. You might find it life-threatening. I don't want guests! There is something wrong with the island. There are dark spirits that will get in your head and write your book…I mean, my book. There's something really wrong here. I'm not sure of myself anymore. You will wish you never came. You will find yourself in mortal danger. And I am going Looney Tunes."

"I shouldn't like that."

"Mortal danger, or Looney Tunes?"

"Both, but I'm coming anyway."

"Okay. Have it your way. Come at your own risk. I'll be here drooling by the time you get here."

"I don't think so."

"There's a water taxi service. Take that to Gnarled Pines. I'll be waiting for you in the lodge. You won't miss it. You can see it before the boat reaches the pier. Take the steps on up to the top of the island. Be careful, they're wobbly and dangerous. They're not stable. In fact, they're not stable at all; nor am I. You'll see. By the way, I did read your review, but you may have missed the point of the book. In any case, nicely put."

"Okay…we'll discuss that when I get there." End of transmission.

"What a beautiful woman!…to hell with the emails…I don't care…Jesus Aitch!…my agent!" Adam went into his email account, clicked "compose" and began writing to his literary agent. *"Dear Mari, I don't know what's happening, but I can tell you that I am neither dead nor missing. I am in Maine staying on a godforsaken island called Gnarled Pines. I should have told you before coming here. It didn't seem important at the time, but if I had, you could have sent a search party. It's a scary real place, Mari. Gnarled Pines is not just a regular island. Well, I'm sure you read all about it by now. I'm told the book is doing, or rather has done well, very well. I know this doesn't make any sense to you because it doesn't make much sense to me, but I'm still writing the novel whether it is already written and published or not. It'll be awhile before it's finished on my end. I'm not crazy. Trust me. I will explain everything when I get to New York. Sorry about missing the tours. It seems the world goes on without me. Ah, there's a lesson learned. It just goes round and round. Try not to be too confused or angry with me. Best, A.J. P.S. Every day I am on this island a year passes where you are. I don't think I've aged any. That's a plus."* Adam stuffed the computer into his backpack and headed for Mariner's Mart.

After piling boxes of Ding Dongs on the counter he gathered more food items to take back to the island. BUT, his credit card had expired. "What year is this?"

"What year?"

"Doesn't matter. Forget it." Adam recognized Captain Ahab behind the counter. He had grown older. A two or three day red stubble. Tired eyes. The corners of his lips were beginning to turn downward. His finger nails were bitten back into the skin. He wore a silver wedding band. He appeared sad and distant, and on a closer look, very much older. *"I should never have painted that imaginary picture of Captain Ahab's home life, in the first place. Did I make that happen? I used to make things happen. Maybe I still can. It's been awhile."* Adam looked down at the pile of Ding Dongs on the countertop and thought about how much he was going to enjoy eating them. "Didn't you used to captain a water taxi?" Adam asked through a friendly-enough smile; the kind of smile that, after running into an old friend, you suddenly see a complete stranger and disappointing memories, and you want to get away—that kind of smile.

"*Yessiree*…until some big company outta Portland put us outta business. You call, they come, you pay right outta your bank account. Sorta like those Uber people."

It was natural for Adam to be empathetic, even with strangers. He recognized a sad young man's wanderlust and said, "That's too bad."

"Is it?" Captain Ahab asked.

"Well, you were put out of business. Isn't that a bad thing for you?"

"*Ahh*, me. Maybe so, but I make more money here. Progress, ya know. Waddaya gonna do about it? I read your *Gnarled Pines* book."

"Did you now?…I hope it didn't disappoint."

"Hell, no! It scared the bejesus outta me. It was a little gory in places, but I liked it."

"That's a good thing. That's what it's supposed to do—scare the 'bejesus' out of you. That's the thing, isn't it?"

"It sure is, Mister Goodblood."

"I'm amazed that you recognized me after five years. *Ah*, probably the photo of me on the dust cover. There was a photo of me on the back of the book, wasn't there?"

"I don't remember. I bought it in paperback. Couldn't afford the other. I recognized you 'cause you look the same and you're wearin' the same clothes."

"Oh, dear."

"No problem. That's sixty-seven ninety-five."

"The price of things have really gone up since I was here last, haven't they? Not that you had anything to do with it."

"New owners. Five years of progress. Things go up."

"Thank you."

"No problem."

Adam paid the man, gathered his purchases and headed back to the boat. The next thing Adam was conscious of was that he was in choppy waters on his way back to Gnarled Pines. *"Damnit! I forgot to tip the attendant. Maybe I should turn the boat around. Nope. It ain't gonna happen. I don't think I know how, anyway."*

As Adam approached Gnarled Pines he saw a figure standing on the pier waving, beckoning him—it was Charon. The closer Adam got to the pier the more difficult it was to breathe, his heart pounded until it felt like it would explode, a torrent of sweat poured from his forehead, and it was salty as the ocean.

GNARLED PINES

Edward Crosby Wells

FIVE

Adam was sitting on the steps of the lodge porch when he spotted Samantha Flores from the "Denver Post" hauling a white canvas shoulder bag that was bulging-full, forcing her to lean to one side from the weight of it. Adam wore a clean-ish T-shirt that he had worn only a few times since it's last laundering (there were no laundering facilities on the island, just the kitchen sink). His knee-length shorts may have been worn a few more times. He put on his happy face as he walked in his nearly worn-out flip-flops to greet the reporter mid-way.

"Well, now that you're here, I'm glad you came, Ms. Flores. Here, please, let me carry that." She lifted the bag from her shoulder and handed it to Adam who cheerfully took it. "Good God! What have you got in here? You carry this thing around? I'd have a heart attack before I made it a hundred feet."

"Then I'll carry it for you, if you'd like," she said through a lovely smile.

"I hyperbolate. Sorry, Ms. Flores. I'd probably make it more than a hundred feet."

"*Ouch!*"

"*What?*" Adam was concerned.

"*Sam.* Just plain ol' Sam. *Wait.* Not yet. Maybe we should know each other a little better before I'd appreciate you calling me that."

"What? *Sam?*"

"There you go, you went ahead and said it, didn't you? So, I guess we're familiar enough now. You'll just have to call me Sam from now on." Sam smiled, and almost inaudibly, she chuckled and extended her hand, "Glad to meet you in person—even if you are dead. You look very well for a corpse, I should add."

Adam laughed. He was beside himself. *"Wow. I love this woman! Her straight forwardness…her style…her sense of fun…her sense of humor…everything. And I only met her a minute ago. Sometimes people connect instantly. It's like a reunion, of sorts."* Adam hadn't picked-up on her charm during their computer conversation, nor could he have imagined the erotic sensation he would feel when meeting her in person, nor did he expect the heart-pounding shivers that shot throughout his body. *"Those lips! Can she see me shivering?"* Adam could not have imagined how difficult it would be to keep his knees from buckling just from the sight of her tall graceful body—he found amazingly arousing. Her black hair glistened under the brilliant yellow sun in the clear blue sky with not a cloud in sight. He did not anticipate the beauty of her mocha skin, which he imagined to be sublimely scented by Nature Herself, and he imagined it would feel silken to his touch. Adam trembled from the thought of holding her breasts while he placed his mouth upon each perfect nipple that hardened under his tongue, drooling at the thought of running his tongue over every inch of her perfect body, moving his hand upward between her thighs and feeling her warm, moist…. *"Oh, God! I hope she can't read my mind."*

"So, Samantha…*ah*, Sam, if you believe what I told you the other day, and I know you don't, but if you did you would know that while you're on Gnarled Pines, the rest of the world speeds on without you. Or maybe time is slowed to a crawl on this island, while the rest of the world just goes along as expected. You really shouldn't be here. You're taking a brave risk coming to Gnarled Pines."

"Risk? Let's call it a challenge." Sam smiled, showing her even white teeth.

"They should have put it in the lease. It would have been a deal-breaker."

"Who they and what?" She asked.

"The Agency that leased it to me; they should have let me know at the get-go about the time thing. I was faxed a contract to sign. I did and that was that. I had leased Gnarled Pines and I guess I didn't take the time to read the contract closely. But, I'm reasonably certain there was nothing in it about stepping out of time…letting time slip away without you. You know, I should have been suspicious then and there; five years of my life, and the clock keeps ticking. I haven't processed any o' this yet. Well, it hasn't actually been five years of *my* life, has it? It's five years of everybody else's life. I keep looking for a sensible, scientific explanation, but nope, I'm still looking and waiting; waiting to wake up and find this is all a dream."

"And you expect me to buy any of this?"

"No. Reporters believe in facts; but I believe it, because I know it, plain and simple. There is more to what we call time than we know. Time is not a fact anyway, I think it's an idea. I mean it happens. We measure it. But we created it."

"Please don't get all crazy on me."

"Sorry. I'll behave. You know, I never had contact with a real person from The Agency. I should have known better."

"Shouldn't we all? What is The Agency?"

"I don't know. Some sort of evil cabal, for all I know. A grown man and I make a bargain with an agency I know nothing about, other than what they wrote in their online brochure."

"You may be a tad bit gullible, you think?"

"Much more than a tad, I'll tell you that. There was a woman in our building…back in Brooklyn Heights when I was a kid…she used to say to me, 'Trust is your mitzvah, Addy.' I don't even know what that means. Missus Cohen was fond of telling me things like that; about myself…things I had no idea what she was talking about…she never said anything about the dangers of gullibility, and misplaced trust."

"She probably had a good reason for that."

"*Hmm,* probably. Can't think of one offhand."

"I feel obliged to repeat that I really don't believe a word of your story."

"Which story is that?"

"Your time out of time story. I'm not trying to insult you, you must know that, but I want to be clear about my inability to believe that."

"Understood. Clear as crystal."

"Okay. Settled. We'll mention nothing more about time. At least, for now. I'm just so honored to interview you in person, Mister Goodblood."

"I thought we moved beyond surnames."

"We have. Sorry, Adam. Or do you prefer A. J.?

"A. J. is strictly for the byline. It's Adam."

"So, Adam, I truly expect time to be as it ought to be by the time I return to Denver."

"I thought we weren't going to mention it anymore."

"Hmm…." Sam removed her sunglasses, scanned her environment. Her eyes were wide with surprise. Sam suddenly exclaimed, "What's with those trees!?"

Adam chuckled. "I haven't the foggiest. I can't decide if they're dead, dormant or what. They're why this place is called

Gnarled Pines. Of course, you know that. *Duh.* Sorry. I imagine them reaching out in the night and grabbing me for a midnight snack. I've never touched a branch. In fact, I don't go too close them—night or day."

"Maybe we should go out together tonight. There's safety in numbers. I even brought a powerful LED flashlight. I always take it camping."

"You camp?"

"Love to. There's no place to camp better than the Colorado Rocky Mountains. Love hiking, too."

"You're a woman after my own heart."

"Am I?"

"*Ah*...in a figure of speech."

"Of course."

Adam felt an urgency to change the subject. "*Yup*...maybe this island ought to have been called Mangled Pines."

"I can certainly see why."

"Please, come inside. There's no air conditioning, but the breeze is cool after dark. Although dark comes pretty late in summer, doesn't it? Don't answer. But when the breeze comes, it does a pretty good job of airing-out the lodge. I prepared the bedroom for you."

"*The* bedroom? I thought I might need to setup my tent."

"So, that's what you've got in that bag, a tent?"

"Yeah. Girl Scout. Always prepared."

"You were a Girl Scout?"

"Of course not. *Yuk.*"

"*Hmm*....There's only one bedroom in this huge lodge and it's all yours. There used to be guest cabins scattered throughout the woods, but they appear to have gone to ruin over the years...*like everything els*e. Besides, I rarely sleep in bedrooms, including my own, and I never slept in this one. It's true. I find bedrooms lonely and sad when I'm in unfamiliar territory. So, I sleep on the couch. Maybe it's a mental disorder, I've got so many, like an abandonment issue, or maybe an issue with my mother, although I'm pretty sure that's not it. Maybe an issue with my father. He was gay. I thought it exotic. Anyway, one doesn't feel so alone when sleeping on a couch, that's all. So many people sat on it before me. All that energy. All those atoms. Those piece of others left behind. There is something oddly comforting about that. Too much information? Strange, *huh?* Sorry. So, how long do you plan to stay. I mean, how long before you need to be back in Denver?"

"*Wow*. You're something else."

"What do you mean by that?"

"You love to talk. That's a good thing; unless one has nothing to say. There's no such thing as too much information. I must be back in Denver day after tomorrow. This trip's on the paper's tab. Beyond that I don't get paid. We can do the interview and take pictures tomorrow, if you don't mind."

"Of course. I don't mind at all."

"Then let's just take what's left of today and get to know each other."

"Sounds good to me."

"I really must know why you chose to come to such a bizarre place, Adam. I'm sure you could have written your book without actually coming here to do it."

"I'm not so sure. But it just seemed a fun thing to do…at the time."

"I know your work, Adam, and I really like that."

"Nice of you to say. Thank you."

"Your writing's a lot of fun. I love how you mix humor with the macabre. *The Thing in the Crypt* made me laugh and it scared the hell out of me, at the same time. I don't remember being scared with *Gnarled Pines,* but it got me thinking about things that scared me—I don't know, but I liked it. Maybe a genre of its own. I guess it kinda makes sense that you chose to come to a place like this, to absorb the atmosphere—like you absorb people on the couch. Still, being here feels a little daunting. But a month? I'd go bonkers. It's a great setting, if you like living in a Dali painting, but it's not a place where I'd want to be alone, or framed and hung on a wall. That's all."

"I understand that. Besides, I've already gone bonkers."

"Have you really? *What fun!*" Sam blurted.

"And let's change the subject, why don't we."

"*Yeah.* How do you see your role in writing?"

"I don't understand your question, Sam."

"What's your purpose? What do you want to accomplish?"

"Sam, I don't have a clue. I'm just an entertainer. I do a performance, like stand-up, and I pray for applause."

"*Ahh*...applause. Tell me...why on Earth didn't you stay on the mainland when you were there? If you really believed what you told me about the passage of time, why didn't you take the chance to get away then and there? I would have gone back to Denver in a heartbeat and never looked back."

"Damned if I know, Sam. I should've. I don't know... confounded, I guess. I only came back for some important things, thumb drives, a place to bring my Ding Dongs. I bought the store out and needed somewhere to store them...and then the interview with you, of course."

"Ding Dongs?"

"Small cream filled chocolate cakes dipped in yummy chocolate that hardens. They are made by the gods."

"I'll have to try one."

"They're like potato chips…you can't eat just one. Besides they're kind of small."

"I'll remember that before I get started." Sam's smile turned into a frown. "Adam, do you really believe we're out of time right now…at this moment?"

"I thought we changed the subject."

"I know, but it still bothers me."

"Okay, I do believe we're really out of time right now. In fact, I know we are. But, I have a conflicting theory that I need to reconcile: if time only exists as an idea, which I'm pretty sure it is, and if a single day on this island is one year on the mainland, then time isn't an idea, it's a fixed phenomenon. But that doesn't make sense to me. I mean, on this island."

"Amazing. You don't appear to be insane, but…."

"But I must be, *huh?*"

"Maybe, but I was going to say that you seem safe enough."

"Enough for what?"

"For not doing anything untoward."

"*Ah*, thank you. 'I hear the best asset of a serial killer is their ability to seem safe enough not to do anything untoward, Miss Flores.'"

"Now, you're scaring me."

"Sorry. That was a line from *The Scarecrow.*"

"Inspector Trudeau says it."

"*Holy cow!* That was my first novel, and you remember it. You're something else, lady."

"I work at it. And, Adam, just because it was your first novel doesn't mean I read it way back then. I may have been too young for you, back then."

"Back then…way back then? *Ouch!*"

"I didn't mean it quite the way it sounded. Let me make it up to you."

"I like the sound of that."

"I just happen to have a few lovely bottles of red wine and some stinky cheeses in that bag that appears to have already shortened you under its weight."

"Really? That's terrific. I mean, it's not really terrific. I mean, I'm already short enough. *Squat.* Some might say squat."

"I wouldn't."

"Good. So, what kind of wine is it, Sam?"

"I have no idea…don't know a thing about wine. All I know is that it's red, cheap, and the guy in Argonaut said it was good stuff. Dry, he said. I'm usually gullible—about *little things*—but what the hell, you only live once."

"So I've heard." There must have been an angel passing through since there was an unusual length of silence before Adam continued. "*Gullible* is a lot like trust, Sam."

After Sam took a bit of time to ponder the his assertion, she said, "Maybe. But maybe gullibility is a kind of ignorance, and trust is a kind of faith."

"Stop! My head is about to explode!" They both chuckled, but neither knew why. Adam liked this woman—"*attractive, funny, open-minded, honest, natural*"—and the list goes on.

They stood by the porch of the lodge when Sam looked back at the ocean and was awestruck, "*Oh my God!* This is breathless. Nice. *Really nice.*"

"You should see it after dark," said Adam, with more than a little anticipation in his voice.

"I plan to, Adam. The two of us. Just you and me…and a flashlight."

Adam was fully aroused by her, *"That was a bit forward, wasn't it. The two of us. Just you and me. The flashlight."* Adam thought he saw a wink, a wee bit of a wink, but definitely a wink, and a grin like the Cheshire cat. That could have been a "come-on" line. Yet it clearly wasn't. The flashlight was a downer. She certainly didn't strike him as a shy woman. *"'I plan to…the two of us. Just you and me.' But then there was that goddamned flashlight. Talk about mixed signals! Was it with carnal intent, or was it meant to be ambiguous, or was she just having fun with me? Was there something sly about the way she said it? Something plain out forward? Had there been an alternative meaning to it? A simple phrase in another situation would mean nothing more than what it said. Maybe that was it. But then there was that goddamned flashlight!"* Adam's libido went into overdrive. He hoped she hadn't seen the physical evidence of his excitement while in overdrive, and yet he hoped she had. Adam knew, because he could visualize it, that the night held something special, he could sense it, he would cause it by visualizing it, then creating it, and it would be thrilling—just like in the brochure. *Thrilling.*

"By the way," Sam said. "I couldn't find a water taxi. Apparently, they discontinued that service over a year ago. You could phone something like a Lyft boat, but I never got an answer when I called. Luckily, there was this guy I met in the coffee house who offered me a ride in his motorboat. He was a little iffy, but I took him up on his offer anyway."

"You got in a boat with an *icky* guy? A stranger? Why would you do that?"

"I said *iffy*, not *icky*."

"Oh my God…*iffy's* even worse than *icky*. In fact, it's a whole lot *ickier*."

"That's not a word."

"It's a word. Guarantee it. Google it." Adam chuckled.

"He told me he was the lighthouse keeper here on Gnarled Pines. He said he worked for you."

Adam's heart stopped. A bolt of lightning shocked him. "For me? No! He does not work for me. He may think he works for me, but he does not work for me."

"Okay. I get it. But why would he tell me that?"

"Beats me."

"Anyway, he seemed safe enough. Turned out he was benign—just *iffy*."

Adam's heart rose into his throat, the palpitations were suffocating, each breath became more difficult than the last, he had to think about his breathing, choose each breath deliberately, or, he felt, he would surely suffocate. The blood drained from his skin, leaving him pale and cold. He felt that he might faint. He fought it.

"Adam?" Sam was concerned. "Are you okay?"

"I will be." Then after taking a deep breath and slowly letting it out, Adam said, "I was thinking, if we left the island together we'd be out of time, but we'd have the same time in common. That would be something, wouldn't it?"

"Indeed it would." said Sam, "I think you have a point there. We'd each have the other to remind us we're not alone; that we share an unknowable event in common. *Nice.*"

"Not being alone with what you know and knowing there is only one other who would not scoff. *Yup,* nice indeed. It's a story only the two of us would believe. I suppose, the day would come when we'd blend in with the folks in our new time; we'd adjust to it, accept it, and our secret would no longer matter. No longer the need to share it. And, best of all, we'd appear much younger to the people we already know. Time must be flexible."

There was a silence when they caught each other's eye and stared for what seemed an eternity, but, like everything else, eternity ends.

"*Hmm.* Are you lonely, Adam?"

"Where did that come from?" Adam was stunned.

"I don't know…it's in the way you say things…you're cautious…cautious people are generally people who are not used to having others around."

"I don't know if that's astute or not, but it feels like it might be. I don't believe I'm cautious around people who make me comfortable enough to make me feel safe enough to be myself. Although, I think it's more thoughtful than cautious. In the end they're probably both interchangeable "

"See, that's a perfect example!"

"Anything else, Sam?" It was not a friendly question.

"*Well*…with all the books you've written, there really isn't much out there about you, other than what's on the dust covers. I did a fair amount of research and found zippo. Just the usual publicity crap; you were born in Brooklyn, had a normal childhood, never married, no arrest records, no love-interests either, I suppose, and *blah, blah, blah."*

"So you assume, Sam."

"I said suppose."

"*Suppose, assume, so what's* difference? That doesn't make me lonely. That makes me grateful. I simply want to write my books. One needs to be alone to write. It comes with the territory. I like writing. It's fun. It's what I chose because I have no choice. I'm in the company of myself and I like myself…pretty much. I'm also in the company of fictional characters who come alive for me; who come alive *in* me, then they are released, and free to go onto the page. My life is pretty much all about writing. That's who I am. If you want to know me, read me. When I am alone with it, with my writing, it is exciting. For me, it is transcending."

"Transcending what?"

"The day to day, I suppose. Not having to answer to somebody else, no boss."

"*Hmm.* So, transcendence is like having a life." Sam scoffed.

"You think I don't have a life?"

"*Oh*…I think you have a life…I tend to overstate things, sorry…but I do think you have a limited one."

"That's absurd. You cannot imagine the excitement of it. You came to interview me, not to give me your opinions of me. You don't even know me and you presume to…."

"*Wait, wait, wait,*" Sam begged. "I'm sorry. I tend to provoke. I'm a natural provocateur. I have a degree in provocateurology…is that a word?"

"It is now."

"I said it all wrong...*ly*. I meant that *all* writers must live *much* of their lives in solitary. Anyway, my degree is in journalism, so I guess provoking comes with the territory. And I certainly was presumptuous. Of course. I misspoke. The last thing I want to do, Adam, is to get into an argument with you. I respect you and I like your work. I think, since I've pretty much read all your books, I may have developed an unfounded familiarity with the author. I'm sincerely sorry and I apologize."

"*Wow.* I'm a sucker for sincerity...and with a lack of caution. Be as familiar as you like. And my narrator should't be confused with me. The narrator is also one of the characters. I think that's the fun of it." Adam gave a friendly smile. A warm smile. A smile that says, *"I like you. I really, really like you."*

"*Too funny.* You're an interesting man, Mister Goodblood from Brooklyn. But, be careful of the butterfly net."

"Thanks, but I don't think they use butterfly nets anymore. In fact, I don't think they ever did. Maybe they did, but I don't think so. The idea must have come from somewhere. Where was I? Oh yes...I think everybody can be found interesting. It's a matter of committing oneself to listening. Everybody has their own story. We all have cause to wonder about the butterfly net man. I'll tell you, Sam, probably most of my conversations with others are annoyingly superficial. It's all party-talk. I suppose it's the environment. I mean, in a party. Most people are afraid to let themselves go; afraid to fly, so to speak. The lion's share of my real conversations seem to take place in my head, in my work, you know, with my own invented characters. Consequently, they are studied, contrived and manipulated. There is little spontaneity. It's polished into seeming that way. So, in the end, how much honesty is there in the written word? But damn, it's fun to play with the alphabet. Are you going to quote me on that?"

"*Hey!* Let's have some fun."

"You ought to quote me on that."

"*Okay.*"

"I thought we already were…having fun, I mean. I know I am. So, what do you have in mind, Sam?"

"Wine and cheese…for starters. No crusty bread…*oops*, I forgot." Sam made a funny face and then, *wink, wink.*

Adam, thinking her funny face beautiful, softly said," You're antagonizing, but I think I'm falling in love."

"Think about something else," Sam chided. "We need wine, wine. wine. And guess what I forgot?"

"Cheese?"

"*Nope,* I forgot to bring a cork screw."

"*Ut oh,* ain't got one here, Sam." *"How could she forget a cork screw? She seems obsessively organized. Surely that came in the journalist's bag of tools. Not the cork screw…the obsessive organizing…an important tool. Oh God, I want to touch her. But she did forget the crusty bread, too."*

"My bad," Sam sighed.

They sat for awhile trying to figure a way to open the wine bottles. Suddenly, Sam jumped up, laughed, and said, "I forgot, they're screw-caps! Told you they were cheap." They laughed, and they laughed until it hurt; they laughed until they realized they hadn't anything to drink yet, and yet they were having so much fun anyway. Then, they ate an obscene amount of cheese and Ding Dongs; and they drank cheap wine directly from a bottle with a screw-cap. It was there, somewhere along their way toward the bedroom, that things began to blur, and then everything faded and vanished.

* * *

Sometimes evil appears abruptly and unexpectedly; and there it is and there is no way of confusing it with anything other than what it is. Other times, evil exposes itself gradually and subtly; bit by bit it is revealed between mouthfuls of lies and deceptions. There, too, are times when evil can be physically felt. The body senses evil and, without always recognizing it for what it is, one is either repulsed by it, or attracted to it.

Charon and Mona sat at the dining table making plans to keep Arthur Baumgarten from becoming any more powerful than he already was—a petty demon of little consequence.

"The trees are quickly turning blood red. Soon they will bleed and new powerful spirits will be born. And you, Miss Mona, you will be reborn with powers you never thought to imagine," Charon told Mona.

"What about Arthur?"

"What about him?"

"You know he's coming for me, Charon."

"I'll take care of Arthur."

"He can still hurt me."

"He can, but he won't."

"I'll need protection."

"Arthur is no match for me, Miss Mona. Soon he will be no match for you. Your powers are growing and until you are reborn, you are under my protection. After that, you will be powerful beyond what you can now visualize. He wouldn't dare get in your way."

"Where is he now, Charon."

"Most likely, back in Manhattan, dead, summoning an army of petty demons as we speak. You must not worry, Miss Mona. You already have enough strength to defeat any army of petty demons that Arthur could possibly conjure."

"Hmm. He was here for the seance."

"Arther himself?"

"I think so…yes."

"Arthur vowed his soul to The Agency. He may have his fun for awhile, until The Agency is done with him and casts his spirit into empty space. Arthur willingly made his pact with the devil."

"He hated me."

"Of course he hated you. He had reason to hate you. He hated your brilliance, Miss Mona…he hated your strength. He deserved your betrayal…it was a magnificent betrayal. You are to be applauded."

"Thank you, Charon."

"You are only beginning to shine, Miss Mona."

King Butcher decided to show the ghost of himself to Charon while he stood at the end of the table, listening. Charon could see King's ghost plain as day. Mona, however, was not aware of his presence. Charon was amused by King's eavesdropping since he knew that King had no way of communicating anything he heard to any of the other guests; at least, not yet. Charon knew that King's spirit was trapped on the island, unable to leave, and a threat to no one.

"And Goodblood?" Mona asked.

"The Agency will never allow Goodblood nor the girl to leave Gnarled Pines."

"The girl?" Mona asked.

"She joined him today. I brought her over myself. I am not sure if she is host material, or food for the dark souls." Charon and Mona laughed uproariously. "Goodblood is an interesting case. He's developing the ability to take form here, while remaining in his own time. That, I do not understand, but I'm sure The Agency does. They must have a plan for him. That has to be why they summoned him here. He is here, Miss Mona."

"You mean here? Now?"

"Yes. He is sitting on the couch having a cup of coffee."

Mona glanced at the couch and there he was. "What the… how? Charon, what is this? How is he doing that? Can he hear us? Why is he here?"

"Good questions, but I have no idea to any of them. There is no knowing and there is no telling what The Agency has in mind."

"You can see me!?" Adam shouted. Mona wasn't the only one who was shocked, so was Adam himself. He dropped his cup of coffee on the blue mirror tabletop, breaking the cup, and leaving the glass fractured. "*Oh, wow!* I am so sorry about the coffee table. *Jeez,* I hope I don't have seven years of bad luck. Would the seven years start from now, or in my own time? Oh, well. Can you really see me? Can you hear me now?"

"Of course we can." Mona was smugly matter-of-fact. "Why are you here? What are you doing here? What the hell do you want!?"

"So many questions all leading to the same answer. Research for my book about Gnarled Pines, and you, of course. You and your entourage," answered Adam.

"You broke my coffee table top!" Mona was angry.

"I am sorry, but you startled me."

"And you startled me, but I didn't break anything!"

"I'm truly sorry. I wish it had never happened. I broke my cup as well. I'll miss it. And I'm really, really sorry about your coffee table. It's beautiful, by the way."

"Was."

"*Forgive me.*" Adam pleaded.

"I don't know that I can…or want to. In fact, I am certain 'forgiveness' is not in my nature. You're an ignoramus…and that in itself is unforgivable."

Adam had enough of her attitude and quickly change his own, "Get off it, lady! You can stop acting. Your act has nothing to do with you. Nothing to do with the real Mona LaBaron; the one who is degenerating as we speak. Too bad you actually believe yourself. You're a mask of yourself—a veneer over nothing. You're tedious, Miss LaBaron, although I know you think yourself cunning and clever, you're boring and predictable, and worst of all —you are so sad and lonely, it pains me. I know you better than you know yourself."

"Nobody speaks to me like that!"

"As you can plainly see, I am no body." Adam faded and was gone.

"You see, Miss Mona, for all our concern, that man does not exist."

GNARLED PINES

Edward Crosby Wells

SIX

Adam was deep within his dream; but to Adam, as far as he could tell, he was not asleep; so how could it be a dream? Therefore, as far as he could tell, it was not a dream; and when it was not a dream, when his body, mind and spirit were fully here and now—Adam remembered. He saw, from a swiftly passing understanding, that souls had come and gone through him his entire life, leaving pieces of their spirit-matter that added to his own, changing him gradually, sometimes for the better and sometimes not so. Adam saw, while living in his dream, that he too had unknowingly passed on his own influential spirits into the lives of others. Adam saw, in his swiftly passing understanding, that he had never been a singular self, but that he was the embodiment of countless selves from womb to the present; and doubtlessly into the future, as well. Adam reasoned that he was not, nor could he ever be, alone—he was every person who ever entered his life.

Adam had taken material form in nineteen twenty-nine. He observed, firsthand, the evil in Charon and Mona as they conspired under the chandelier over the dining table in the lodge. Adam observed no evil in the spirit of King. From observing Adam's past and present presence the theatre folk learned, as they traveled back and forth between two aspects of reality, that they could see their future, and with that knowledge, perhaps they could change it. Every Fourth of July for a hundred years the Broadway troupers were forced to relive the regrettable fate that awaited them on Gnarled Pines. They came to understand that Mona was not only the affected bitch she had always been, who overacted to an impossible and acutely obvious degree, but that she had also become, most alarmingly, a mortal threat that needed to be dealt with posthaste. Their destiny haunted them and they knew that, year after year, there was no way to change the events of their Fourth of July on the island of Gnarled Pines. Until they find a host to take them off the island, their predestined, damnable, lamentable fate would remain unchanged.

Adam awoke before dawn to find himself spread-out naked on the bed and lying next to Sam. He threw his dream aside and racked his brain for memories of last night, not the dream, before the dream, while all the time fearing the worst: a remembrance of regrettable memories. What he had not forgotten were merely bits and pieces, scraps and fragments of moments; a puzzle of scattered and lost pieces. There were smiles, moments of laughter, on the sofa sitting inches apart. She called herself a "half-breed." He thought it a terrible thing to say. She laughed. She confessed it was said for shock. More laughter. Her mother was Irish. Her father was Mexican. She had a happy childhood, until it soured when she turned old enough to understand the fear in her father's eyes, the sadness in his disposition—he was undocumented. Adam wondered about his selections of memories; fragments really; perhaps there is a chance that some of them might come together in moments of silence, like something you tried to recall yesterday but waits until today to come to mind; memories that would never ever be complete; and comprehension becomes less and less a possibility.

* * *

Once again Adam awoke. *"What the…there was something going on with time."* He was certain he was reliving another day. *"Yesterday…maybe today again…maybe tomorrow…no…that's not possible. Is this a goddamned 'Groundhog Day' thing?"* The sun was pouring through the bedroom window. *"How did I sleep so late. Okay. The wine. Yes, we drank wine. I drank too much. That's it. It must have been the wine. How long did we stay up talking? Did I talk too much? I usually talk too much. She must hate me. She thinks I am stupid. I talk too much and I say stupid things. I hate myself sometimes. Jesus Aitch! There's Sam! She's naked. What am I doing here? I'm supposed to be on the couch. Oh, God! I don't remember! Why can't I remember?"*

* * *

And, yet again, Adam awoke. He found his shorts and T-shirt bunched on the floor near the foot of the bed. He quietly put them on, afraid of waking Sam, afraid to look her in the face, afraid of her reaction. *"Would it be regret? Would it be disappointment? Would it be happy? Would she smile? Would her smile be forced and fake? Would it be the face of a stranger? If it did happen, was it good? And would she remember? Remember. Remember. Remember what?"* He would just have to wait until she awoke for an answer. He felt numb as he sighed, left the bedroom, and cautiously closed the door.

Adam went into the kitchen and discovered that two of the bottles of wine hadn't been opened. *"I certainly could not have gotten drunk sharing only one bottle of wine. Jesus Aitch! I'm going Looney Tunes, bonkers crazy."*

Sam awoke, lying on a pink chenille bedspread. Last night the room had been dark, little to see. But in the morning, Sam caught shafts of sunlight abuzz with fine bits of dust and particles of creation floating in the light of a hot July morning. Splinters of sunlight bent over the Art Deco dresser beneath an oval mirror splattered with black patches where the stuff that makes a mirror reflect was gone. Narrow streams of sunlight illuminated the dresser's surface where it shone on a frog in a bottle.

The frog in the bottle was considered, by Mona LaBaron, a prized possession. She did it for an eighth grade science project. Once, Mona was heard to say, *"That frog reminds me of myself; it reminds me of Poughkeepsie. I had grown beyond the constraints of my environment. I desperately had to get out and go to New York City, where I have always belonged."* The bottle once contained lilac toilet water from Gimbels department store. It was a present from Mona's father—a medical doctor with his office in their home—after returning from one of his frequent trips to New York City. *"Gimbels…oh my…this is special…this came from Gimbels."* In all, the bottle was approximately six inches tall. Its bottom widened into a bulbous chamber about two inches across, narrowing dramatically as its slender neck rose three inches to its crest, where it was sealed with deep scarlet fingernail polish and covered with an uneven thickness of yellowed white wax. On the very top of the cap, in a waxen impression, clearly and purposefully embedded, the fingerprint of an eighth-grader remained. Inside the bottle was a yellow-tinged liquid in which a green frog sat on its floor with its nose pressed firmly against the glass to one side, and its feet pressed equally firmly against its opposite side.

The frog in the bottle did not make one bit of sense to Sam; at least, not one she wanted to know, not one she wanted to understand, because if she did it would be painful and angering. *"How did Mona manage to get a frog that large into that little bottle? Its throat is barely wide enough to slip a pencil down it."* On that sumner-sunny morning, in the portentous atmosphere of the lodge's bedroom, it struck her; she became cognizant of what she did not want to know. *"Mona didn't put it in there when it was a mature frog. Of course she didn't. How could she?"* Sam's heart sank from the ugly realization, the fear, the struggle, the suffocating death of the frog in the bottle. *"What kind of person was Mona LaBaron? Who would do a thing like this to a live creature?"* The answer, of course, was Mona LaBaron—she was that kind of person who would do a thing like that. Sam did not want to dwell on it, nor did she want to stare at it. It repulsed her. She was pained by it, but it was too late—she could not take her eyes off it. She was mesmerized by it. *"This is obscene,"* Sam told herself. The frog had grown in that bottle from a tadpole. It grew until there was no more room for it to grow, and then it died; not unlike the child who fell down a funnel-shaped hole in the ground until reaching the juncture of entrapment; unable to move, the child can go no farther. Spectators gather, they cry, they gawk, some fall to their knees and pray, some simply watch unattached and uncaring; but the child is beyond the point of rescue and old enough to comprehend the oncoming pain of a protracted death. The child cries for the comfort of sleep, and soon—but not soon enough—the child's tears roll into silence. *"That frog reminds me of myself; it reminds me of Poughkeepsie."* The shaft of sunlight danced upon the bottle with the body of the frog drowned in formaldehyde, and as the sun continued to rise, narrow streams of daylight slipped through the window blinds and stabbed the cobwebbed corners of the ocean rock and pine wood walls.

    Sam heard the sounds of Adam being carefully busy, trying to be quiet in the kitchen. She told Adam only yesterday—*"Was it yesterday? The day before? When? How long have I been here? When did I...?"*—that she was a vegetarian. Had Adam known when he was shopping, he would have gathered groceries with the restrictions of a vegetarian in mind. He would not have bought the bacon, the sausages, the cold cuts, the pre-formed hamburgers, muffins, rolls, sliced bread, the canned stew and, of course, all the Ding Dongs in the store; all in preparation for entertaining his house guest; a house guest who invited herself; who insisted on coming to the island despite repeated warnings; who was a goddamned vegetarian.

"Never figured she'd be a vegetarian. Who would?...you'd think she'd tell me a thing like that...in advance. You'd think anybody would. I'm angry...of course I'm angry...I have a right to be...not crazy-angry...not that kind...not at all...but more like doubly miffed...and goddamned embarrassing. Number one: thoughtless, or absent-minded? Boy-o-boy, I'm doubly miffed... triply miffed." Embarrassment hurts in inexplicable ways.

"Better be coffee!" Sam yelled. She got out of bed, dressed, went to the dresser, picked up the bottle with the frog in it, looked at the dead body, felt its terror-stricken existence, shuddered, then put the bottle back in its place. *"Mona...how pitiful. I would hate being you."* Then she headed for the kitchen.

"Such a peaceful night. That bed's way too comfortable. I might not want to go back to Denver," she told Adam while wrapping her arms tightly around him from the back, resting her head on his shoulder.

"She likes me," thought Adam, and then he said, "When I heard you coming, I was ready to ask if you had a good night, but I guess the answer is yes, and a beautiful way to answer, indeed." Adam turned to face her and he saw everything he thought he had ever wanted. Finally. Later in his life. Later than he would otherwise have liked. But now was as good a time as any. Now he was ready

Charon stood outside the cabin, listening to them, playing with time, smiling and giggling. Well, giggling is a gross exaggeration. Charon had to envision the shape of a smile, since he never actually had one. He had been known to giggle when in the presence of Mona. It took Mona two summers to figure out that the smothered and manic sound he made, was the sound of Charon giggling.

* * *

The gathering in King's cabin had resorted to plotting ways to escape the island. Willy suggested that they murder Mona and Charon, but something of that nature would need an unanimous vote, and he and Reggie were the only two in favor.

"Death to the two of them!"

"Save the world from evil and bad acting!"

"Very funny, boys. We're not going to kill anybody." Florence chuckled. "Now let's find a way to get off this island without resorting to murder." After a moment for all to think, Florence continued. "Maybe someone could swim to shore."

"That's ridiculous, Florence. I saw how high those waves were, crashing to shore."

"The waves are not like that everyday, Reggie. Sometimes the ocean is smooth as glass."

"I could swim to the mainland. Then when I get there I'll find somebody with a boat to come back and get you all away from this godforsaken place," Ídolo suggested. "I am the fittest person here. No insult, Hudson, but I'm a trained dancer which makes my body perfect for it. The mainland doesn't look all that far from here."

"Well, it is! Don't be stupid, Ídolo. It's nearly impossible to see the mainland from here," Reggie warned.

"I agree with Reggie, but only when the light is right; otherwise, you can see it plain as day." Willy explained.

"I'm in perfect shape, too," Hudson piped up.

"In your own mind, dear boy." Reggie snickered. "Drugs, arrogance and stupidity are already beginning to take their toll. I say that with a generous portion of actually caring, Hudson."

"I love to swim," Hudson pouted. "I really do."

"Of course you do, Hudson, but you'll drown before you get a hundred feet from shore," Annabelle chided. "We love you just too darn much to allow something like that to happen. I know you're high on the courage of cocaine, but your body may not share that same enthusiasm."

"Cocaine makes me stronger than I look. I don't know why everybody's so keen on Ídolo. He's not the only one here who can make it to the mainland. He's not the only one here with a good body. I have one too. Ask Mona."

"I'm sure you do. No reason to ask Mona. You could show me yourself, when I get back from the mainland. It would be my pleasure. I would make a study of it." Ídolo felt bold. Hudson felt electricity. They both smiled.

"I don't see what dancing has to do with it." Hudson gave a firsthand example of his foolish arrogance—enhanced by drug-induced certainty.

"Like the woman said, you should be seen and not heard, Hudson," Willy berated.

"You think I'm stupid. All of you think I'm stupid. Well I'm not! You don't think I'm stupid, do you, Florence?

"No. Of course not." Florence said.

"Neither do I. I would never...." Ídolo desired to touch Hudson, to embrace him, to let him know that all he needed were better influences, and that he himself might be one. "I think you're smarter than you know, Hudson; and I certainly don't think you're stupid."

"I do...sometimes." Willy offered.

"Me too...sometimes." Reggie chimed in.

"It hurts, you know. I got feelings too." Tears swelled in Hudson's eyes as he said to Ídolo, "Thank you. Thank you, Ídolo," and then his tears fell.

Annabelle said with a soft and soothing voice, "Hudson, don't take everything so seriously, so personally, and don't take any of us seriously—especially those two old geezers." She gave an exasperated scoffing at Reggie and Willing. "We're theatre people. We love to play characters, but sometimes we lose our way, we forget ourselves and become the character we're playing, like Mona has. She cannot help herself. Anyway, cheer up. None of us think swimming ashore is in your best interest. Nobody here wants you to drown. I think I speak for all of us when I say we genuinely care about your wellbeing—and your feelings. Each of us loves you in our own way."

"I don't...sometimes," Willy mumbled.

"Stop being provocative, Willy," Annabelle chided.

"If anyone has a chance, it's Ídolo," Florence announced. "But maybe swimming was a bad idea. In fact it certainly is a bad idea. I take it back. Forget it. Gone. Never said."

"But I could do it, you know? If I wanted to." Hudson interjected once again.

"Of course you could, Hudson, I know. But think how angry Mona will be when she finds out. There's no telling what she'll do. Especially to somebody in her employ." Florence told Hudson while holding his hand.

"You're right. I forgot, Florence."

"Of course you did, Hudson, but it's okay."

"Thank you, Florence. And thank you, Annabelle. And thank you very much, Ídolo."

"Oh, God! You're making me nauseous! Hudson, please get out of the center of the room."

"I'm not in the center of the room, Willy."

"I rest my case, dear boy."

"It's way too far to swim, Ídolo," Annabelle said. "The mainland is farther away than you think. Only a fool would try. Remember how long it took us to get over here by boat? Imagine swimming all that distance. Nope, it's a terrible idea."

Ídolo said to Annabelle," I don't see a better idea. I can't stay here. I'd rather die out there than stay on this island one more day. *One more hour.*"

"That's a foolish thing to say, Ídolo."

"Foolish or not…I'm going to do it."

And thus it was decided, despite all the warnings, Ídolo would swim to the mainland. The only matter undecided was *when.* Ídolo needed a calmer ocean before taking the plunge to Turtle Run; however, an increasing wind was causing ripples to rise into serious waves. The sky was darkening, a storm was most likely on its way, and with the threat of lightning strikes, swimming was impossible for Ídolo to attempt.

"Please don't do this, Ídolo," Florence begged. "I'm sorry. I should have kept my mouth zippered."

Then the subject was changed. For their own good, for their own protection, for their peace of mind from the evil they saw coming, it was decided that they all stay together and move together as an army, side by side. At the heart of that decision was the old adage: There's safety in numbers. To avoid putting their lives in peril, their course of action was to act as they normally would, which shouldn't be difficult for a group of theatre people; seasoned troupers all. That was the final order of business. They exited King's cabin *en masse* and walked like soldiers towards the lodge.

"Are you sure we shouldn't just kill Mona?"

"Yes, Willy, we're sure."

"Well...let's not rule it out."

Arthur came around from hiding behind King's cabin. He had been listening to their conversation. Arthur had come directly from the morgue slab to the middle of the island, so naturally, except for the toe tag, he was naked. He had been holding-up in one of the empty cabins farther back within the gnarled woods. He was now wearing Reggie's gray slacks, white shirt, and no shoes— stolen earlier in the day when everybody was in the lodge, including Charon. Arthur decided to remain out of sight until the time was right to show himself. He hoped he would recognize the time when it is right. While Arthur was headed to his cabin he suffered an angst moment, brought on by wondering about the shelf-life of a cadaver.

Meanwhile, back in the lodge, "They've just left the cabin. How stupid do they think we are? They have no idea of what is in store for them. Plotting ways to get rid of us...and to get off the island...but only in their dreams, of course," Mona told Charon, after testing one of her new powers—astral projection.

"*You see,* Miss Mona. Doesn't it feel good being able to go wherever, whenever your name is mentioned? You can be easily summoned, go unseen, and easily leave. I witnessed them in the cabin too, Miss Mona, but if any of them try to get off Gnarled Pines, they will not get more than ten feet from shore before they will be painfully swept back against the rocks. It will certainly kill them. Are theatre people generally that stupid, Miss Mona?"

"Absolutely not!"

When the troupers reached the lodge, an army armed with hope and little else, they entered the pungent atmosphere where mid-afternoon shadows cast themselves upon the floor and over the furnishings, to the top of the fireplace mantle where the frog in the bottle rested. All were certain that Charon was not human. Mona had changed, she was no longer the Mona most had come to know. From a distance she could easily be mistaken for human, but on a closer observation her humanity was questionable at best. Her playful banter, frequently sharp and stinging, and her affectations that were unwelcome more times than not, had turned as cruel as daggers; cold-blooded and demoniacal. Mona's disadvantaged guests decided she was possessed; that something iniquitous had definitely happened to her around the time of the seance. Her humanity was on the brink; of what was yet to be determined.

"I see you all chose to join us." Mona greeted the group snarkily. "You've all missed lunch. There might be some leftover crab salad and some other delightful tidbits, if you're starved enough for leftovers containing warm mayonnaise and shellfish. It's been sitting out awhile. *Mea culpa.* But, that's what happens when one is late for lunch. Charon and I shouldn't be required to wait and starve ourselves, now should we? I'm confident that every single one of you understands my position. If not, you ought to.

Since you all have decided to hate Charon and me so very much, you should know we feel the same towards you, and we are in a position to do something about it. You can scoop up the leftovers for yourselves."

"Pretentious bitch," Willy said under his breath, but just loud enough to be heard by everyone.

"The queen of bullshit," Florence offered—just loud enough.

"At the moment, it's only you we hate, LaBaron, but I imagine we will all learn to hate Charon just as much. Perhaps, even more than you, were that possible." Reggie did not speak under his breath, but nice-and-loud and ready for battle.

"Hear, hear." Willy cheered. *"I fucking love theatre!"*

Charon, who was sitting next to Mona, rose, stood at attention, stared directly into the eyes of Mona's guests, looking at one person at a time, choosing who would be the next to sacrifice. Who would be his next kill? Who would flinch and show their fear? Who feared death the most? It was mortal fear that attracted Charon the most. Like a wild beast, Charon could smell fear. He could taste it, and it was delicious. The fear of the victim added to the thrill of torturing. For Charon, fear always trumped pain. His face screwed up into something misshapen, something grotesque; something so repugnant Annabelle could not look at him without experiencing jolts of electricity piercing her body—she was surely being electrocuted. She heard the pounding of her own heart, causing her to need to consciously and purposefully breathe; until, finally, with one enormous sigh, she managed to pull all the air in the room into her lungs, then let it out ever-so-slowly, concentrating on the process, managing her breathing until it managed itself. Annabelle listened to her heart as its pounding began to go downtempo; and finally, with enmity, she mustered the gumption to stare straight back into the eyes of his evil screwed up face and say, "Mister Charon, I don't see what you have to do with anything. The problem between Lady Macbeth and the rest of us, is none of your business. You are a servant, are you not?"

Charon's face screwed more tightly, a tinge of blood-red flashed in his eyes. His face turned ashen. Not one inch of flesh showed anything close to the color of live human skin. Charon was bloodless. His hands curled into fists. He pulled himself upward, stretched like a wooden soldier, and whispered into Mona's ear, "I will deal with them later." He turned and walked out, stiff like Boris Karloff.

After the sound of the door closing ever-so-gently, everybody exhaled; followed by a moment of silence and disbelief before Annabelle scoffed and said to no one in particular, "Was that an answer, or what?"

"You hurt his feelings, Annabelle." Mona spewed ridicule. "And here I thought you were above hostile displays of your natural unctuous self."

"I could kill you, Mona, if I thought I could get away with it." Annabelle may well have meant it.

"You needn't worry about getting away with it, my dear Miss Lovelace. I am afraid you will find that quite impossible."

"Will your pretentiousness never cease?" Florence asked, rhetorically.

"Florence, one day I may regret our ever having been friends."

"I already have."

"For God's sake, I can't stay in here!" Ídolo headed for the door.

"Where are you going?"

"For a walk, Mona. Is that allowed, your highness?"

"I would be careful were I you."

"Well you're not me, are you?" Ídolo walked out of the lodge and slammed the door with the added force of rage. He then set out for the rocky shoreline of Gnarled Pines to reassure himself that it would be too dangerous to swim today. When he arrived at the water's edge, and after telling himself he could make the crossing, he was unable convince the voice within that knew he could not. Yet, nonetheless, Ídolo determined that there was no longer any threat of a storm, although there plainly was; that the sky was clear and blue, although it was clearly not; that the ocean was level, although it was far from it. Invisible arms engulfed him and whispered, "*Why not? You can't stay here another minute. You said it yourself. The water is smooth as silk. Let the warmth of the ocean embrace you. Let it wrap itself around you and make love to you. It's time to go.*" Ídolo felt heavy hands pressing down on his shoulders, and the familiar voice of Charon, *"Time to go!"* He felt himself being pushed forward. *"Do it!"* Ídolo took a deep breath, leaned forward, and dove into the violent, raging waters of the Atlantic ocean.

Back at the lodge the venom continued. "*Et tu,* Hudson?" Mona asked, sourly.

"Huh?" Hudson was truly puzzled.

"*'Huh'* from the mouth of an expensive piece of meat.... '*Huh!*'"

"Jesus Christ! What the hell is wrong with you!?" Willy was irate."You've gone too goddamned far, you…you…you piece of shit!"

"You will pay for that, painfully, Willy. *Painfully.*" Mona warned.

"Well…not by your hands, LaBaron."

Willy stood, laughed at Mona's absurdity, and hurriedly headed for the door, when Mona said, "Your shoelaces…."

Instantly, Willy who was wearing loafers, tripped over himself, fell and screamed from excruciating pain in his right leg. Through his screams, Willy managed to yell out, "This is your fault, LaBaron! You did this! Who the hell are you!?"

"*Moi?* How could your clumsiness possibly be my fault? I'm just one of Broadway's award-winning actresses. I'm a star. That is what I am! So, *chop, chop,* who knows what to do with a broken leg?"

SEVEN

Adam sat on the porch in a tan wicker chair waiting for Sam to do her "formal" interview. Although, what could possibly be formal after last night's animal sex, and this morning's passionate sex. However, the problem being: Adam did not quite remember having—animal or otherwise. He thought he remembered, but then again he couldn't be sure. At least, he was pretty sure, more than a bit sure, especially about the sex they had that morning; he prayed he did not disappoint; that is, if he hadn't been dreaming. Adam was between worlds and could not think of a thought that wasn't questionable; his consciousness wandered hither and thither. That said, the idea of a formal interview would seem staged and dishonest. It's difficult to communicate with honesty in an awkward situation; when one is between two worlds. *"I remember waking up in a dream...then into another dream...before waking up into now...if this is now...the final now. Too easy to forget which time to believe...which dream to believe...which reality to believe...which now...when everything can disappear at any moment by waking up yet again. Christ!...she oughta finish her bath...come out...sit next to me...enjoy the clouds...roaming... morphing...on a powder blue ceiling. That's an honest way to conduct an interview...an honest moment...over a cup of coffee... or tea...."* Adam sat watching from the wicker chair, as the blue and white panda transformed into a dragon's head, and then into a man's face, then a clown. All was *déjà vu*, something from childhood, from the crib. Breasts of a woman like pillows, white clouds of cotton candy, bright clouds that didn't know what to be, how to be, how long to stay before meandering into the sky, wayfaring, reshaping, a magical performance, tricks of light, vaporous clouds, unpredictable illusions before parting into spheres like tumbleweed billowing into extinction; vanishing along with the magician; sitting in a wicker chair, staring at clouds.

Doubtful ruminations concerning death and immortality haunted Adam, until the spirits of Ídolo and King showed themselves to him; then Adam's doubt turned into the magical, the wondrous, then disbelief, then belief, then the joy of integrated sensations that pumped through his veins and diffused throughout his body. An awareness embraced him with a sense of liberation, overwhelming him with the idea of beautiful freedom. There *is* life after death! Adam felt fearless—until, he descended and his feet touched ground. He began to think about the others who were still alive in another time on Gnarled Pines one hundred years ago. He didn't want to feel their pain. He didn't want to see their pain. He knew it would be too grotesque to watch, and too excruciating to endure for Mona's guests who were condemned to die in the most abominable of ways, every Independence Day—year after year—for one hundred years.

Adam also knew that he was obliged to do something; his conscience demanded it. To continue believing he was the kind of man he told himself he was, he had no choice but to put his beliefs into action. He believed that he was on Gnarled Pines for a bigger reason than working on his next novel. The Agency was responsible for his being there, they had a plan that involved him playing a pivotal part; but it was becoming apparent that The Agency's plan was not the plan that Adam would have chosen for himself. It was not his plan, it was not his purpose, and certainly not in line with how Adam saw himself. *"Maybe,"* thought Adam, *"it was a higher power, a power greater than The Agency, that brought me to Gnarled Pines? Maybe I am the power. Wishful thinking? Magical thinking? Looney Tunes? Absolutely bonkers!?"* He didn't come to Gnarled Pines to commune with demons, and certainly not to be used by the collective known as The Agency. Adam's higher power was his conscience, and his conscience told him that he had a chance, for the first time in his life, to do something real, something good, something beneficial, something that would change the lives of others in a positive way; something redeeming. But Adam hadn't any idea for what it was he could do. He was, however, sure that if he gave it enough thought he would figure something out. He always does. Now, there was only to begin.

When Ídolo and King appeared on the porch, Adam was naturally surprised, no shivering heart-stopping shock kind of surprise, just surprised. He had already met these men in a dream-state. It struck Adam, while thinking about the alternate reality of nineteen twenty-nine, that there might be a possibility of more, many more, countless more unseen dimensions swirling around him at all times long before coming to the island and that they were only a blink of an eye away. He thought he might one day reach out and touch the space that was occupied by nineteen twenty-nine, or any other moment in time. With that in mind, Adam pondered the possibility that time happens all at once, like an amorphous invisible creature that he unknowingly wanders through, is a part of, and that there was nothing linear at all about time. Aging, he thought, might have nothing to do with time itself, that time was simply the force that allowed existence, and aging was more a matter of gravity. Then, everything slipped away as quickly as it had come to his consciousness and he forgot whatever insight—if indeed it was insight—that there might have been, as his thoughts turned to whether or not he and Sam had sex last night, or again that morning. There was, of course, the wine. The wine could certainly explain his forgetfulness; but then, so could the malevolent sorcery of the island itself.

Adam could now talk with Ídolo and King, face to face, under the sun, in his own here and now, in his own reality; and unless one happened to walk through them, none would question their solidity. Adam, having had the pleasure of meeting Ídolo and King while he was in a state of astral projection, when they were sentient in nineteen twenty-nine, felt certain that they had brought with them the evidence, and the optimism that came with it, of a world filled with potential possibilities; a world in which there was no death—only change. Adam was thrilled that he could now get a first-hand account of what truly happened on the island of Gnarled Pines nearly a century earlier.

"Damn!" The recording app on Adam's cellphone didn't work. *"Nothing works on this godforsaken island. Up a creek without a paddle…in the doldrums…lost in time. It's maddening! I need to get out of here…off this island…away from the disorder…the chaos of my mind."* In awe, Adam listened to the accounts from Ídolo and King while all the while taking mental notes to transcribe at a later time.

King spoke: "Adam, all of us have been watching you since you arrived. We tried to communicate with you when you first stepped on Gnarled Pines, but we couldn't. We could only reach you while you slept. We are able to materialize now because our times have synchronized for the first time in a century. All of us are in nineteen twenty-nine and in your time, as well. You can only see us here in your time after we have been murdered. It's all happening again, Adam…*now*…the killings. The others will join us after they are dead…once again…for one last time….and then we will be free of the bondage of nineteen twenty-nine. Year after year we have suffered the consequences from having come to Gnarled Pines. Every Fourth of July we come alive and Charon and Mona LaBaron orchestrate their deadly drama…again. But this year you are here on the island…in your time and also in our time…both at once. It must be for a reason. This has never happened before…certainly not since nineteen twenty-nine. You have a role in this, Adam; a destiny, if you will. *I believe that.* You're not here by accident. The Agency brought you here for a reason, but it was a reason for their own benefit, not yours."

"Yes, but I may have a reason of my own," Adam said. "I saw an ad for Gnarled Pines. I needed an idea for a new book. It caught my interest. I decided to pursue it. I made the choice. The Agency may have been presented the opportunity, but it had nothing to do with my choosing to come here. At least, I like to think that. I like to think I still have free will."

"I hope to share your optimism," Ídolo said. "There is one thing I know for sure: it is going to be a different future for all of us."

"Something to look forward to," King agreed. "Most likely it has something to do with you writing a book about us, and everything to do with you being here when our times intersected."

"We think the ruler of the dark souls may want your book to be written the way The Agency wants it to be written, Adam," said King.

"Yes," agreed Ídolo.

"But why? I can't make any sense for that." Adam was bewildered.

"We think the dark lord is using you to promote The Agency's own devious cause," Ídolo said.

"Your novel may not be the novel you think you are writing." King proposed.

"Nonsense. I read it, at least what I've written so far, and it's exactly what I intended to write. Although I don't actually remember writing it." Adam was bewildered. "But nonsense all the same."

"Nonsense? Adam, the fact that we are here was 'nonsense' a day ago. Nonsense is something that you cannot make sense of until the day you do. You may hear what you expect to hear, read what you expect to read, but you may be blind to the message. Sense is something we must make for ourselves."

*"Wow…far out…*you guys are too much. You really are. So tell me…tell me why?*"*

"Who knows?" King answered.

"The message, Adam, might be spellbindingly evil," Ídolo offered.

"Spellbindingly? Way too spooky, fellows."

"Yes, it is…spooky and hypnotic, Adam." King said.

Ídolo then gave his account of what happened before he was killed: "When King went missing, we didn't know what to think. But we knew something was suspicious. We got together in King's cabin to talk about our misgivings, our fears, how we might protect ourselves from Mona and Charon. We were certain that they might be possessed by something evil. Now, we're just plain certain! They are the walking personification of evil. Be careful, Adam. Charon is here, right now in your time, on this island with you."

Adam frowned and heaved a sigh. "I already know."

"So, we're in King's cabin and our first order of business was who burgled Reggie's cabin. Someone stole a pair of pants and a shirt. Who would do that? None of us could come up with a logical answer. None of us would fit into his clothes anyway, so we moved on. I, stupidly, volunteered to swim to the mainland and find a boat to come back and pick up the others. I don't know why I offered to do that. I didn't really want to do it...it was only something I offered in the heat of the moment. I wanted to be taken seriously, I suppose. People who are like me...you know exactly what I mean...are not taken seriously, and that's a fact. I was infuriated with Mona LaBaron when I decided to give it a try...to swim to the mainland. I wasn't thinking straight. I see now that I was hurting myself just to spite that bitch. Senseless, right? Well, that's me, I guess. In mindless moments we throw our good sense out the window, don't we? Anyway, I stormed out of the lodge and walked down to the shore, trying to blow off some steam. There were nothing but rocks, everywhere I looked—*rocks*. I never saw so many rocks in one place in all my life. Looking up from the shore, I saw that the entire island was crumbling into the ocean. Maybe it should...in fact, it *really* should. The shoreline has certainly changed over the past hundred years. I undressed and walked to the water's edge. I took a step or two, barely got my feet wet, when I felt Charon push me into the water. Then a wall of water rose and was moving at full tilt towards me. There was nowhere to go. I tried, but I couldn't move. I was trapped...and then, it hit me...as high as a two-story house, maybe higher... huge...it hit me! I was hurled back against a boulder where my head exploded. How could that have happened? Only small waves rolled over the ocean from here to the mainland...most of the time...just small waves, unless there was something extraordinary, like a hurricane, or something they call a nor'easter up here. But this? This was impossible. Inexplicable. Where did such a thing come from? Not from Mother Nature, that's for sure. It was conjured by a demonic force. Next thing I know...I'm looking back at my body. I lingered...I stared at it...I was amazed...I wasn't in my body anymore. Charon suddenly appeared from nowhere. I followed him as he dragged my body to a tunnel on the north end of the island that led to the lighthouse. He didn't see me. I didn't want him to and maybe that's why he couldn't. He continued to drag my body along the rocky floor of the tunnel. When the tunnel opened into a large room filled with rotting bodies and body parts scattered about a gust of wind so powerful it nearly blew my body across the room. The wind came from over the ocean, through the tunnel, and erupted into the space where Charon laid my body on a makeshift table...a bloody board supported by a pile of rocks on either end of it. I watched as he fondled my body...touching me...smelling my flesh...slowly, running his hands down my chest. Kissing me...not me...only my body...on the lips, then his tongue slid down to my nipples. Then down my body, over my belly...and then he pulled my legs apart... he lifted my genitals...cupped them in his hands...put them into his mouth...he moaned and cried...but his eyes remained dry. He laid my body on the floor of the cave and raped it...forcing his giant prick into me...into the body, not mine...not me...brutally... savagely. I was dead and still I winced with disgust. When he had satisfied himself, he unceremoniously lifted my body back onto the table. Next thing I know he's holding a saw...the kind for sawing trees...and then...my arm...my leg...they're not mine anymore... their just things...it was too horrifying. I couldn't watch anymore. Next thing I know, here I am...right here in front of you...in a different time and place. It won't be much longer, Adam, before we're all here in this future with you. If you stay, that is...please stay...wait until we're all here. When you spoke at the seance, a couple of us thought that you might be the host."

"The host?"

"The person who will come and take us off this island." King answered. "Otherwise, we will remain trapped here, in Hell, forever. We only need to get a hundred feet or so away from this island before we're released from the effect of the demons within the gnarled pines. That's all it takes to be released from this prison. But we cannot do it ourselves. We hoped you'd let us in and take us away from Gnarled Pines. Once we are in a safe distance we will say 'thank you' and 'goodbye' and go wherever we like. You just have to let us in."

"Let you in?" Adam was flabbergasted. "*Let you in?* I don't know what you mean by '*let you in.*'"

"We're spirits, we don't weigh anything—you only see us because we want you to—we hoped you might let us possess you. Not in a bad way. You won't even know we're there...unless you want to. We would only share your body until you deliver us beyond the point where The Agency no longer has any power over us. You could be our host. You've hosted many spirits before, Adam," King said.

"What?" Adam exclaimed.

"Everybody has. You just don't know it. They come, they go, and they leave a bit of themselves behind, a residue of themselves; people, books, maybe a song, or a poem...the spirits within them share a portion of themselves. It's how we grow, Adam...seed by seed...memory by memory...and with the help of many you become fully alive...wholly alive, Adam." King explained.

"I've actually thought that myself, King."

"Because it's true, Adam. Truth lies within you. Listen to me...closely...please. Do you really think you are your body? Adam, you only possess your body for a length of time. Your body does not possess you. *You* possess it. You animate it. You are not your body, Adam, and we are proof of that. If you will be our host, we'll remain silent and you won't even know we're there." King said, hoping Adam was truly their host. "*Honest*. Should you be our host, you will not know we are there."

"I see," Adam said, bemused.

"I died by my own hand, Adam," King said, "but I was being manipulated by Charon. We all were. I thought about suicide, but I don't believe I would have gone through with it. I had a lifetime of hiding...and after being exploited, exposed and humiliated by Mona LaBaron, I went back to my cabin, took out my razor, but then I thought better of it. And then I felt the presence of Charon behind me...he grabbed me...he held me tightly...he forced my hand with the razor to my throat...he ripped my throat. I had no control. He was too strong...too strong for me to fight back. Later on, he dragged my body to the cave under the lighthouse. My body was mutilated by the time he got there. Then, he tore it apart, threw the pieces into a vat of rotting corpses... where it will rot until it's ready to feed the demons in the trees. You have got to get off this island, Adam. If you die here, you will remain here with us. Held captive in Hell. The gnarled pines are about to give birth in our time and your time, as well. They will be the most evil spirits ever to inhabit Earth. They are black spirits who will possess every person in a position of power, every person who reads your book…they're hiding in the pages of your novel, Adam…and when they are released, the reader will help The Agency to bring about the end of this world. They're spirits of corruption that will go everywhere on Earth to destroy whatever they will—it is in their unnatural nature. The Dark One put all the seeds of potential evil spirits into those trees tens of thousands of years ago, to keep them safe while they mature and are released. Evil does not suddenly appear. It must be nurtured. After the dark spirits are born, the cycle begins again for another hundred years… and then a new generation of evil is born…every hundred years… over and over again."

"*Wow!* You guys are really doing a number on me. How do you know all this?" Adam asked.

Ídolo jumped in and answered, "We know all this because we've seen it play out before…in nineteen twenty-nine and then every year right up until now. We watched. We listened. And we took note. Adam, the most powerful of those spirits have already influenced your book…they have made changes that you are not aware of. We cannot repeat this often enough. You must believe us. *Oh!* And be *very, very* careful around Charon. He is capable of anything. The darkest of the dark spirits—the Dark One—is his master and performs all manner of evil through him. The Dark One is the most wicked spirit on Earth. Some people call it Satan…but it doesn't have a name…it is the name of its host. It can possess you, change you, turn you into something foul and evil, without you knowing it. The Agency brought you here to use you, Adam."

"We'll see about that. Perhaps my choice to come to Gnarled Pines was an unconscious decision to thwart their evil plans." Adam was defiant.

"Adam, here's something that ought to interest you. Charon oversees this island in both my time, yours, and every other minute there is between," King said. "He doesn't need to go back and forth. He's in every dimension of time at once…every dimension there ever was, is and will be. He moves through time at the speed of thought. Charon lives everywhere. He's the oldest thing on Earth, Adam. He's not human. He's omnipresent."

"*Jesus Aitch!* That certainly interests me alright."

Ídolo added, "Like King said, Charon is everywhere. He was created to ferry souls to their fountainhead; the home the souls create for themselves during their lifetimes; the fountainhead is the consequence of every deed committed in their lifetime. After awhile, out of rejection and boredom, Charon willingly gave his soul to The Agency. There aren't just a few souls in those trees, Adam. There may be tens of billions. When they enter this world, it will be the beginning of the end. The world will be out of balance. Evil and good keep each other stable when one balances the other, but when evil overwhelms good everything goes kablooey…the globe will be transformed into a sterile, depraved malignancy…in chaos…then dead…exactly like this island."

"*Oh, God!* I get it. I get it. *Enough! I've heard enough.*" Adam raised his voice in anger and dismay. "*Wow.* You sure know how to scare a guy. *Yup,* you sure do."

Sam came out from the lodge. Ídolo and King disappeared.

"Adam, are you talking to yourself?"

"*Um*…Sam, I'm…just talking out loud…to a couple characters in my book."

"*I see*. Well…actually I don't, but hey, go for it."

"It's my process, Sam."

"Whatever works. Ready for that interview?"
"Nope."

* * *

Mari Glaze of the Glaze Literary Agency told Sara, her daughter and partner, about the email she had gotten from A. J. Goodblood. "If it actually came from him. Although, it did come from his email account. 'Though it could've been hacked. Strange. Sounded like he was on drugs, or he'd finally gone over the edge; he always was a bit *different.*" Mari couldn't make sense of it. She thought about flying up to Maine to see for herself. So, she Googled the island of Gnarled Pines.

"I Googled Gnarled Pines, Sara. It's a real place, alright. It's off the coast of a town called Turtle Run, in Maine. The island's been abandoned for years. Apparently, Gnarled Pines was the scene of some pretty grisly murders back in the nineteen-twenties...twenty-nine, I think. Anyway, a bunch of Broadway theatre people, nobody I ever heard of, were murdered. Well, if the critics don't get ya...a serial killer will. Too much? *Sorry.* Gallows humor. They say it was haunted right up to the day it was destroyed by a fire...and it was that same day an earthquake toppled the lighthouse and it fell into the ocean. All the trees on the island went up in flames—they were considered sacred or something, anyway the wind blew their ashes out to sea. Now the island is nothing but a huge rock jutting out of the ocean...and it's completely inaccessible. After the earthquake, rocks and boulders fell away from the island and made it impossible to get near it. *So*...there goes my trip to Maine. Sure could go for a lobster or two...on the waterfront...watching the lobster boats doing their thing...gulls squawking, or whatever it is they do, besides crapping all over the place...hauling up, unloading, then dropping the lobster traps back in the ocean. It's interesting if you never saw it before. Sam took a lot of pictures. This was before you were born. When I had a life. I mean, a different life. Not that there's anything wrong with this one. Forget it. Anyway, remind me and I'll dig around for those pictures. Most of them are still on slides. I think there might be a couple on my facebook account. Ever been there, Sara?"

"To your facebook site or to Maine?"

"Maine, of course."

"Gay Pop and I went up there four or five years ago. Ate lobster and little necks every day we were there…right there on the pier…and we were there for an entire week. Haven't had any since. Sick of them."

"I don't remember that. Where was I?"

"Australia," Sara said.

"*Hmm.* Anyway, when we were there, Sara, Sam and I climbed Mount Katahdin. Fabulous view from up there. The email was definitely a hoax. Right?" Mari asked.

"Somebody got hold of Adam's account and is spamming or scamming or something like that."

"Sure sounds like that."

"You said Goodblood told you in the email that he was still writing *Gnarled Pines.* Isn't that certifiable?"

"Maybe. I researched the timeline when he was supposed to have been up there, and it seems that he was most likely there during the time of the fire and earthquake. He may have been killed there. Burned alive."

"For pity's sake, get that image out of my head right now, Mother."

"Sorry."

"Didn't he send you the flash drive with *Gnarled Pines* on it?"

"Yes. And it was proofed and finished right here. Although, it wasn't actually sent. It was hand delivered. Don't you remember that weird guy?"

"What weird guy?"

"Five years ago! Early July, as I recall. *Yeah.* Right about now. This guy walks in and hands the IT guy a thumb drive and said it was from A. J. Goodblood—all formal and stiff-like. And then he disappears. What's his face said he literally disappeared."

"That explains why that IT guy isn't here anymore."

"Fired 'im. Drugs probably. Here's the thing, Sara." Mari took a deep breath and hesitantly said, "I don't know how to tell you."

"Of course you do. Just tell me."

"After I Googled the place, I got down A. J. Goodblood's book and flipped through it…and…*ah*…and I discovered….have you read *Gnarled Pines* lately?"

"No," Sara answered. "Why would I?"

"You should. I skimmed through it and found…you're not going to believe this…."

"What? What am I not going to believe?"

"It's really disturbing,"

"*What?* For God's sake, spit it out!"

Mari spat it out as fast as she could, "This is the thing: The book keeps changing every time you read it. Everything that's in the book is happening now. *Us. This conversation.* It's in the book, Sara. Look at this," Mari said, reaching across her desk, picking up

Gnarled Pines and opening it about midway and holding it out to Sara.

Sara did not take it. "Later, Mother. I haven't the time right now…in the middle of editing R. L. Perkins' new book."

"Any good?"

"It's great."

"You *must* read *Gnarled Pines* now! I bookmarked the pages. You'll see that…well…like I said, you're not going to believe this…this conversation…the one we're having right now…right this minute…*it's in it!*…word for friggin' word."

"You're not making sense, Mother."

"This conversation you and I are having right now, word for word, is in Goodblood's book."

"Are you still seeing that psychiatrist?"

"This isn't funny! Take the goddamned book and see for yourself!"

"Bullshit. That's not even close to possible." Sara laughed and grabbed the book. She began to read the page that her mother put her finger on. Her eyes grew wider. "*What?* What the…? This isn't…*what is this…?"*

"I don't know, Sara. I really don't know."

"I need to sit down."

"So sit. It won't change anything." Mari patted the seat of the chair next to her desk.

Sara sat. "What should we do about it?"

"What do you mean?"

"There's something wrong here."

"Of course there's something wrong here."

"We've been hypnotized," Sara reckoned.

"By who?"

"By the waiter in the coffee shop downstairs. Or maybe we've been drugged!"

"No." Mari said.

"No?"

"No."

"I think I'll go home early today," Sara said.

"*Yeah*....maybe tomorrow."

"*Yeah*...tomorrow." Sara was definitely shaken. "Maybe it'll change by tomorrow."

"Change into what?"

"Damned if I know, Mother." Then she slammed the book shut.

* * *

For now, the island and the lighthouse were still intact. The trees were still there, their branches were beginning to move and creep along the floor of the woods, some already rose their bloody limbs several feet from off the ground. Their muffled buzzing continued to drone, announcing the imminent nativity of inhumanly cruel spirits ready to divide the people of Earth with pure hate; hate that will break every rule that people live by; and then the chaos where dark spirits thrive.

Willy was flat-out on the lodge floor whimpering, sobbing, angry and in pain. "*Jesus Christ!* Somebody do something. *Quick, quick!*" Willy cried.

"Surely one of you must know what to do with a broken leg, other than cutting it off, that is. Although, it would seem easier, wouldn't it? *Chop, chop!*" Mona smirked with menacing satisfaction.

"*Goddamnit!*" Willy screamed. "You're a dead woman, LaBaron! It needs a splint, kids! What's goin' on? Man in pain here. Reggie? Where's Reggie? *Oh, my God, it hurts, Reggie!*"

"I'm looking for something to make splints with, Willy," Reggie answered, while frantically running around the lodge trying to find something that would do the job. Reggie stopped at a tall three-legged table where an expensive-looking cobalt blue porcelain vase was on display. He knocked the vase to the floor, shattering it into half a dozen pieces.

Mona screamed, "That's my vase, you ninny!" Pronouncing it *vahz-z,* of course. Mona continued, "Do you know what that's worth, you stupid clown!?"

Reggie didn't care and he didn't say a word. He lifted the table high over his head, then smashed it on the floor. It took him three smashes to free two legs.

Mona screamed again, "That's my table, you oaf! What in hell do you think you're doing!?" Reggie took the two table legs over to Willy. Annabelle went to the front window, pulled down the curtains and began ripping them into strips. "Those are my handmade Battenberg lace curtains, Miss Lovelace! You might not recognize the finer things in life, but I do!"

Annabelle paid Mona no mind and joined Reggie who was kneeling next to Willy. He placed the table legs on either side of Willy's leg. Annabelle handed Reggie the strips of cloth, and he quickly wrapped the leg tightly in place.

"*Ouch, goddamnit!*" Willy screamed.

Florence stood nearby wringing her hands. Hudson walked back and forth, stopping occasionally, then walked in circles before, once again, walking back and forth in a straight line. Willy continued to scream and moan with pain. Mona sat at the head of the dining table and did nothing other than to say, complacently, in a low dull voice, *"Bravo. Better than Kurt Weill."*

Charon walked into the lodge holding Ídolo's sandals. "It appears that Mister Ídolo decided to brave the ocean and swim ashore, after all."

"I thought he said he wasn't going to do it today. The water was too choppy, or something like that." Hudson disclosed."

"Well, he changed his mind, didn't he?" Mona said—it wasn't actually a question—to Hudson.

Florence, who was pretty much in a daze since Willy tripped and fell, mournfully said, "I pray he makes it."

Mona said, contemptuously aloof, "Despite your silly prayers, Florence, he ought to make it. He's got frog legs."

Abruptly, Florence lunged at Mona, wrapped her hands around her neck and squeezed as tightly as she could. Mona easily freed herself from Florence's arthritic fingers, and forcefully pushed her the entire table's-length away. Mona's eyes flashed with scarlet glitter and everybody saw them. There was absolutely no longer any question in anybody's mind—Mona LaBaron was definitely something else; evil through and through; something to be feared. Then, Mona said in a deep voice that didn't sound like it belonged to her, *"Listen, old woman, you're worthless, not fit for dog food, and you'll soon be dead, anyway. Sit down and be still!"* Mona saw the fright in her guests's eyes and said, "For Pete's sake, kids, my eyes get red from ruptured blood vessels. Annabelle should never have pulled my precious curtains down. Now the sun will fade everything in here. *Philistines.*"

Nobody was buying her story about her eyes because nobody had said anything about them—nothing about them turning red. Not a single word. Could she read minds, too? The air turned to ice. No one spoke. They hadn't yet found words to express their mixed emotions; they were speechless. No one moved; they were disconnected from their bodies, and any of its possibilities. No one breathed; their lungs hadn't time to think about the lung's need to breathe. Their hearts stopped in the time it took to miss a beat. Time had suspended. Willy, Reggie, Annabelle, Florence and Hudson could see, but they didn't recognize a single object, not its color, not its function. They saw all their world contained in a frozen nanosecond; without a past, without a future, without an awareness of the now. They were suspended in the ice of time. They ceased to live in the material world.

It was the sound of Mona's laughter that melted the ice and brought breath back to life. Charon and Mona LaBaron were in charge. There was no doubt about that. Life, as the Broadway troupers knew it, no longer existed. They were on the edge of a precipice—one step away from nonexistence. They didn't know what to do next. Stand and look like idiots? They were already doing that. Close their mouths? In time they would. Slowly back-up towards the door? That crossed their minds. Scream at the top their voices? They didn't want to bring more attention to their fear than they already had. Get on their knees? Thespians do not get on their knees. Lay prone and submissive? They never saw that as an option. Make crosses with their fingers? That was absolutely absurd. Throw things? They would need to move to pick up something to throw. Their positions were fixed. They were statues made of flesh. They certainly could not accept this moment as a manifestation of reality. They did not know what to do after the shock. The jolt that is needed to recognize and respond to the clear and present danger right in front of them, staring back at them, was yet to kick them into action. These two people, Mona LaBaron and Charon, if they were indeed *people*, were profoundly ungodly, and their mission was in no way anything close to performing *good deeds*.

So what did the Broadway troupers finally do? They snapped out of it and then they pushed and elbowed one another. Each tried to get ahead of the other. They walked over a screaming Willy on their way out. And, after they had cleared the door, crossed the porch and were down on the ground, they heaped shame upon themselves. Head-bent, eyes-closed shame. In time, their heads slowly lifted. What else could they do but face their shame; feel it, live it? Slowly they began to look askance until each eyed the other and all any of them could see in the eyes of another, was guilt. They were not that kind of people, they told themselves, but they were. They were that kind of people—and they hated themselves for it. In the face of a common enemy, when all are guilty of inconsideration for their fellow human beings who were suffering the same fate, when all are prisoners in the same boat, they finally come to feel an invisible bond with one another; and they all felt relief. And where was Willy? *"Oh, shit!"* Had he been trampled to death while crawling towards the door, painfully dragging two legs of a three legged table? *No*. He had been moved to the couch where he was stretched-out and asleep. And what about Hudson? Hudson never left the lodge; he ran to Mona and clung to her tightly.

"I'm sorry, Miss Mona."

"Sorry for what, Hudson?"

"You know. Meeting with those people who had nasty things to say about you."

"Did you say any nasty things about me?"

"No. Of course not."

"Of course you didn't. I never thought you did."

"Is there any more…*you know*…."

"It's called cocaine, Hudson."

"Yes…that. Is there any more of it?"

"In the bedroom. In the tin on the dresser. Did you get that?"

"Yes. In the bedroom, on the dresser, in the tin."

"Good boy. While you are in there, stay in there…and mama will join you in a couple minutes."

"Yes, Miss Mona. Thank you. I love you, Miss Mona."

"I know you do, Hudson. You must. You cannot help yourself. Now go and snort up your stuff, get undressed, and I'll be right in."

As Hudson passed Charon on his way to the bedroom, he looked up at him and said, proudly, "I'm hung like a horse."

"I am told," Charon envisioned himself grinning.

"Go, go, go, Hudson. Get ready for your mama." Then, she said to Charon, "Why don't you go help the boy?"

"I see no reason why not to help," said Charon, in a dull slightly cheerful tone.

Hudson scurried into the bedroom. Charon followed, removing his thick leather belt en route. He sat in the blue overly-padded velvet armchair in the corner facing the bed, eyeing Hudson. *"Like a horse. Lucky boy,"* Charon smacked his lips and his eyes flashed red.

"Thank you, Mister Charon."

"Get ready, boy."

"Yes, sir!"

"Quickly, boy, quickly."

"Yes, sir!" Hudson removed his sandals, slipped his suspenders over his shoulders, took off his shirt, his knickerbocker shorts, stood in his urine-stained underwear while facing Charon and showing off his steadily inflating prized possession. "How is that, sir?"

"Nice. Very nice."

Hudson grabbed the tin on the dresser, opened the lid, dipped his index finger into it and came up with a tall mound of cocaine that he put under his nose and with one large snort the cocaine disappeared.

"Now get on the bed and stretch out…face up. Spread your legs and arms," Charon demanded.

"Yes, sir." Hudson obeyed, and quickly stretched out on the bed."Take off your underwear."

"Would you like me to do it slowly, sir?"

"Get them off, boy. Now!"

Hudson's prized possession slapped his belly and reached his navel.

Charon bent over and picked up four strips of leather from the floor next to the chair. He rose, went to the bed and proceeded to tie Hudson's wrists to each head post, and his ankles to the foot posts.

"Are they too tight, boy?"

"No, sir?"

Charon went to each bedpost and tied the leather straps yet more tightly, until he saw Hudson wince and heard him stifle a cry. "How's that, boy?"

"*Um*...good, sir. Thank you, sir."

Hudson lay spread-eagle, in pain, expecting Charon to touch him, but he didn't. Instead, Charon opened the bedroom door and whispered to Mona, *"He's ready."*

EIGHT

Noon, and the interview never happened. Adam tried to explain to Sam what was actually going on; that evil spirits were incubating in the gnarled pines; that he encountered two timelines separated by nearly one hundred years; that time had slowed down on the island; that every day on Gnarled Pines was a year on the mainland. He told her how he was being counted on to save the souls of those who had been murdered on Gnarled Pines during an Independence Day holiday in nineteen twenty-nine and every year since, and he told her how he would be their host. He also told her, with a cautious degree of embarrassment for sounding absurdly delusional and self-focussed, if he hadn't already, that he might be able to save the world in the process, or at least make it a little less dangerous place; although, he hadn't yet come up with an idea for doing that.

Sam saw no reason to stay on the island any longer. She was anxious to get back to Denver. She was too uncomfortable being around a man who was obviously disturbed beyond neurosis. She had nothing to take back to her editor other than the story of a hermit falling apart on an island in the Atlantic; nothing to justify the expense of the trip. She was angry.

Adam and Sam walked briskly towards the pinewood dock.

"And you are sure you're not coming, Adam?"

"Yup."

"You do know how to get to Turtle Run, right?"

"Of course. What kind of question is that? I'm an old salty sailor, matey. Don't worry. I'll get you there in one piece. But I gotta come back. I told you I'm needed here. There are people depending on me."

"Ghosts?"

"Yes...ghosts. And maybe the whole world."

"I wish there was something...*damnit!*...you're exasperating. Please let it go and come back with me. You need...." Sam was quickly stopped.

"*Help.* Is that what you were going to say?"

"Maybe. You do seem to be under a great deal of stress, Adam."

"Of course I am. Haven't you heard a word I said."

"I heard you, Adam. But you're not making sense. That's why you should come back to Denver with me. Going home may be just the thing you need right now."

"I can't."

"Of course you can."

"I may not have a home anymore. It's been five...six years."

"*For Pete's sake, Adam!*"

"I gotta stay, Sam."

"You don't really believe that 'host' crap, do you?"

After a pause to think about it, Adam exhaled and said, "I do."

"And the time difference?"

"*Yes.*"

Sam sighed. There was nothing further to say. Adam was unreachable, delusional, simply out of touch. Perhaps, she could send a professional to help him. *"Yes, that's what I'll try to do. There must be a shrink in Turtle Run. Maybe police...ambulance...something."* She had hoped for a romance, but that got dashed. Now, all she had was a whole lot of *"nothing further to say."*

When they reached the dock, Adam looked for the tow line to pull the boat out of its miniature lodge, but the tow line wasn't there, and neither was the boat.

"CHARON!!!" Adam yelled to the sky, in anger.

"What's going on here, Adam?" Sam worriedly asked.

"He's not going to let us off the island, Sam. There's more I haven't told...."

Before another word was spoken, Charon came charging down to the dock. "What is your problem, Mister Goodblood!?"

"The boat is gone." Adam was irate. "What did you do with the boat, Charon?"

"I did not do anything with the boat, Mister Goodblood. Are you sure it is gone? Maybe you parked it somewhere else." Charon's idea for impersonating guiltless-innocence didn't exhibit any truthfulness.

"Do I look like an idiot to you!? It's gone! The boat is gone and I want to know what you've done with it. I know you used it to shuttle Ms. Flores to the island. It's all strangely unusual when you think about it, isn't it?"

"Should I think about it?"

"If you are able."

"Mister Goodblood, your hostility is not appreciated. You chose not to go to the mainland to bring your guest back to Gnarled Pines. You chose to leave Miss Flores abandoned in a coffee store in Turtle Run. A dreadful place filled with disagreeable people. There is nothing strange or unusual about it. I did you both a service. You should know, Mister Goodblood, that I have every right to use the boat. You only rented it...The Agency owns it. Should you look in your lease you will see that I am correct."

"In small print, again?" Adam sarcastically replied.

"Small is relative, Mister Goodblood."

"What did you do with the boat, Charon?"

"Nothing, sir. I did nothing. It was there the last time I saw it."

Adam was puzzled. *"What?"*

"Maybe you did not tie it up right and it floated out to sea."

"You were the last person to use it," Adam accused.

"Oh, look," Charon shouted. "There it goes." Charon pointed to the south end of the island.

Adam caught a brief sighting of a boat floating out of sight, but there was no telling if it was the boat in question, or if it was another boat. "Now what!?"

"You tell me, Mister Goodblood."

"Mister Charon," Sam interrupted their accusations, "Why don't the both of you shut up!?I need to get to Turtle Run. I have a job to get back to and I don't want to be fired. So, you don't happen to have another boat…a backup in case of an emergency, do you?"

"I do not have another boat, Miss Flores. I am grieved to tell you that it just floated away. It must not have had a proper knot."

"Jesus!" Adam's tolerance was being tested, and he was failing. *"Now what? What do you expect her to do?"*

"She is not on the lease, Mister Goodblood. You forfeited your right to have guests when you signed the lease. So what I expect her to do is no concern of mine. She is not on the lease. Now, I could show you how to tie a bowline, Mister Goodblood. It should only take less than a minute…or more. But you no longer have a reason to know how, now do you? We might be able to put together a raft. There is some old timber in the lighthouse. You will be charged for the boat, Mister Goodblood." Charon turned, marched double-time up the hill, and was swiftly out of sight.

"What have you done, Adam?" Sam asked. Her anger was showing.

"Whatayah mean by that? I haven't done anything, Ms. Flores. There's no reason to be hostile. Besides, you shouldn't be here. I did not invite you. I told you to stay in Denver. You didn't listen. You wanted to play reporter. So you just barged into my life. I was doing just fine before you stuck you nose in...."

"Fuck you."

"*Yeah*, fuck you too. By the way, when you heard me talking to myself...I wasn't talking to myself. I was having a conversation with two spirits. I don't know what it will take to convince you that I'm telling the truth. Ya know...I don't care anymore. You're a very rude person, Ms. Flores. Do you usually think everybody needs mental help when you don't happen to believe them? Actually, I do know what it will take." Adam called out, "King, Ídolo...please help me here!"

"Adam...you're out of your...."

King and Ídolo materialized on the dock.

Ídolo spoke, "Miss Flores, please don't be frightened. Our souls are stuck on this island. We cannot leave Gnarled Pines on our own. We've been here since nineteen twenty-nine. Adam has offered to be our host. You've chosen to stay and be our host, haven't you, Adam?"

"Yes I have and I am proud to be of assistance," answered Adam.

"Excuse me," Sam said to Ídolo. Stupefied, she looked at Adam and said, "I need to lie down."

"Of course you do. I'll help you back to the lodge. Unless you think you can get up those steps all by yourself."

"*It's me.* Oh my God, it's me, Adam. I'm the one going insane."

"Nobody is going insane, Sam. At least, not today. You've put me down and you've made unpleasant insinuations. Now you can see for yourself. Now you know."

"I'm sorry, Adam. I really am. I'm afraid. I don't know…I don't understand any of this. What's going to happen to us?" Sam was choking up and about to cry.

"I don't know, Sam. I guess that depends on us. All I know is, we need to get the hell off this island, but now is not the time."

"We're waiting for our friends to be murdered," King remarked.

"What!?" Sam was stunned.

"Yup," Adam said. "We can't leave the island until the others join us."

"They'll all be here soon," Ídolo affirmed.

"Adam," Sam said weakly, "I really need to lie down." Sam began to swoon. Tears ran down her face. She tried to lie on the deck, but Adam wouldn't let her. He straightened her up and steadied her while gently helping her up the hill to the lodge.

"We'll talk later," Ídolo whispered.

* * *

The front door to the lodge opened sluggishly. Laughter poured from out the bedroom. A naked, hollow-eyed Hudson stepped into view. He stood frozen in the doorframe for the time it took his body to realize it was not dead. Hudson cautiously closed the door, and, with legs trembling with indecision, he walked across the porch while watching molecules of sound vibrating to the rhythm of the electrical buzz throbbing in his head. Hudson reached the porch steps, grabbed the railing with one hand and held what was left of his prized possession in the other—it had been bitten off and eaten. He stood expressionless, tightly squeezing it in an unconscious effort to keep it from spurting blood; although, blood continued to spray between his fingers. There were welts, raised high and repulsive, disfiguring the length of Hudson's body from having been beaten with a leather belt which left perfect engravings of its buckle. There were savage bites covering his chest, one of his nipples was torn away, bite marks continued down his chest; deep, easily defined imprints left by teeth covered his bloody thighs; gouges from fingernails dug and ripped into his back; his back and buttocks were covered with handprints made of feces; pieces of his buttocks had been eaten away. Hudson stood transfixed at the top of the stairs, not knowing where he was. There is an ironic sadness in his coming out of the lodge alive, but with a soul too damaged to stay alive. He was an unconscious being in a brain-dead body. The sound of Mona's laughter was seeping out from under the bedroom door.

Annabelle, who had been hiding in Florence's cabin, came running towards Hudson, reaching him just in time to save him from tumbling down the porch steps, then he collapsed into her arms. She steadied and guided him back to the cabin where Florence was waiting and shivering in the July heat.

Trembling with fear, empathy and love for Hudson, Florence asked, "Hudson, are you alright? I mean, will you be alright?" He did not answer, but continued to stare vacantly into the whirling mixture of molecules. "Hudson," she asked, "can you hear me? Do you know where you are?" Hudson opened and closed his mouth, tried to moisten his lips, gibbered something, and passed out.

Annabelle said with disgust and urgency, "We need to clean and bandage these wounds quickly. And we need a wet towel to wash off all this shit. What kind of people are they?" Without another word, Florence took off for the lodge, ran up the stairs as best she could. Hoping her knee would not give out, she limped across the porch, threw open the front door, walked in, and tore down the one remaining curtain. She then took it into the kitchen, pumped cold water into the sink, threw the curtain and a nearby dish towel into the water and folded them—in the manner of folding bread dough—just long enough to drench them. When she came out of the kitchen, holding the dripping curtain and towel, she saw Mona, arms akimbo, standing in her way. Florence bellowed, "I'm not afraid of you, bitch! I don't give a fuck what the hell you are, get outta my way!" She forcibly pushed Mona aside, then limped to the door and left. Mona's response was, *"Bravo you."*

When Florence returned to the cabin, Annabelle was kneeling on the cabin's floor holding Hudson, with tears running down her cheeks, she looked up at Florence and shook her head from side to side. There was nothing to say. Hudson was dead. In the stillness, Florence covered Hudson's body with the wet curtain, then knelt next to Annabelle and cried.

Meanwhile, Reggie was hiding behind the gasoline tanks in the back yard, shaking and crying, waiting for the right moment, waiting for the gumption to go back into the lodge and help Willy to his cabin. He felt guilty hiding-out while his best friend was still in the lodge, but he knew that he must rescue Willy as soon as he conjured the strength to face the monster Mona had become.

Mona came to the door and shouted, "You kids can all come home now. *It's teatime! Come, come...it's truce time.*"

"Go to hell," Florence shouted back. "When we get off this island, you're going straight to Sing Sing, if one of us doesn't kill you first!"

"That's nice, dear. Thank you. In the meantime, our dear Charon will give our beloved Hudson a proper Christian burial, while we all have tea and toast. *Chop, chop! Tea's on!* We'll talk about prison another day."

Annabelle cried out from inside the cabin, "You're completely insane! Hudson's dead and you're talking about tea and toast! You're a murderer of the worst kind. You and that creature killed a kid. *Christian?* What a joke! What is wrong with you people?"

"He wasn't a kid, dear one. He was twenty-one."

"She's fucking crazy...possessed by something evil. Satan maybe," Florence said through tears and hatred.

"We're going to get killed, aren't we?"

"Not if I can help it, Annabelle."

Annabelle struggled to get off the floor. Florence helped her stand. Then Annabelle stepped out of the cabin and screamed at the top of her lungs towards the lodge, *"WHAT IS WRONG WITH YOU PEOPLE!?"*

"Not a thing," Mona responded. "The dear twenty-one year old man-boy died from too many drugs. Booze and cocaine; they made him beg for more. *Beg, beg, beg! More, more, more!* We were just playing a little game and he went overboard. Totally harmless. *That's it. That's all.* It was entirely his own fault. *Ah,* the passions of youth. He was twenty-one. *More, more, more!*"

After a moment to register what Mona had just said, Florence yelled, "Died from drugs? How did you know that we lost Hudson?"

"I know everything," Mona answered. "Besides, he's not lost. He's dead, you worthless old piece of shit!"

"And you know a lot about shit! You make me want to vomit, LaBaron!" Florence was beyond irate.

"Of course I do," Mona was smug. "C'mon, children, it's truce time. Teatime. *Chop, chop!*"

Reggie had heard enough. He could no longer restrain himself. He jumped up from behind the gasoline tanks and briskly walked to the front of the lodge, stood at the bottom of the porch steps, fearlessly looked up, faced Mona with her inappropriate smile, her penetrating red eyes, baffled by her enigmatic transformation, he bellowed,*"What…are…you?"*

"I'm an actress, darling. A goddamn tour de force."

"*Hmm*. Where's Willy!?"

"Where you left him, clown. You destroyed my little table for nothing…not to mention my priceless vase. Willy didn't break a leg, you buffoon. He pulled a muscle and you all made such a fuss. Just a muscle, you *performing baboon!* Charon gave him a little sleeping pill and a massage and now he's right as rain." Mona glanced into the main room and summoned Willy, "You can go out now and play with your little friends, sweetie." She turned back to Reggie, "I guess he's not mobile at this time. You'll need to wait. You people almost trampled him to death. It was all your fault. And he had all that pain you all caused."

"I'm getting my friend, whether you like it or not!"

"Well, let's see. I don't like it. But if you must, he's on the couch. You could throw a little water in his face or slap 'im. *Go, go, go.*" Mona sneered.

Reggie walked into the lodge, went over to the couch and shook Willy. No response. He shook and shook again and still nothing. "Water," he said to Mona, pointing to the kitchen.

"Be my guest. Certainly you don't expect me to get it?" Mona pointed to the kitchen.

Reggie got up and walked sideways to the kitchen. He didn't trust Mona, so he did his best not to turn his back on her.

"I hope you don't plan to tear down the kitchen curtains." Mona was smug.

"Just a glass of water," Reggie said while re-entering, carrying a full glass of water.

"And now you'll ruin my couch. You don't care. *Peasant.*"

Reggie emptied the entire glass of water on Willy's face. Willy stirred and mumbled, then went back to sleep. After some pulling and tugging, Reggie managed to rouse and drag Willy past Mona, across the porch, down the stairs, and towards the woods before Mona shouted, *"You're welcome!"*

Reggie said to the non-responsive Willy, "She's disturbed, Willy. You're going to be all right, old friend. *Damnit!* Wake up... *please.* For the love of God, please wake up." Reggie could not hold back his tears.

Together, they disappeared into the woods of unnatural pines. Mona's response was to yell toward the bedroom and advise Charon, *"It looks like tea for two. Chop...chop."*

Reggie, Annabelle, and Florence were dead certain that their lives were in mortal peril. They knew they had to take strict precautions to stay alive while they waited for Ídolo to come back and rescue them. The shame they felt earlier had turned into a shared, numbing fear which allowed them to mutually suspend acknowledging the death of Hudson. *"Mourning gets in the way of the pursuit of survival. What's done is done and mourning will not change it,"* they told themselves in one way or another, consciously or unconsciously. They were facing death and they knew that from then on, their every choice would determine whether or not they would continue to stay alive. Willy was still asleep. They gathered in the woods to assess their chances for getting off Gnarled Pines alive. No one actually knew why Mona was acting so bizarrely. All they knew was that she was dangerous, a murderess, most likely insane and, more than likely, under the evil influence of Charon.

"He has her under his spell," Annabelle said.

"*Christ!* We gotta get off this island!" Reggie stated the obvious, while continuing to support Willy.

"We should kill them," Florence offered.

"Now you want to kill them. A little late," Reggie scoffed. "That's gonna be difficult, Florence," Reggie warned. "I don't believe either of them is human."

"What I want to know is why did Mona bring us here?" Annabelle asked.

"That's the question," Reggie said.

Not any of them knew the answer to Annabelle's question. But there was an answer and that answer was: When Mona made her pact with The Agency, officiated by Charon, there was the provision that she must make an offering of seven people for the purpose of feeding the unborn demon souls. This was a fragile time for the dark spirits, since, nearing the end of their gestation The Agency needed Charon's constant attention, day and night. The trees needed to be fed much and often. Human bodies needed to be gathered at short notice, processed and distributed around the trunk of every tree; having plant food available on a moments notice was necessary; and The Agency needed more than the bodies Charon would be able to hunt down and haul over from the mainland. Having fresh food available at any time, day or night, brought comfort to The Agency.

After an anxiety-ridden meeting in the heart of the woods, the four unanimously decided that they needed a permanent place to hide. They were also aware that there was no place on the island to hide without being seen. They concluded that their best chance would be somewhere along the shoreline. Perhaps, they might find a nook, a cranny, or possibly a cave where they could hide while waiting for Ídolo to return with a boat to take them to the mainland.

Silently, they walked through the woods, then followed the edge of the island to the stairs that led down to the dock and the shoreline. Reggie held Willy tightly as they slowly took one step at a time. When they reached the bottom they looked to the north and to south of the island, until they finally decided to walk northward —the rocks appeared to be less forbidding. Reggie continued to hold Willy while maneuvering him over the dangerous terrain. *"Wake up, Willy...please...wake up...Jesus...what did they do to you, Willy?"*

Willy began to breathe more regularly. He opened his eyes and began to take small steps. Reggie said nothing, he only cried.

Arthur Baumgarten followed them, taking pains not to be seen as they sought a place to hide. Arthur was empathetic to his stranded friends; he knew that every possible hideaway would be too easily found; that the forbidden cave that went up into the lighthouse at the northernmost end of the island was no place for them to be discovered. Arthur was aware of Mona's metamorphosis into something worthy enough to become the eternal partner of Charon. He had not been blind to Charon's spending the last couple summers courting Mona. Arthur didn't care. He didn't care because he had his own assignations with the girls provided by his friendly, accommodating procurer in the Bronx.

What The Agency, through Charon, had to offer Mona were powerful sinister potentials; magic that Arthur could never give her. The Agency promised much, but much of what? That was in the fine print and yet to be determined.

Arthur's flesh had begun to swell and rupture, bloody tendons and bones hung from the uneven lacerations in both wrists; he hoped his hands would not fall off. He stank exactly like what he was—a walking, rotting corpse. His lurking about Gnarled Pines would soon be limited by the strength and direction of the wind blowing across the island; otherwise, Mona or Charon would easily pick up the scent of him. Although, there was no reason to believe they hadn't already. When Charon boasts that he knows everything that is happening anywhere on the island, it's safe to assume that he does.

Surreptitiously, Arthur followed his friends as they looked for a place to sequester themselves among the rocks and boulders. He watched their despair, felt their frustration, and witnessed their inability to connect honestly with one another. There was an unaddressed presence that lingered about them, that followed them and haunted them—the name of that unspoken presence was Hudson Sky. Arthur watched as they avoided the very thought of

Hudson by blinding themselves to anything other than the rocks beneath their feet. Arthur internalized and visualized their inability to look directly into the eyes of another, and he could not help but feel the pain and disgust of facing the horrors that were brought upon Hudson. Arthur knew that for them to see those horrors in their mind's eye, to believe them and to face them head-on, would undermine their ability to address the reality before them— maneuvering the rocks below in their search for a place to hide. Arthur could emphasize with the numbness they felt, and he knew they could never fully imagine the horrors committed upon Hudson and still remain optimistic to any degree for their own future. They walked over the trail of rocks hunting for sanctuary, and all the while they continued to keep their distance from making any real contact with one another as each turned the proverbial blind-eye to the thought of Hudson Sky, the ghost that walked beside them.

  Arthur did not regret, nor did he feel guilt for how he lived his life. He had no ax to grind with God, and, he assumed, God had no ax to grind with him. He hadn't a clue for where he'd be going after he rotted away, or if he were going anywhere other than an endless sleep. *"When you are dead the memories of your life are more sweet than they actually were when you lived them."* Arthur mused. *"It is not the unhappy, or the unpleasant memories that are the first to surface when you are dead; it is the pleasing moments, the tender moments; it is that one single moment you wish you could live and relive forever. When you are dead, you remember the life you never lived. When you are dead, you ponder on what it might be like to go back, to make better choices, to be kinder, to follow through with those many untaken opportunities. When you are dead, you wish you could live life over again with different parents in a different place, in another country, on another planet, perhaps. When you are dead, you remember reasons for staying dead, so you pray that you will never need to do life ever again. When you are dead, you find that you are in control of nothing, but are controlled by vagary and chaos. When you are dead, you wonder why you never loved yourself—and then you realize that you might have changed your world; that is was always within your power."* Arthur continued to follow his friends while working up the courage to gently dash their hope for the return of Ídolo. He knew that he had to tell them the truth. He knew that in time he must. Until then, Arthur turned and went back to the lodge.

Mona and Charon were in the lodge making their plans for the birth of the dark spirits. Mona was looking forward to sharing her endless unnatural life devoted to corruption, destruction, chaos and Charon. In the end, all Mona was, all Mona had, was a single point of view; one of endless points of view watching the universe though other sets of eyes. Mona felt cheated by having only one viewpoint from which to look down upon her world; so she decided that her point of view was the one and only point of view, the right point of view to look upon the reality that spread out before her. Mona decided she was God. But Mona was the god of nothing. Mona was no longer there. It was the spirit of another who controlled the animation of her body; she only observed from a distance.

"Would you like to feed the pines with me?" Charon asked. "You could help me prepare Ídolo and Hudson. The spirits will enjoy their sweet flesh. Together we can make the most delectable ambrosia for the dark spirits."

"I would be honored, Charon."

Arthur listened from outside the lodge. The duo disgusted him. He had to find a way to help his friends. *He had to! He must!*

"When you are dead you forgive. *I do not want to watch Mona suffer; it would be sad, pitiable; she was already a damned spirit. What is there to say, Mona? There's nothing of you left. When we met, I fell head over heals. You were fun-loving. Spontaneous. A force of nature. You made others feel better about themselves. Your talent! I wanted your talent on my stage. I wanted you. Only the best for an Arthur Baumgarten production. We were great friends, you and I, Mona. And then we were happy lovers. And then we were just friends. And then we weren't anything. In the end...nothing...well, here I am. When you are dead, ruminating is useless—nothing can be changed. When you are dead, all your choices have been made. What happened to you, Mona, was not only your own doing, but Charon's doing, as well. This island, these trees are the powerful dark spirits that have taken possession of you, Mona. When you are dead you wait...you wait until you are not.*"

GNARLED PINES
Edward Crosby Wells

NINE

Adam asked Sam, while massaging her shoulders with gentle hands of familiarity, "Are you okay?"

"I'm okay," Sam answered half-heartedly. "I'm just trying to get my head around all this...you know...ghosts...ghosts?...*Jesus Christ!*...they're real...they're *really real,* aren't they?"

"*Yup,* they're really real, Sam."

"Then, no. *No.* I am *not* okay, Adam. I'm not one bit okay. I'm sorry. I am sorry about how I acted. I was a bitch, wasn't I?"

"*We-e-e-ll.*"

"I should have believed you, Adam. I thought you were crazy."

"I am."

"You know what I mean...*ghosts.* Who would have thought? *Ghosts.* They can't hurt us, can they?"

"Relax. Catch your breath. Ghosts can't bite." While Sam sat in an over-stuffed leather armchair, Adam continued to massage her shoulders—her warm smooth golden skin. Her shoulders, her breasts, her belly, her thighs, all tasted like desire on a mid-summer day in a clearing in a green woods where life chirped, buzzed, and fluttered on rainbow wings; and you knew you were a part of its design. The scent of her was nothing but the fragrance of herself. The scent of her hair perfumed the air with subtle whispers of gardenia. Adam's hands caressingly glided like ten tongues licking up her neck, lithesome and slender. His hands slid downward, lingered on her pulse, then continued on to her shoulders; and the massage began again. "Feeling better?"

"I guess."

"Relax. Nothing to be afraid of...however..." Impersonating Bela Lugosi's Dracula, "maybe *I* vill bite you... bwa-a-a-a."

"*Yeah*...ya think so, *huh?* And I never said anything about being afraid. Your Dracula sucks, by the way. Pun intended."

"Now wait a minute! That's my best impersonation."

"Then, I'm speechless. You've proven yourself to be too much, Mister Goodblood."

"*Really?*"

"That's one of the things I like about you." Sam answered, coyly.

"That I'm 'too much?'" Adam asked, trying not to seem too eager, or fishing for more. He could wait. The time wasn't right. He didn't want to give himself entirely away. He wasn't sure he was ready to open up again only to be dashed once more; at least, not yet—even though he wanted to. "Are there many other things you like about me?"

"A few." She answered, matter-of-factly.

"A few? That's promising...I guess."

"Should I have said one of a whole pile of things?"

"*Hmm*...I'm not sure I like the sound of that." Adam laughed quietly. "Sam...why do you think you have such a problem with ghosts?"

"A problem?"

"You know what I mean. Why can't you let yourself go and accept that they exist; especially, since now you can see them plain as day? You can't un-see a thing once you've seen it, Sam. You know that as well as I. You'd have to look away, pretend there's nothing there, or stick your head in the sand like a dodo bird."

"Ostrich."

"Okay, ostrich."

"I'm Catholic."

*"Huh?...*Practicing?" Adam asked.

"Out of practice."

"Me, too." Adam confessed.

"Catholics don't believe in ghosts," Sam said with apparent authority.

"*Ahh*, but Catholics certainly do believe in ghosts, Sam. Ever hear of the Holy Ghost?"

"That's different, Adam."

"How?"

Sam thought a bit, and found herself confused. *"Okay,"* she thought, *"I know it's not the same...or maybe it is. He's...he's...oh, God...do I want this man?...I don't need this man...I don't need him every day...every night...it's not about his money...'though it'd be nice...God forgive me...is it him?...maybe it's him...it could be him...I hope it's him. We both live in Denver. Convenient. Can love happen in less than a day?...of course it can. I think it can...maybe it can't. Oh, God! I don't know. Already I see he's predictable...in a fun way...most of the time. Okay...the Holy Ghost...or the Holy Spirit...parochial school...it was Ghost. Maybe it was Spirit. Everybody's got a spirit...or a ghost. Hmm. So sweet. I thought he was gay...guess I was wrong. I wonder what he thinks of me...if he thinks of me...after the way I behaved. His hands...they feel so good...don't stop...I do want you...I'm sure of it...but there are the ghosts...maybe they're watching...the ghosts...oh, God! Help me."*

But what Sam actually said was, "Adam, I don't know. It's hard to let go...to walk into...well, into another reality. I'm trying. Honest. I just don't know. Help me out here."

"*Uhh*...what about Casper the friendly ghost?" Adam continued massaging her shoulders.

"He looks like a dumpling," Sam chided.

"*Hmm*. Casper does not look like a dumpling. He's supposed to look friendly. Dumplings look like dumplings. But these ghosts are real people, Sam. I mean, they were real living people, and now they're real ghosts—as real as real gets...for a ghost."

"They could be dumplings disguised as real people, Adam. Ever think of that?"

"Now that you mention it. They could be dumplings from the past. No. From outer space. Space dumplings."

"*Oh, God!* Get outta here. Go get yourself a Ding Dong, Adam."

"We ate 'em all."

Sam exhaled. She breathed regularly. She felt better. "Keep eating those Ding Dongs and you could be a dumpling, yourself."

"*Ha, ha, ha*. And here I thought you liked my hot little belly."

"Little? Well...sorta."

"*Sorta! Sorta?* She said *'sorta.'* Now I know you're feeling better.*"

"A bit." Sam admitted.

"Just a bit?" Adam asked, jocularly. He gently squeezed her shoulders, signaling that the massage was over. He came around and sat in the chair opposite her. "You gotta feel a whole lot better than 'just a bit.'"

"Maybe a wee bit more," Sam smiled, tentatively.

"There you go. I saw that smile, kiddo."

"I'm stranded on this island, Adam. With ghosts. That wasn't a smile. Maybe just a tiny droll grin."

"Nope. It was a smile alright. Like a Cheshire cat."

"Where are we going with this?" Sam asked, resigned.

"As far as you like."

"*Hmm.* What I really want to know is, what are we going to do, Adam? How are we going to get off this island?"

"That's *the* question, isn't it? And the answer is: I don't know yet. I'm thinking about it. But…I need to tell ya, you should be more afraid of Charon than ghosts. Charon is a mass murderer. A serial killer. Charon is evil through and through. *Period.* He did something with the boat, Sam. He hid it. I'm absolutely positive." Adam's worry showed on his face. "I think he knows I'm going to help the ghosts when they all get here. So, he hid the boat."

"Why? Why would he hide it?" Sam showed her worry.

"To keep us here, Sam. To keep me from helping my new theatre friends. Charon can be in at least two timelines, at once. Of that I'm certain."

"Huh?"

"He's here and he's also in nineteen twenty-nine. And who knows how many other timelines?"

"And you know this how?"

"Because I've been to nineteen twenty-nine and he was there; the same Charon. Oh, Sam, there's so much I need to tell you."

"*Wow.* Don't freak me out again, Adam."

"I don't want to, but we need to deal with a different way of seeing things. I did try to tell you, Sam. You read my book, right?"

"Which one?"

"*Gnarled Pines,* of course."

"I reviewed it."

"Yes. And now you're in it. You already know ghosts are real. Now, you gotta accept that the reality on Gnarled Pines has little to do with the reality on the mainland. Even the speed of time, or how it is experienced, is different here. You really should have known all this before you came. I tried to warn you."

"*Okay, okay.* Don't harp."

Adam said in a soothing manner. "I didn't die, disappear, or whatever, Sam. I'm here, aren't I? I've only been gone a few days."

Sam closed her eyes, shook her head, and said, "I didn't know. Had I known what I should have known then, I certainly wouldn't be here now."

"No, you wouldn't…you wouldn't be a part of the book, either. I certainly wish you had listened to me."

"*Yeah*…me too, but I didn't. For Pete's sake, Adam, I get it. Look at it this way, If I hadn't come I wouldn't have met you."

"*Ahh*…there you go, being nice again. Now is the time we kiss, Sam."

"You're funny."

They leaned toward each other and kissed. What had begun as a quick peck on the lips, became a passionate, prolonged kiss.

After a bit, Adam said softly and sincerely, "You really are way too nice. And way too beautiful."

"So are you, Adam.

"Too nice, or too beautiful?"

"Take your pick.

"How about hot and marvelous?

"*Yeah,* how about it?" They kissed some more, and as Sam moved away, she soulfully asked, "What's going to happen to us, Adam?"

"To us?"

"To you and me."

"All I know to say is, if it's meant to happen it will be a beautiful thing."

"I like the sound of that."

"The sound of my dulcet voice, or what I said?"

"You silly...." And they passionately kissed some more.

After they came up for air, Sam said, uncomfortably, "I've been having headaches since I came to this island. They don't last long...a few minutes, that's all, but they're really sharp and painful. It's never happened to me before. I think it must be something in the air."

"Maybe it's me." Adam smiled.

"Stop being silly. Of course it's not you."

"*Um*...then it must be the energy emitting from the trees. If you get close enough to them, and I don't advise that, you can hear an electrical buzz. If that's not unnatural enough, I believe they are the source of the different reality on this island...our reality... now...which is not the same as it is on the mainland. That could be what's giving you headaches."

"I don't understand any of this, Adam."

"Neither do I. What I do know is: there are at least two timelines; the one here on this island and the one on the mainland. I know that with absolute certainty. We are not in sync with the time on the mainland. So, either the time here on Gnarled Pines is snail-pace-slow, or the time on the mainland is going super fast. I think it's the former. In fact, I'm almost sure of it. It really has to be that time is screwed up on Gnarled Pines, and not on the mainland. It makes less sense otherwise. How that is, who knows? Certainly not me. There are at least two physical dimensions. That I also know. There is here, right now, and there is nineteen twenty-nine—both happening as we speak. Somehow, both dimensions have intersected. People are being murdered in nineteen twenty-nine by a Broadway actress with the name of Mona LaBaron, a really nasty bitch, and also by the evil Charon; the same Charon who brought you over from Turtle Run. How he is in two places at once—if you think of time a place—I haven't a clue. All I can say is, it is what it is. The ghosts who are here on Gnarled Pines were murdered in nineteen twenty-nine. And sadly, Sam, there will be more.

"Murders?"

"*Yup*. Mona invited seven guests to Gnarled Pines for the Fourth of July back in twenty-nine for the purpose of feeding them to the trees. The spirits in those trees feed on flesh and blood. They're about to give birth, both here and now and in nineteen twenty-nine, to millions of degenerate spirits; serial killers and Hitler-type monsters who will possess humans around the world. Their goal is to corrupt, cause chaos, create dictators, and maybe end the world. Sam, don't freak, promise me?"

"*Jeez,* Adam…alright. I promise to try. But…but, I think I'm already freaking out."

"*Don't.* You need to keep your wits about you if we're going to survive. Charon is planning to kill us, too."

"*What?* Okay, now I know I'm freaking out."

"I mean, he's going to try. Just try…but he won't. We need to find a way to see that he doesn't, and we will. I can see his machinations at work. I know how dangerous he is. Just tell yourself that we're going to survive this. Believe it! Just believe it and we'll find a way, Sam. *Believe it.*

"God help us."

"We've got to help ourselves, Sam."

"I thought you were Catholic?"

"Out of practice."

Sam's reluctance to accept this new state of affairs could be heard in the trembling of her voice. Nonetheless, she blocked-out much of what Adam had told her, tucked it away in a room in the back of her mind, shut the door, took a deep breath, exhaled, then gave her mind permission to change the subject. "Well," Sam began, "if they are friendly ghosts and not dumplings, and they aren't going to scare the bejesus out of me, maybe they could help us."

"Maybe they could."

"Then, why don't you introduce me to them?"

"The ghosts?"

"Yes, the ghosts."

"I'd be glad to. Thought you'd never ask. They're sitting right over there on the couch."

Sam looked in the direction of the couch and saw King on one end, Hudson in the middle, and Ídolo on the other end. "Oh, my God!"

"Say Hello, Sam. Like I said, they're not going to bite."

"Hello," Sam said, shyly, before making a broad smile and saying again, with sincerity, *"Hello."* Her reluctance was wearing off.

With their voices overlapping, Ídolo, Hudson and King said, "Hello."

"Sam," Adam stood and moved away from the chair, "let me introduce you to King Butcher. King is, by the way, on a U S postage stamp." King smiled proudly and nodded.

"Oh my goodness! I know you." Sam said with great enthusiasm, "I know you from my Women in History class. I can't believe I'm getting to meet you. Oh my god! This is fabulous. You are one brave person, Mister Butcher. Everybody ought to follow your example. You taught me to stand up and be myself, to be whomever it is I am, and with no apologies. As it it turns out, I pretty much like who I am...most of the time."

"Thank you, Sam. Please, just call me King. You're not…"

Sam cut King off, "No. I'm not. But it doesn't matter. I mean, it wouldn't matter one bit if I were. I've thought about…but no. In one way or another, your bravery affects all women. Men as well…I suppose…well, it oughta. I am honored to meet you, Mister Butcher…*uhh*…King."

"You do know I'm a ghost, right?"

Sam chuckled. "Of course."

Adam shouted, "*Hallelujah!* She believes in ghosts." Everyone laughed.

"I certainly do." Sam was ecstatic.

"Let me introduce you to Ídolo." Adam beamed. "Ídolo was a famous dancer on Broadway. He was featured in the *Ziegfeld Follies*."

Ídolo waved and said, "Hello, Sam. It is a pleasure to meet you."

As Sam was about to say something, Hudson jumped in and said, "I'm Hudson Sky. Just call me Hudson. I'm…I'm…well, I'm in the theatre." Hudson was no longer a mangled body. Now, he was back to his former glory—presumably along with his prized possession and from the way Ídolo was cozying up to him, the odds were that Ídolo would be the first to find out. Hudson continued, "I'm not on a stamp, of course, but I'm going to be in Mister Goodblood's book and that should make me famous, too." King and Ídolo chuckled.

Suddenly, Hudson became urgently serious. "You gotta help the others, Mister Goodblood. They're still back there and hiding from Miss Mona and Mister Charon...I don't know what his last name is...or maybe that is his last name...then I don't know what his first name is. I guess it doesn't matter. They're evil as evil gets, Mister Goodblood. Miss Mona's not Miss Mona anymore. She's gone. They get pleasure from...I can't tell you what they did to me...what they made me do. It's too disgusting to say out loud. Maybe I'll tell you when we're alone, so you can put it in your book, if things like that are allowed in books nowadays. But if you do put it in your book, I'll be even more famous, won't I? I sure got a story to tell, I'll tell you that."

"Bet you do," Ídolo swooned.

"Thank you, Hudson," Adam said.

"You've got to help our friends, Mister Goodblood. *Please*."

"I will if I can, Hudson."

"You need to host us, Mister Goodblood."

"I've already decided that I would, King."

"Go back. See what's happening. Maybe then we can figure out something...*please*." Hudson pleaded.

"I've got to sleep in order to do that. But there is nothing I can do to save them from what will happen to them. Their fate is not going to change. We will wait for them here. They'll only have to go through the pain once more. You'll all be together again, you'll see."

"Are you going to sleep now?"

Adam held Sam, "Sam, I must do this."

"I know."

Adam kissed her before heading into the bedroom. Suddenly, he came rushing back. "*Sam!* Do you know the name of the author of the book in your Women in History class?"

"No. It was a text book. It just contained excerpts from the works of women writers. I do seem to remember it was from a book titled *Running From Evil*, or something like that. The author was…was… I think it was Annabelle something."

"Could it have been Annabelle Lovelace?"

"*Yes*. That's it."

The three ghosts jumped up from the couch with jubilance from the good news.

"*Holy shit!* Annabelle escaped! She found a way off the island alive. I never found the original source for the Gnarled Pines story. That was it! This is the bomb! God bless you, Annabelle Lovelace." Adam could have jumped up and down, but he didn't.

"Adam, did you just say 'the bomb?'"

"Sorry. I never said that before."

"Please, don't say it again."

"Easy-peasy." Adam rushed back into the bedroom.

Sam remained in her chair and began a conversation with the three ghosts without fear, disbelief, or a thought to their actually being ghosts—not Holy Ghosts, of course—but certainly fantastic ghosts, the ghosts of real people.

Charon stood outside the lodge, listening and making plans. He could do nothing with the ghosts, but he will kill Adam and Sam, of course—one way or another.

* * *

Adam awoke and found himself in the company of Mona LaBaron.

"*Ahh,* if it isn't Mister Gooseblood come to pay us a visit." Mona's greeting came with an overdose of fake hospitality.

"*Goodblood.*" Adam corrected.

"Of course it's Goodblood! Do you think I'm a raving idiot?"

"I think you might well be, and I also think the world might be better off if you weren't in it. Your death would be cause to celebrate."

"So unkind…*tut-tut-tut.* Right to the blunted point. You should be afraid of me. Why aren't you afraid of me, Gooseblood?"

"Why? Because I'm not here."

"But Charon knows where you are."

"Yes, I've already gathered that."

"Then I gather you came to talk to your little friends."

"You mean those you haven't murdered yet?"

"*Wake up!* Go write your ill-informed book about how Charon and I are going to kill every last one of you. You do know your book has already been written and published, don't you?"

"So I've been told. I don't understand it, but I've been told. I don't know how it ends, yet. Do you?"

"I just told you. It ends with everybody dead. You don't remember your own book? Maybe it wasn't you who wrote it. Maybe it's not worth remembering. Maybe you're dead already."

"Maybe it's for the best that I don't remember, anyway. That way, the book is subject to change."

"I will tell you this, Mister Gooseblood: The Agency wrote most of it. What are those words you like to use...*wow* and *yup?* Unquestionably, wow and yup right back atcha. Take a walk through the woods, kiddo. That's The Agency; the collective who wait to be born, both here and whenever it is you are. You came to see what you could do about your little friends...to help them if you could."

"*Yup.* That's pretty much it."

"There is nothing, Mister Gooseblood, absolutely nothing you can do to change anybody's fate. You should already know that. I heard you admit it. You might as well go back to your own time and wake up. You do realize that you and your girlfriend from Denver will soon...what's the word for it...*Poof*...?"

"May I ask you something, Miss LaBaron?"

"If you must."

"I'm wondering why time passes more quickly on the mainland than it does on Gnarled Pines? Do you happen to know?"

"I don't happen to know. Is it important to you?"

"Kind of."

"Then you need to ask Charon. That is, if he's not standing over your sleeping body right now, this very minute, and about to suffocate you with a pillow, darling."

Adam hated Mona like he never hated anybody in his lifetime, hated like he never thought possible, but he could not help finding her amazingly amusing. He saw her as a performance piece; a highly insecure character spun from a medieval melodrama.

Charon came from out the bedroom with an answer. "Because time goes slower on the island. That's it. That's all. You need to accept things as they are, Mister Goodblood."

"That's not an answer. That sounds more like a threat." Adam expressed dissatisfaction from Charon's ill-considered explanation. "It's not an answer at all. The question was *'why,'*" Adam muttered. "But thank you for not calling me Gooseblood."

Charon's expressionless indifference was palpable. He turned and marched back into the bedroom.

"Who are you, Miss LaBaron?" Adam asked, feeling quarrelsome,.

She flew-up her arms in a grandiose way. "I am an actress, darling."

"Before this current performance, I might have agreed. Who are you? *Really.* I have been dying to know…maybe 'dying' was an unfortunate choice of words. I've read so much about you these past few months. I became a fan of yours…for awhile, anyway…and then…well, I guess I read too much about you. More than I ever wanted to know."

"And your question was?"

"Who are you?"

"Little ol' me? I'm just a girl from Poughkeepsie, New York who went to Vassar. What else is there to know?"

"Nothing more. I know enough. You're boring me." Adam resigned to not asking her again. That was it—the last time.

"I was brilliant on the stage, Gooseblood. I was envied and I was admired. I was loved by my adoring audiences."

"I read that, too. It's a shame you didn't remain on Broadway. How did you go from Vassar to here…to now…after you were so brilliant on the stage?"

"Just lucky, I suppose. All aces. "

"Yes, I thought something like that. *All aces.*"

Mona became abruptly serious. She visibly shifted from one mental state to another; a state seeming totally different; one that might cause one to mistake her new act for real, for actually finally being herself, baring her soul—it was that kind of serious. She became more self-possessed, less Mona LaBaron. "I was drawn to Gnarled Pines. This is where I was reborn. This is where I am meant to be. The last time Arthur and I came up here, two spirits were born prematurely and they had nowhere to go. They were weak and they never could have made it to shore; so, we became their hosts. Arthur hosts one soul, the weaker of the two, and I host the stronger one. When the soul that I host grows stronger…."

Out of the blue, Mona's appearance remolded into something unmistakably malevolent, yet august, lofty and remote. Her cheerless eyes turned scarlet. Her voice became deep, dark and commanding. It was a man's voice: *"I grew stronger from eating Mona's soul. She is still here, for now, what's left of her. When she no longer exists, I will fully exist. This body will be completely mine. I like being a woman. I want to be the partner to Charon that Mona never could have been. She was a woman too shallow for Charon, too stupid to exist. I shall change all that. When the rest of the Broadway food are rotted flesh, and fed to the trees, millions, maybe billions, of us will be born—in more timezones than you can count. We will find hosts the world over. We can go anywhere on Earth in an instant. Mona was the perfect host. She was ripe with four of the deadliest profanities: pride, envy, lust, and greed. I should add, she was void of any self-respect, capable of embracing filth and the most vile of acts, she is my playground, defenseless and compliant. Who could ask for more? The souls that will soon be born will hunt down and possess weak human souls, most of them are; heads of state, presidents, dictators, corporate executives, the corrupt, the thieving rich, and on and on. When they are ripe for possession we begin to change the world. We possess them not just because they are profane souls, sweet and delicious, but because they welcome us and we make them do very bad things. Extremely horrendous things, and they enjoy it. Charon and I will remain on this island and tend to the trees for the next hundred years...and this takes us to you."*

"Me?" Adam asked, breathlessly.

"Yes, you are a man I would love to possess. Although, when I say 'love' it means something entirely different than when you say it. Maybe, 'relish' is a better word."

"I'd go with 'relish.' You wouldn't like possessing me. I have too much hate for your kind."

"My kind? Mister Goodblood, you could not fathom my kind. And all that hate you say you have for my kind is exactly what makes you so delicious. I hear the word 'hate' much more than the word 'love,' especially when it comes to judging others. There are so many of your kind who judge others, but swear they don't actually hate any one of them...the thrill is in the judging. Judging is a powerful activity, Mister Goodblood. It makes humans feel better about themselves. It's such a beautiful dark power. They swear to their imaginary god that they only hate some of the things that others do, and some of the ways they think, but not...no never, do they admit that it is the actual person they hate. They hide

behind the lies they tell themselves. It is said that the things a person does, defines who that person is. Liars, liars all. You got to love them and taste their hate. These humans are delicious! I could eat them alive. I do not judge others. I know them for what they are, Mister Goodblood. They are food for the gods. And, in fact, we do eat them alive."

"I try not to judge others, either. And I wouldn't want to be eaten; at least not while I'm still alive. I tend to think that what people do is their own business."

"How do you know you are alive?"

"I have faith. I believe I am."

"You make me salivate, Mister Goodblood. Consider this: Under the tyranny of dictators, hating the actions of a tyrant without also hating the tyrant himself is not only not possible, it's downright stupid. Everybody hates in one way or another. It makes them feel lighter than air...whole and complete...invincible in their self-empowerment. Dictators are our favorite hosts. I could eat every one of them, slowly, from the inside out. Some I have, actually."

"So...you kill the soul and become the body."

"Something like that, but only until I get bored and move on to another. Maybe a man's body next time. Maybe yours."

"The life of a true sailor."

"Ask yourself about your truth, Mister Goodblood. You hate other humans. I know you do. I can smell it. You hate me. You hate my kind."

"Yes. I do. And I've hated others. So I hate. I'm not perfect. What human is?"

" Not a one, Mister Goodblood. Here is my truth: When you and your lady friend are fed to the trees a new generation will

be born and we will feed on profane souls everywhere. Feeding on your soul might be dull, I suspect. It is the profane souls who will host us without giving it a thought. We make them rich and we make them powerful. We turn them cruel and brutal, and they begin devastating wars; they bring about chaos and death...more to celebrate. Dictators all! When you become fodder, Mister A. J. Goodblood, you will not be missed."

"What the hell am I doing? I'm talking to the devil!"

"You give me too much credit. There are no devils, Mister Goodblood, just the unfortunate we assist to joyfully behave badly. It is always their choice. Always. We only help and nurture them. We enter only by invitation."

"If there are no devils, then why Mona's devil face?"

"That, Mister Goodblood, was a gift from The Agency at her request. We cannot, nor will we ever, be seen other than by the actions of our host. We are invisible. We are primal. We are forever.

Then the voice became, unmistakably, that of Mona. "...I will become stronger and I will have powers you cannot imagine. And that, Mister Gooseblood, is who I am. Just a girl who went to Vassar."

"*Wow.* I think I actually do hate you, and it's truly personal. Thank you for your honestly, Miss LaBaron."

"My honesty? Are you sure of that, darling?"

In an instant, Adam found himself on the rocky shore of Gnarled Pines. He saw Mona's four remaining guests hunting for a place to hide. They did not see him. When Adam spoke they did not hear him.

"It's useless, Mister Goodblood. You're wasting your time."

Adam turned to see who it was speaking to him. He found himself face to face with Arthur Baumgarten. What he saw was literally melting flesh under the hot July sun. "What the…are you Arthur Baumgarten?"

"I am. At least, I was. Now I'm dead. A zombie, you might say."

"A zombie. Of course. I can see that. If you don't mind my asking, why are you here, Mister Baumgarten?"

"I came to watch Mona suffer. I came to produce the show of my revenge. Now, I no longer care to watch. I would save her if I could, but she is too far gone. There is only a shadow of her former self left. She will cease to be soon; totally non-existent, as if she were never here at all. I mourn her already, Mister Goodblood. My role now is to help my friends find a way to escape this island and to arrive safety on the mainland…back to Broadway. Maybe this is my penance, why I am here…to live in death to help my friends. Maybe there is hope for me yet. Who can say? There is a boat at the mouth of the cave."

"You will be pleased to know that the spirits of King, Hudson and Ídolo are in the future, Mister Baumgarten."

"I know. Remember…there is a boat at the mouth of the cave."

Before Adam could say another word he fell back into himself, awoke, and uttered the last thing he remembered hearing, *"There is a boat…somewhere there is a boat…."*

* * *

Cautiously, yet anxiously, Sam asked, "Did your nap provide any answers?" Hoping that Adam's answer would give her good reason to be optimistic, she took in a deep breath, then exhaled with an audible sigh that said, *Okay give it too me quickly. I'm ready to hear the worse.* But what she actually said was, "You did go back, right?"

"Yes, I went back, but first...this is terrific...I found that I can project without needing to be asleep. All I gotta do is go into a meditative state...easy peasy. It doesn't need to be difficult...just meditate. That saved a whole lotta time, and boy, am I gonna have fun when we get off this island...and we will get off this island, Sam. What was I saying? *Yes*...so I get there in a New York minute and *The* Mona LaBaron...I told you about her—*way beyond diva!* —was right there in front of my face. Nearly scared me to death. I was nose to nose and a foot away from her, and boy-o-boy, she was certainly not ready for her close-up. Her skin was like leather, wrinkled as a Chinese Shar Pei, her make-up was smeared, she had an overbite of sharp yellowed teeth. She certainly was something...something nobody oughta see. She had changed since the last time I saw her. I guess getting what she asked for caused her quick deterioration and I mean *quick*—what an awful price to pay. She had nothin' to offer but a great big pile of arrogance. *However*, while she was being her normal unbearable self, something strange happened and, all of a sudden, I found myself in a civil conversation with a dark spirit, the demon that Mona was hosting, the demon that will take complete possession of her, and soon...no more Mona. She was pretty much just a body possessed by a chatty spirit."

"What are you saying, Adam? I mean, *really?*"

"For real. It was a compelling experience, Sam. Anyway, after that, I found myself on the shoreline and saw the others." Adam nodded to the three ghosts sitting on the couch. "I tried to get their attention, but they didn't see me, and when I spoke to them, they didn't hear me, either. I guess to them I was a ghost."

"So, it was all for nothing." Sam sighed.

"*No, no, no.* Nothing's for nothing, Sam. I can confirm, with certainty, that the others are still alive…o*h!*…and I met Arthur Baumgarten, the Broadway producer. He was a zombie. His, face was melting, but he seemed a nice guy. Thank goodness I was a ghost from the future and couldn't smell him."

"Is this a joke!? What are you doing, Adam? If you're trying to be funny I don't appreciate your sense of humor!" Sam began to show dangerous signs of a vitriolic nature. Her anxiety level was going through the roof. She was about to have a meltdown and she hadn't brought her medication. For moment or two, Adam thought that she might be hosting a dark spirit. Was that possible? Of course it was possible, but not likely. He dismissed the thought without further consideration.

The pines were bleeding and humming louder than ever. Adam knew that they didn't have much time left to get off the island. He also knew that a staggering number of dark spirits were about to be born, and he needed to do something more than just escape—he needed to save the planet from yet more wars and divisive hatred. The last thing the world needs are more damned demons! Adam took time out to have an inner dialogue. *"Save the planet? Now that's the stupidest thing I ever heard. I can't save the planet. It's beyond saving. First, I'd need to save everybody from their own self-destructive ignorance. Yes…that's true…but it's not always their own fault…in fact, it rarely is…have you observed how fiercely they will protect their ignorance? But the planet? Why bother? They've practically already destroyed it. It is probably beyond saving. Stopping the unleashing of the dark spirits seems of little consequence…it won't matter…but, you're supposed to be my conscience, why don't you help me? I never stop helping you, Adam. Never."*

"Can't do much about my sense of humor, but I assure you that it wasn't a joke, Sam. I would never joke about anything as serious as this. We could be killed if we don't figure out what we're gonna to do! So, we're gonna figure this out and figure it out soon. I have no intention of being killed."

"You say these things as though you knew for sure. You don't know. How could you?" Sam's eyes teared and were about to run over.

"We're gonna be all right, Sam? Remember; you just gotta believe. Easy peasy."

Sam snapped back, "I can't!"

"Where did my Sam go? You sound a bit...well...not like yourself."

"What do you know about how I sound, Adam? Really? I don't know you and you don't know me...and I don't know anything about your sense of humor...also, I'm not your Sam. All I know is you're a writer from Brooklyn who acts like a child and eats Ding Dongs for breakfast. So, please excuse me if I can't get my head around any of your shit. I'm falling apart, Adam. I need help. "

"I'm truly sorry to hear that, Sam. I certainly understand. Lean on me. Let me help you."

"You can't. But thank you. I need my meds."

"I can't help you there."

"I know."

"Just relax and don't think about your meds. Tell yourself your strong and you don't need them."

Sam looked at Adam with sad watery eyes. She felt contrite. She sighed and said nothing.

Adam left Sam to sit and pull herself together. He turned his attention to the three ghosts. "You should know that Arthur said he was determined to help the others get off the island. He sent his regards to all of you. I should have told him about Annabelle escaping to the mainland, but I forgot. I believe Arthur was sincere and dedicated to helping them. If we don't meet them here, then there's hope that they all made it to the mainland. We already know Annabelle did, and since she was part of the group Arthur was helping, there's a good chance that they'll all make it."

King lifted his head Heavenward and pleaded, "God, help them, *please*."

Ídolo and Hudson responded with, *"Amen."*

Adam closed his eyes and said, "*Yes*. God help us indeed."

In the nanosecond, before Adam could say another word out loud, he was having an inner conversation: *I don't think Sam considers things long enough to understand anything outside herself. Why is that? I don't know. I think it's selfish...yes...it is... but there's always a good reason for that, too. Really? I don't know what it is. She seems combative...not to mention unflattering... don't like it...don't like it at all. I'll need to keep and eye on her... for her own sake. She's a good person. She has problems. And you don't? Hmm. I did learn something more about what I've been thinking. I've been wondering about The Agency...the dark souls within the pines...the collective...they sort of run things in absentia...that's The Agency. Every one of them can think of where they want to go, and there they are, across the globe...just with a thought. Good spirits can do the same...and they can also settle into the life of a host...share in that host's life without possessing the host...share their thoughts and ideas with the host's natural spirit...remind the host of important things...and best of all, the host and the spirits within can meet through meditation...who are you speaking with now? We can talk and help you figure out how to get off the island. We help you write. You need to listen to us more closely, Adam."*

At the other end of Adam's nanosecond, Sam muttered, "Are you aware that we need a boat to get off this island? There doesn't seem to be a boat. What are you going to do without a boat?" Sam's questions were laced with bitterness, sadness, anger, then anger for being angry, disappointed, frightened, desperation, and a case what-am-I-doing-here? Altogether: fear.

Adam said, "I don't know. And, if you remember, I warned you to stay away from this island. I warned you several times. Blame yourself!"

"*What?* What did you say? I am tired of hearing this from you. So I didn't listen and stay home. So fucking what!?"

"I'm sorry. I'm tense too, you know. Anyway, there *is* a boat, Sam"

"Where?"

"Let me think. I just need to think and wait. It'll come to me. Promise."

Ídolo interjected, "When you die on this island, your soul is trapped here forever, or, at least, until it finds a host. This island is like a spider's web, and sooner than later it's going to get you. Charon always knows where we are and what we're saying. What we need to do is figure a way to keep Charon in the dark, but I don't see a way to do that. And yes, there is a boat."

"Well that's encouraging." Sam was complacent.

"*Yup.* There simply must be a way to keep him from spying on us." Adam knew in his heart of hearts that he was not going die on Gnarled Pines. *No friggin' way!* The idea of it was preposterous. He would not be a victim. He would get off this island, and that's that. When Adam felt this certain of something, anything, he wasn't going to be denied satisfaction. When he knew a thing, he knew it. *Period. No question!*

"Yes, there is a boat, Adam," Ídolo said. "You can't go through the lighthouse, he's sure to stop you, but you can walk along the shore until you come to the entrance to the cave where he keeps it. The rocks are torturous and there are boulders you'll need to climb over. There is no other way to the shoreline than going down to the dock and walking maybe half a mile to the entrance of the cave. Like I said, it's rocky and dangerous. I know this because Charon dragged my body over those rocks while on his way to the cave…*and his filthy workshop.*"

"We need to get Charon somewhere else, get his attention away from us, while we go grab the boat and skedaddle," Hudson offered.

"Exactly, but that's the problem—getting him somewhere else." Adam agreed.

"Charon is probably listening to us and laughing his fool head off right now," King added.

Charon *was* listening, but not laughing. For him, life was a game that always ended in torture and death—exquisite and thrilling. After countless years in exile, no longer the ferryman, Charon was left alone on the island of Gnarled Pines without a reason to exist. When he was given the duties to watch over the spirits in the pines, and to feed them their special diet of rotted human flesh, he felt useful once again. Finally, he had something to do; and having something to do gave him reason enough to exist. His duties demanded unspeakable acts for The Agency. Through time, alone over thousands of years, he lived totally within himself; he was the soul within himself; he grew accustomed to his sordid deeds, until, as the world dashed its way through time, Charon was free to mold himself; and so he did. Charon was his own creation. Charon once again was cobbled together, except this time he had cobbled himself together. As far as Charon was concerned, God was dead! There was only The Agency. The Agency gave Charon a violent lust for the darkest of passions and desires, along with powerful supernatural abilities— such as his inexplicable ability to be omnipresent; and his ability to stop and reverse time.

Exasperated, Sam got up, *humphed,* and went into the bedroom.

"I'm sorry about Sam. She's having a difficult time. I wish she had never come to the island. Maybe she doesn't realize how badly she is behaving? I think she does. The island's dark spirits may be beginning to effect her. I don't think so. I'll go and see what I can do for her. That's a good idea, Adam. Jesus Aitch! When those dark spirits are born they will destroy all the good that is left in the world, and I cannot imagine the evil they will replace it with. Pure evil. We can't leave without doing something about that! Any ideas? I have many ideas. Listen to me and we'll figure something out. I've never let you down before, have I? No, but sometimes I tend to panic, you know? I do know, Adam. I certainly do."

GNARLED PINES

Edward Crosby Wells

TEN

The rocks beneath the feet of Mona's remaining four guests were unforgiving. The cool balm of the rising water beneath their aching feet warned them that the ocean was gathering strength enough to hurl them against the side of the island where powerful waves had heaved and crashed for millennia, carving out the cliff's sold rock wall beneath Gnarled Pines one minuscule fragment at a time. Over the years, Arthur walked this trail of rocks, rocks smoothed by the ocean along with rocks recently torn from the cliff, still jagged, dangerous, and waiting for the ocean to shave their barbed edges. At every opportunity, Arthur escaped the hurly-burly of Manhattan to trudge upon the forbidding shoreline as a feat of personal satisfaction—danger has its attraction—on an abandoned planet at the other end of the universe, with only the voices that came from the ocean, the sun, and from the rocks themselves to accompany him. On many a warm evening along the island's shore, Arthur would reach out and scoop up sparkles of moonlight as they flickered upon the swelling ocean that warned him to scuttle back to the lodge before high tide; warning him to mind each step; warning him how each maneuver must be carefully watched and well thought-out. Atop the island of Gnarled Pines there was but one warning: *take care to avoid what will inevitably kill you.*

Losing balance, now and again, the remaining four guests continued to stumble their way over the rocks; the rounded rocks that were painful on the arches, the jagged rocks that could pierce the arches, rocks that grew hotter under each step, and as they moved along the rocks became larger and more challenging under the scorching sun; and if that were not enough, the ocean's mist was scant solace.

Florence and Annabelle held hands for support. Reggie and Willy also held hands as they followed behind. Willy had finally regained consciousness from what Mona shoved down his throat to keep him quiet while she and Charon savaged Hudson. Reggie came back to the land of the living when Willy finally opened his eyes and smiled. Reggie could hardly contain his delight to see his best friend finally able to stand; albeit, with Reggie's stable and caring support. They stumbled on until they reached the large and imposing boulders that forced them to stop and consider their situation and—most of all—to take a much needed rest in the shade provided by those Boulders.

"My stomach, Reggie. My stomach aches something awful."

"Here, sit down, Willy."

"The pain. Oh God, Reggie. It burns."

Reggie called to the women. "What in hell are we doing? I don't want to climb over those. And why should I? *This is it!* Willy and I ain't moving. There's nothin' to do, and there's no place to hide." Reggie roared. "This is as far as we go, damnit! We're too old for this shit. *No more.*"

Florence agreed emphatically. "We need to rest and gather our strength. That's all, Reggie. We just need to rest awhile. Soon you'll feel differently. For the time being, this place looks safe enough to me. If we get behind a couple of those boulders up by the cliff's wall, maybe Charon won't find us…or maybe he won't be looking for us…maybe he doesn't care anymore. No, that's not likely…can't be likely…not likely at all, Reggie. He's gonna find us if he wants to…when he wants to…oh, shit!…he's gonna kill us." Florence showed her rising temper. "*No!* No, no, no! He ain't gonna kill us. He ain't gonna kill me. He ain't gonna kill any of us. I won't let that happen. You can bet your bottom dollar on that. I didn't live this long, work so hard, to end this way. None of us did. I won't have it!" And she sounded like she meant it.

Reggie was solemn, "What's the use, Florence? What's the point of going on? What's the point of anything, anymore? Ídolo isn't coming back. He's dead. There's no way Charon would have let him off the island. He's dead and that's that, Florence."

"What an awful thing to say, Reggie. Of course he's coming back." Although, if one were to listen closely they could hear certainty wavering in Florence's voice.

"No," said Reggie, resigned. "He's not. We might as well face it. We are prisoners on this island and there is no way to escape. Face it, goddamnit! We ain't gonna escape this godforsaken place, Florence."

"Not with that attitude we ain't." Florence expressed with all the conviction she could muster, which was not all the conviction it would take to convince herself that there was no longer any reason not to be doubtful and afraid. "I'll tell you somethin', Reggie: fear's a kick in the ass! It pushes us to giddy-up and go."

Annabelle stood motionless; the realization of their situation had overwhelmed her and drove her farther into the isolation of herself; slipping away into the soundlessness and darkness that consumed her. She said nothing. She felt nothing. Then, something happened: *"There's something…dead…there's something…someone…dead…all over…it's finished…a life ends…*

is it mine? Excuse me, sir. Do you know where am I? You're no*where, ma'am. Nowhere? I can't be nowhere. How did I get here? Over the rocks. What rocks? What is everybody talking about? No...don't tell me...I don't want to know...not yet...when I'm ready. Please...please. Can you help me? I'm not supposed to die...not yet. I have so much to do...so many parts to play...I haven't danced down a staircase yet...each step lighting up as I tap my way down...a magical entrance...followed by the girls in the chorus. It isn't fair. It just isn't fair. Please help me, God."*

Willy raised his head and began to say something to Reggie, but just as he was about to utter his first word he violently gagged, chocked-up, and was unable to breathe. As he gasped for air the sound of his wheezing and smothering grew more loud, more desperate.

"Hey, buddy," Reggie held Willy tightly. "Let's get you comfortable." Willy continued to fight for air. Reggie was frantic. "C'mon, buddy, breathe." Willy's only response was to die in Reggie's arms. Reggie slowly lowered Willy's head to the rocky surface. Blood rolled from Willy's open mouth and down his cheek. Reggie saw Willy's blood smeared on his own arm. Reggie rubbed his arm and it felt like sandpaper. Then, blinding flecks of light stung as they pierced Reggie's eyes, causing him to squint before focusing on the tiny lights that he recognized, through mounting tears, as reflections of ground glass ablaze in Willy's blood under the unforgiving clarity of the sun. *Willy's blood!* Reggie jerked from convulsions that rumbled through his body. He felt he would explode with anger; tear himself into shreds that would fly into the cosmos. Willy's heart stuck in his throat and prevented him from saying a single word; not one word; not the word he wanted to say; *help. Help.* Annabelle and Florence knelt next to them while hot, salty tears flooded all their faces.

"I swear to God I'm going to kill her! Hear me God! I'm going to kill her!" Reggie screamed heavenward with such ferocity that if there were a God, God could not help but hear him.

Arthur Baumgarten could no longer remain silent. Arther knew that it was time to make his presence known. Unnoticed, he walked up and startled them when he said, "I am so sorry, Reggie. but it will do you no good to kill her. She's not Mona, Reggie. Mona is already dead. And whatever she has become cannot be killed by you, or any other mortal. Otherwise, I might have murdered her myself."

Florence could barely believe her eyes. *"Arthur?"*

"Yes."

*"Wha…*what happened to you?" Unnerved, Florence asked.

"Please, don't be frightened. Problem is, my body's dead, but I'm still in it…walking."

"Oh my God." Florence was dumbstruck.

"Reggie, you need to know," Arthur began, "Willy continues to live in spirit. There's nothing religious about it. It's just the nature of things. Willy is a hundred years in the future along with Ídolo, Hudson and King. They are with that Goodblood fellow you met at the seance."

Reggie took a deep breath, wiped his eyes, looked up and winced at the sight of Arthur. "A zombie?"

"I suppose you could call me that, but I don't walk around blindly and eat people, if that is what you mean."

"Good to know," Florence said.

Reggie said, as tears rolled down his face, "What do you mean when you said Willy continues to live?"

"He isn't dead, Reggie. He's still on the island, but a hundred years in the future. He'll be fine, Reggie."

"Bullshit, Arthur. Bullshit!"

"No, it isn't, Reggie. I swear to you, he's happy and making plans to escape Gnarled Pines with Mister Goodblood."

"And I'm supposed to believe you? What a crock!"

"I'm sorry, Reggie. I truly am." Arthur tried to console him, but Reggie wailed.

Annabelle looked up, steadied her gaze upon Arthur, then turned away as if what she saw never registered. *"Please...please tell me this isn't happening."*

The sight and scent of Arthur Baumgarten's rotting flesh began to permeate the air beneath Gnarled Pines.

* * *

After a hundred years of sleep, the pines were demonstratively alive. They dragged their bloody branches, scraped them over the rock-hard surface, droned more loudly, gradually rose and stretched their heavy limbs above the island's floor, until gravity grabbed hold and forced them back down with one quick snap. Soon, the trees will gather enough strength to rise high as the lighthouse and flail their arms in a dire dance throughout the deadly woods, and without the nuisance of gravity. Soon the pines will drip thick red blood and scream as they give birth to countless dark spirits that will rise and disappear as they begin their voyage around the globe, seeking eligible hosts who are amoral and vulnerable to the furthering of their own evil inclinations; eligible hosts have never been in short supply in any period in the history of humankind. Throughout the world the dark spirits will find their hosts and when they do they will set about to deepen their evil and change their hosts into personifications of pure depravity—each with immoral and malevolent intentions to escalate the corruption of humankind; humans, irresolute, angry, unhappy, filled with rage and lust, who feel cheated of everything they do not possess, have always been easy-pickings for the dark spirits.

The eagerly awaited hundred-year birth of the dark spirits will bring new atrocities. There will be a stock market crash, and another; a great depression filled with hunger and death, and another; another world war, another holocaust, the dropping of nuclear bombs, unending wars in the Middle East, unending savagery, children caged and dying along closed borders, new and deadlier tyrants, failing democracies, more chipping away at human decency, more disregard for humanity, more ways to kill large segments of the world's population who are deemed dangerous, inferior, or they have something someone else wants; more reckless uncaring for the survival of planet Earth, the rise of American dictators, pandemics from manmade viruses, a weeding-out of the underclasses; and more and more of every vile possibility. Every hundred years new enemies of humankind appear; enemies of Godliness, of whatever one may call the good in the miraculous nature of existence.

Surveying their Lilliputian sovereignty, Charon and Mona stood on the catwalk surrounding the lighthouse lantern. Mona was leaning over the railing; the blue enamel veneer peeled off against her palms as she listened to the rhythm of the pulsating pines, hearing their soothing hum that increased and expanded her senses with pure eroticism. Mona experienced a perpetual orgasm; the climax ending the Forth of July fireworks that she and Teddy, Teddy somebody, a schoolmate, they sat and watched the fireworks, his arm salty with sweat languished around her shoulder while the fingers on the hand of the other sweaty arm crawled up her leg and gave her shudders of anticipation for something, something that was coming, though what, she had no idea; but she felt her world explode and she hadn't yet reached puberty. It was on the bank of the Hudson she lost her virginity and she has been trying to find it, to reclaim it, trying to experience the ecstasy of her very first time, but she could not. The boys under the bleachers, the boys in the bushes, the men who took her to their own place, or under trees, in graveyards, in sleazy motels—she loved every one of them. She especially liked motels where she felt free to be more aggressive, to be in control, to be in a place where she could fulfill her unspeakable and depraved desires, to be in a place where she could leave motel rooms a vulgar mess for somebody else to clean. She did not want it to ever end, she wanted to go higher, to feel the presence of a man, any man, and her desires finally brought her to Charon. His limitless black desires mixed with hers and she realized that she still had more to learn; more first-time explosions from depravities she hadn't imagined possible until Charon who would fulfill her desires as no man had ever done before. The hum of the pines effected her in a way that encouraged her ravenous pursuit to discover new realms of abominations.

  Charon leaned over the railing with his body firmly touching Mona's. The hum of the pines filled him with visions of Plato, Socrates and Aristotle. He knew them all. They enjoyed the trip across the river. Most don't. Most fear the next shore. Most fear change. His passengers each gave him much. Most, through their foreboding and anguish, gave Charon a glimpse of the essential human spirit, which gave him the tools to self-construct in their opposite image. Then, at the height of his fulfillment, Charon ended. He was thrown into limbo where, other than a dull and constant pain, he no longer existed; until he awoke on the island of Gnarled Pines.

Charon stood straight and said, referring to the last of Mona's guests, "They are on my beach."

"A pile of rocks, you mean." Mona corrected.

"My beach. Rocks or not, it is my one and only beach," Charon chided in his generally tedious monotone; a tone of his own design without a wisp of emotion. "It is all I have been given. I am bound to my kingdom in the Atlantic. Surely, you understand my attachment to my humble dominion."

"Yes. Of course. Forgive me."

"There is nothing to forgive, Miss Mona. Now we have each other and we will create a world in our own image."

"I like the sound of that."

"Baumgarten and the final three have gotten together. He is helping them search for a sanctuary from us, Miss Mona, but there is no such place. I do not know why they try the impossible. None the less, they do—they try the impossible over and over again. Humans seem destined to persist in hopeless efforts. They run and hide and fight to survive their unavoidable fate. The nature of fate is its inevitability. On and on and they never stop. They are tenacious. Their desires and quests are made of daydreams and the unobtainable—which only drives them towards the certainty of an uncertainty they spend a lifetime trying to avoid: the end of dreams. It is the sum of themselves that matter in a lifetime; but, when looking back at the end of dreams they are forced to see how nothing in their miserable lives ever mattered. In the end, most succumb to their essential flaw—panic from the fear of change.

That brings us to those still on the beach—my rock beach, Miss Mona, my shoreline. I have lived on this island since whenever. I do not recall coming into being on Gnarled Pines. I simply awoke here. But before I came to be here, I was an invaluable ferryman. I was *The* Ferryman. I began with the original Adam himself; the result of a single atom exploding. I was the one and only Ferryman. Now I am here. A gardener to gods. Here is as good a place as any other. Here is where we are. Here is where I breathe and walk and talk and live. Tell me, Miss Mona, what do you think we should do?"

"Should do?"

"With the final three. What pleasantries have you in mind to expose their last essential fatal flaws? Roasting them and watching their blistering skin bubble and burst? That's been done to death. Tying them down and eating them while they watch us chewing what is left of their lives? That's worth considering. What is your pleasure, Miss Mona?" Charon asked in an officious monotone manner; as if he were a waiter in a hamburger joint handing her a menu.

"I will consider what's fitting for each of them. You call me 'Miss Mona' even though you know she no longer exists. Why is that, Charon?"

"Because when I look at your body I see Miss Mona. I cannot see the color of your spirit otherwise. Do you want me to stop?"

"Charon! No. I was only wondering. I like being called Miss Mona. I enjoy being in the body of a woman. I like to feel my own vagina. I will be her for as long as you like. Besides, I have her memories. I can be her whenever you want. I want to be a woman. I want to be *your* woman. On this island you are all I want. I think somewhere there is a piece, a speck, a shadow of the consciousness of Mona LaBaron left. Yes, I believe so. I will do whatever it takes to satisfy you. I like being called Miss Mona, Charon."

"That would please me. I will continue."

"Then I shall be your Miss Mona, every time."

"Good,"

"What about Baumgarten? What is he doing here? What can we do about him? I still feel too many of Mona's absurd emotions. I do not want him here, Charon."

"There is nothing we can do, Miss Mona. Baumgarten was brought back for a reason by an uncommonly powerful spirit. It is not a spirit that I have encountered before. I have heard of it, but I have not seen it. It is not a dark spirit. It is a spirit that has become more and more powerful over the millennia—it is to be avoided. Baumgarten is untouchable, predestined, and he is already dead."

"Such a pity to know there is nothing we can do to him. *Ahh*, the pleasures I could feel with his body now." Mona sighed.

"Why did you hate him in life, Miss Mona? I don't want your memories of him to get in the way of our fun."

"It won't. I promise. I don't know why I continue to hate him," Mona confessed. "Maybe what is left of the life of Mona knows...but not me. Although, it must have been something once...the residue of all that hate...some reason I had all that hate...or Mona had...so it must have been for something real, but after awhile one gets used to a thing and forgets the reason for it. It gets easier to continue rather than to look back and chance seeing that the fault may have been your own. Who wants to see that? That's Mona talking. I am certain she does not want to remember something she chose to forget. I wish I hadn't brought her up.

Humans are consumed by the pretense they call love, only because they can hate what is contrary to it. It is hate they feel most strongly. Hate is the motivation that allows them to maintain the pretense they call love. They are an unknowable paradox, humans are. "

"Maybe. What have you decided about the final two?"

"You mean three, Charon."

"No. Reggie his being taken care of."

"That narrows the choices. It must be something out of the ordinary. We won't do them both at the same time. Fun that will linger. It must be memorable."

"We will make it memorable. Do not forget, Miss Mona, that we can take the boat ashore and bring back any body we like."

"Thrilling."

"Death should be slow." Charon said, deviously. "It should always be slow."

"Of course." Mona smiled back with equal deviousness. "And shockingly original."

"Did you notice that the body of the one who was called Willy is no longer there, Miss Mona?"

"No. Where did it go?"

"While they were all focused on Baumgarten and not on Willy, they did not notice when I went down and ferried his body away in far less than a second. Unfortunately, I had to forfeit the pleasure of dragging his body back over the rocks—I do enjoy maiming a body first, getting them juicy and ready for ripening—but this time it called for expediency. I took it directly to the workroom, below the lighthouse. And that's where I took Reggie."

"I never saw you leave here, Charon."

"That is what I was formed to do. That is what made me The Ferryman…quick and quiet, then on to the next. You probably blinked when I stopped time. I can move through time and change it if I like. I'll teach you how to play with it. I've ferried tens of thousands one at a time in less than an endless part of a second."

"You can do that?"

"I did do that…once." And if Charon could sigh, this is where he would. "Would you like to see where I work, Miss Mona?"

"Of course." Mona answered while conjuring visions to satisfy her exquisite desires; and her favorite vision of all—the tender purity of Hudson, a profound joy. While she pictured Hudson, unreserved gratification raced through her body in cascades of carnal fulfillment.

"Come," beckoned Charon. "I will show you another kind of pleasure, beyond anything you ever imagined."

"I would like that, Charon. I would like that very much."

After managing the constant downward steps of the spiraling staircase, there was still the descent into Charon's workplace. Upon arriving, Mona breathed-in deeply, taking in the fragrance of Charon's fetid air for her first time. In a wide trough caked with dried blood, left by countless cadavers, lay Willy's body, already stripped of his clothing and ready for surgery. All this was pure ecstasy to Mona—to the thing inside Mona's body.

"Here," said Charon, handing Mona a nine inch boning knife, also covered with dried blood. He pointed to the body's throat, "Insert it here. Then pull it down to here." Charon instructed, indicating the navel.

Mona took the knife, sniffed it, licked it, grinned, and placed the tip of it on Willy's Adam's apple and with one quick thrust she plunged the knife, dead-center, into it. She giggled and felt consummate delight as she withdrew the knife, licked it clean, then plunged it in again, and then again before she ripped the blade down the center of his ribcage, glided it to his belly button where she plunged it deeply within and jabbed it in and out until gas, pieces of un-chewed lobster, and entrails escaped his butchered flesh. She twisted the knife's blade several times before carving another trail several inches parallel to her prior incision, then back to his throat where she sliced a bloody canal connecting the two parallel incisions. Mona's eager fingers intertwined with Charon's as they dug beneath Willy's skin and peeled it downward; leaving uneven pieces of flesh and fat on the underside of the cadaver's epidermis.

After savoring the sweet flesh of Hudson earlier, leaving blood pouring over her chin, Mona had already developed a lust for the taste of human flesh. The thought of what she was about to do with the still warm corpse of Willy caused her to violently shiver with a wicked passion that filled her with aching anticipation. She gathered a handful of blood and flesh and rubbed it between her thighs, inserted it into herself and squirmed with inexplicable satisfaction. She removed her hand and offered it to Charon. He lifted her hand to his mouth, then sucked and, one by one, licked her fingers clean. Mona unbuttoned his trousers, scooped a handful of intestines out of the corpse, rubbed his enormous member with them, then she knelt and wrapped her lips around it, sucking while masterbating herself with warm intestines in one hand, while her other hand was shoved deeply into Charon's anus. Their screams of satisfaction could be heard on the shoreline and out to sea.

ELEVEN

A dam went into the bedroom and closed the door. Sam was sitting on the edge of the bed crying. Adam sat next to her, put his arm over her shoulder and.... *"Shhh...it's okay."*

"It's not okay, Adam. We're going to die."

"Hold that thought," Adam said while getting up and running to the door. He ran to the dining room table, snatched his composition book and pen then ran back, sat next to Sam on the bed and, breathing heavily, Adam wrote, *"How many times must I tell you? We're NOT going to die. Have plan. Say nothing you don't want C to hear."*

Sam looked at Adam directly and, without a word, used her eyes alone to say, *"Really? You think so? I don't believe."* Or perhaps they were saying, *"Oh God, I pray."* However, what she said to herself was, *"Lost my mind...must've...no...didn't bring my meds...hallucinating...ghosts...he goes to sleep and time travels... should've brought my meds...what did he do with the boat? We're going to die...can't think. They're just words...'I am going to die' are just words. Stunned...if stunned means blank...my heart... pounds...I hear it...feel it...thump, thump...along with that god-awful electric hum from those hideous trees...can you call them trees...it never stops...the hum...never...think...oh God, can't swallow...I can't swallow...think...breathe...deep...yes...there... I'm dead already, aren't I?"* Sam shifted her attention to the frog in the bottle, shivered and said, *"We're going to die, frog...did it take long?...was it painful?...did Mona LaBaron enjoy it?...dying...just like you, frog, I'm dying..."* Death is only a word, nothing more;

neither sticks nor stones, just a word. Death is a word without meaning, you cannot hold it, feel it, or know it until it is and when it is it really isn't anymore.

"*Shhh*...not here, not now."

"We don't have a boat, Adam."

"*Shhh*...don't worry about the boat." Adam wiped her tears with his fingers. "Everything will be fine. You'll see. *C'mon*, feel better."

"But if there isn't any boat...." Sam sniffled.

"No worries. Are you ticklish?"

"No! Don't tickle me."

"Only if you promise to feel better."

"I don't know...."

Adam raised his hands, his fingers made I'm-going-to-tickle-you motions. "I'm coming for you."

"Stop! Stop it! Okay...okay...I feel better. I feel so much better. I cannot tell you how much better I feel."

"Really?" His fingers still dancing in the air.

"Yes!"

Adam smiled and said, "Good to hear it." He pulled her into him and held her firmly.

After a minute or so, Sam looked up with red, watery eyes, and contritely said, "Adam...about before...you know...I'm sorry. I really am. I'm tired...overwhelmed, I guess...and I forgot to bring my medication."

"For?"

"Depression, anxiety. I suffer bipolar rage."

"Rage?"

"It's totally under control. It has been for years...until now."

"*Wow.* But you forgot to bring your medication."

"I wasn't thinking. I was in a hurry to come here. I can hold out until I am either murdered, or make it back home."

"Is there something I can do?"

"Just keep holding me. And keep me alive if you can. And *please* understand I don't mean to be mean to you, Adam. I'm sorry."

"Well...thank you. You made my day."

Adam held her as if his arms could say *I'll never let you go.* He inhaled the fragrance of gardenia—and he kissed her on the head, but not before taking in a deep breath of her essence. *"She's needy. Beautiful, yet so needy. How is that possible? No. This will never work. This happens too many times with me. Maybe you're the one who's needy? Yeah, I'm the one. Always the one...who are you?...who do you think I am...me?...a deeper me?...my conscience?...my subconscious?...just you...only you...I'm talking to myself! Well...maybe...."*

Sam sniveled again, then asked, "Where are...you know... the ghosts?"

"On the porch. They were just joined by Willy."

"Willy?"

"A theatre director—Wilson Woodhouse. I read he was one of the best. Back in the early nineteen hundreds, there was a bit of a scandal surrounding him. I forget what it was. Anyway, nothing came of it. It blew over and he went on to be one of the best stage directors of his time."

"And he's on the porch, too?"

"*Yup.* Mona murdered him. She fed him ground glass."

"*Jesus Christ!*"

Adam lifted Sam's head, gave her a peck on the cheek, reached for his composition book and wrote: *Leave tonight.* Adam held the book up so that Sam could read it, and then he said aloud, "*So-o-o*...have you any plans for the day? Something special? Something to write home about?"

Sam took in a deep breath, let it out, wiped her eyes, thought for a moment, decided to play along, and answered, "I thought I might go down to the seashore and lie in the sun...maybe wiggle my toes in the ocean. Or, perhaps, walk through the woods and hunt for mushrooms."

"What brave ideas," Adam said, dramatically, and then, "I might write for awhile...even though I'm told my novel is already written...apparently helped with some details by a demon. They say, the devil is in the details."

"I have heard that God is in the details."

"No argument from me. I don't see why not." Adam suddenly had a thought and turned to Sam and asked, hopefully, "Was *Gnarled Pines* a bestseller!?"

"Could have been. I don't remember."

"*Is she being coy?*" Adam wondered, then said, "Don't play with me, Sam."

"*Oh*...okay. Pretty good. It was a long time ago. It might have been. I really don't remember, but I'm sure it did well...pretty good."

"*Pretty good!?* Christ! I'm a has-been already."

"Stop begging. We made a shitload of money."

"Music, music, music to my ears! Sam, I don't think there are any mushrooms on this island."

"Okay. I don't like mushrooms anyway." Sam giggled.

"Me either. Never did like 'em. Maybe I'll work on getting back into shape…do a few pushups…."

Sam interrupted him, "Not with that Ding Dong belly of yours."

"*Hah, hah*. Very funny. It's genetic. My entire family—my father, my grandfather, lots of uncles and a couple aunts—all had Ding Dong bellies…some cousins, too."

"They had Ding Dongs in your grandfather's time?"

"It was my Grandmother who gave Hostess the recipe."

"*Bullshit.*"

"*Yup*. That's what it is, alright. I think it was the recipe for Twinkies. I could be wrong. Anyway, I might come down and join you on the beach. It looked so beautiful in the brochure. *Or-r-r*…I have a better idea. You could come up to the lodge afterward, Sam, and let me *join* you," Adam said with a salacious leer.

"*Well, well, well*…you nasty little boy…sounds pretty good to me…to soothe my nerves, you know…better than my meds. Pretty good means 'fucking fantabulous' by the way." Sam said with a sly smile.

"Good to hear. I'm a great nerve-soother. Goes way back. I come from a long line of nerve-soothers, too, on my grandfather's side of the family." Adam bragged.

"Did they all have Ding Dong bellies, too?"

"Not a one."

"So, when was the last time you soothed somebody's nerves?"

"*Ahh*. Let's see…*um*…never. I never soothed a one. Made it up. My bad."

"You stinker!" Sam accompanied her words with a playful slap on his biceps. She jumped up and said, "I'm hungry. Goin' to the kitchen. What would you like?"

"I don't know. What have we got?"

"Well, I'll just go and have a look." Sam sashayed to the kitchen. Opened the cupboards and the ice box and didn't come up with much. She shouted back from the kitchen. "Peanut butter. Baloney. Flour tortillas. *Flour tortillas?*"

"I brought 'em with me."

"Well then, let's see. *Um*...I got it. We're going to have peanut butter and baloney on old flour tortillas. *Yummers....*" Sam yelled. The peanut butter jar fell from her hand and crashed. Broken glass covered with oozing peanut butter lay on the floor. Then the sound of a cup crashing through the kitchen window. Her screams continued as Adam came running and didn't stop until she clutched him for dear life.

"What, what?"

"Careful! There's glass!"

"I see. What happened?"

"In the window. That man! He was staring at me. Just kept staring. Didn't move a muscle."

"Charon?" Adam asked.

"Yes. That's him. He looked like he was dead or something."

"Or something?"

"More dead. I don't know."

There were three loud knocks on the back door that led into the kitchen. Adam moved to answer it, but before he could, Charon opened the door and came in holding the ceramic mug that Sam had used to break the window. The mug was undamaged. Charon put it on the counter under the window. He examined the broken window, made creepy clicking sounds and said, "The Agency will make you pay for that." Charon then looked at the floor and said in his usual emotionless, expressionless way, "There's peanut butter on the floor. Watch the glass. You best clean up the peanut butter now. I'll get to the window tomorrow."

"Tomorrow? Why not today?" Adam asked.

"Today's Sunday." Charon made that creepy clicking sound as he walked out.

"*Oh…*Adam," Sam cried. "It was awful. *That man!* I thought he was going to kill me then and there. So damn frightening."

"*'Today's Sunday?'*"

From outside, Charon's voice was loud and clear when he said, "I am sorry if I frightened you. I did not mean to." Sam and Adam turned to the broken window and saw Charon looking back at them. "I was walking by and I saw something odd out of the corner of my eye. I did not think it was you. I thought you were a stranger, so I took a closer look. That is it. The lighthouse clock stopped in the night. Do you know what time it is?"

"I don't have a watch," Adam said. "And no internet connection, so I couldn't tell you."

"Okay. Time to go." He turned and marched off.

Then everything changed. Time had been reset. Adam and Sam had gone back in time. They were in the bedroom when Sam said, "I'm hungry. Goin' to the kitchen. What would you like?"

"I don't know. What have we got?"

"Let's see." Sam shouted back from the kitchen. "Peanut butter. Baloney. Flour tortillas. *Flour tortillas?*"

"I brought 'em with me."

"Well then, let's see. *Um*...I got it. We're going to have peanut butter and baloney on old flour tortillas. *Yummers....*" The sound of something crashing and breaking. *"Goddamnit!"*

Adam rushed in from the bedroom. "What happened?"

"I'm so sorry, Adam. I broke your *Swamp Bugs* mug."

"They made a movie of that one."

"I didn't mean to. I'm sure I put it away, but it was on the counter, I didn't see it and I knocked it off. I am so sorry."

"It wasn't a bad movie, either."

"I agree. I thought it was pretty good." Sam looked out the window, then looked at the broken mug on the floor. "Adam, I just had the strangest sensation."

"Oh?"

"*Déjà vu*. For a second I thought....So, peanut butter and baloney, right?"

"Sure. Why not? Boy is that window filthy. You saw *Swamp Bugs?*"

"Yup."

* * *

Arthur helped Florence and Annabelle over the boulders, until Florence cried out, "Stop! Help me. My knee. It's out of joint. *Damn, it hurts.* Annabelle help me sit over there." She pointed to a rock about a chair's height.

"Of course. Oh, dear. Sit. Let me see...." Annabelle had recovered from her momentary withdrawal into herself.

"Ouch."

"Sorry. Your kneecap. It's bruised. It'll probably swell. Nothing to do. Wish we had some ice." Annabelle was empathetic.

Arthur walked back to help Reggie, but he ran into some difficulty.

"I'm not going!"

"C'mon, Reggie." Arthur pleaded. "You can't stay here."

"Of course I can. I ain't leaving until I kill that bitch!"

"That bitch ain't Mona anymore, Reggie. She's something else. Something foul. That just ain't Mona. How many times do I have to say it? It ain't Mona and if it's anything like Charon, you won't be able to kill it."

"We'll see about that!" Reggie jumped up from the rock he had been sitting on and ran down the rocky shoreline towards the dock and the steps that led up to the surface of Gnarled Pines.

Had Arthur yelled to Reggie, tried to stop him, it would only signal their whereabouts to Charon. Charon could hear them anyway, but Arthur did not know that. So, Arthur could only watch with much sadness for the fate Reggie had chosen for himself.

The sun had set, but there was still enough light for Arthur to see farther back, towards the dock. A thick black bank of fog just large enough to consume Reggie from view, slid in from off the ocean. Arthur watched until there was no longer any sign of Reggie. Pain and anguish for Reggie seeped into Arthur's moldering flesh, into the heart of him, absorbing the hurt into himself, knowing that in the end he had accomplished nothing other than his testing his own sense for empathy, his ability to learn, his willingness to give himself up, to become one with another and share the burden—to care. Arthur thought: *"Empathy! In the end it's just another selfish endeavor designed to make myself appear better than I am. I'm not fooling anybody. Is this my Hell?"* Plainly, Arthur thinks too much. He was relieved to know that he had chosen survival; that it was Reggie who chose not to survive, but Arthur would move on and live for as long as a dead man can live. Arthur suffered from the persistence of guilt. He believed that the guilt was not by any choice of his own; it was a demon that followed him, taunted him—it always had. Even when he was a kid in Five Points, there was guilt from what he and his gang did to survive. Arthur was permanently damaged by it. He knew then that there was a demon inside him. He could feel it. He could hear it demanding him to make every possible bad choice. And now, the guilt from allowing Reggie to choose for himself. He would not be responsible. There were the ladies to help. Arthur must still have had a soul, he still felt emotions; and even though his body was decomposing, he still took time for self-examination. Despite everything that Arthur had done in life, there was an essential goodness about him that all who knew him saw, except for Arthur. Arthur never saw his own goodness.

Arthur went back to help the ladies who were tired, sweating, bruised and generally out of sorts. Florence was sitting on a large rock and Annabelle was leaning against the towering wall that lifted Gnarled Pines like a pillar rising from out the Atlantic. There would be no going back, no second thoughts after they had reached the moment when they were aware of their real possibility of staying alive. And that moment had come upon Annabelle Lovelace. It swelled her heart, which was beating twice its normal rate.

An edited excerpt from an interview with Annabelle Lovelace, author of *Running From Evil*: "All of this was no fault of my own. I was invited by a woman I shared the stage with once, only once, to celebrate the Fourth of July on a private island off the coast of Maine, all expenses paid. I barely knew her, but I did *know of her. She was a legend. Golly! At first I didn't believe it. It was a joke, right? But okay, I tell myself. Okay, might as well. I accept. I'm going, and there I was, and I was not willing to die there. I would not! I refused to die there! I knew that it would hurt, and it hurt a lot. It was difficult; my choice to live. Choosing to live is difficult for some. It hurts to think about it, to believe it really happened. Still. it hurts to look back, to see they're gone, while I'm still here, a surviver. I didn't know how Arthur was going to pull that off, but I trusted him, maybe because he was dead. I mean, if you can't trust a dead man, who can you trust?*

"Florence. Yes, I liked Florence. I liked her a lot. I was worried about her trick knee, her ability to walk. She wasn't a bully like so many other older actresses can be. I've worked with some doozies. But Florence, she was down to earth, a good soul. Oh, God! Reggie! How could I have forgotten about Reggie? What happened to him? Something did, of course. Something terrible. Something unspeakable. I knew Reggie would die soon. He walked right into the lion's den. There was no way Reggie could have survived. He would die a horrible death, just as Willy had. He would die by the hands of Charon and Mona LaBaron. They were monsters. But Reggie went right on running into their hands. And for what? A fool for love? A martyr for love? What's the difference? Martyrs are fools for love, really. The results are the same. And Reggie loved Willy. He was Reggie's best and only real friend. They were like brothers.

"There I was and it still hurts to think of the others, but I believe it is the hurt that kept me going, that still keeps me going. Now, I see that I am not myself, but rather, I am the self behind myself. I am the one who animates myself. Like God, but I know

I'm not—God, that is. You know what I mean? I feel complete. On and on we go away from something, or towards something. Sometimes we forget where we've been; a convenient lapse of memory. Sometimes we have no idea where we're going. Sometimes we just go and we don't care where. We tell ourselves we headed for something better. And sometimes we give up and we go with the flow of life. That is what I learned while running from evil, and I didn't stop running until long after—a year after escaping Gnarled Pines."

Arthur made hand signals for the ladies to stay in place. He would sneak around the next couple boulders and check to make certain that Charon's boat—a fifteen footer with an outboard motor—was parked at the mouth of the cave.

"Wait here. I'll be back when the coast is clear...and then we can get you ladies off this godforsaken hellhole. *Shh*...quiet. Make yourselves comfortable. I don't know how long I'll be. There might be complications."

"Complications?"

"We might come to fisticuffs."

Annabelle and Florence fell deeper into fear. They watched Arthur until he disappeared around the north bend of the island's shore. It was difficult for them to keep quiet when there was so much to say, so much to hear, if it was only the sound of their own voices, when death could come at any moment, when it is right there next to you, when it can reach out and touch you without warning, without seeing it coming, they could not be silent. "I don't know, Annabelle. I don't know that I want to go on," Florence whispered.

"Of course you want to go on, Flo. You don't want to let down those who love you, do you?"

"No. Of course not."

"Then why let yourself down and give up?"

"*Hmm*. Then, fuck it! We're gonna make it, Annabelle. We're gonna get away from this place. I don't want to remember Gnarled Pines. I want to forget…like I was never here. And poor Arthur, *dead. Jesus Christ!* Arthur is dead. *A goddamned zombie.* How can that be?"

Annabelle pondered a moment before saying, "Redemption."

"What make you say that?"

"I don't know. It just came to mind."

"Hmm." Florence continued whispering. "I want to believe this is all a nightmare. Did you know I was Mona's friend? What happened? What happened to her, Annabelle?"

"I don't know, Flo. She went bonkers. You know, like those people in Bedlam."

"*Yeah,* Bedlam." Florence grimaced.

"She can't really know what she's doing, what she's done."

Florence took a moment to think about what Annabelle had just said before saying, "She's possessed. Can't be anything else."

"Gnarled Pines is no place for any God-fearing person."

"Maybe I'm not God-fearing, Annabelle. I don't fear my God."

"We're going to get on that boat, Flo, and we're going to get the hell out of here and we'll never look back. Believe it. *Belief does the trick.*"

"I'll be looking back on this experience for the rest of my life. Unforgettable, isn't it?"

"So, you've stopped giving up. How good is that?"

* * *

Meanwhile, Reggie opened his eyes and saw that he was in a dank cave. He caught a glimpse of an eyeball on the floor; "*blue,*" he thought. A few feet away from it lay two bloody fingers, both were decomposed enough to clearly see the bone holding onto what little flesh remained. Reggie gasped. He sniveled and smelled the foulest of stenches he thought possible. The stench of death. The stench of decay. The stench of the food for the gods of Gnarled Pines. The scent of Evil. Reggie soon discovered, when he tried to move, that he was standing, that he was chained to a cold wet rock wall spread-eagle, that he was naked, and that he could not move. As he became fully conscious he could see Mona standing nearby, staring at him, smiling, and holding a nine inch boning knife. *"Help me, God. Help me."* Reggie tried to say something, to express his hate, to curse her, but he felt a terrible pain throbbing in his mouth and he could not say a word.

"Hello, Mister Mooner. Looking for this?" Mona held out her hand with Reggie's bloody tongue on the palm of it. "Is this what you're looking for?" She then put the tip of his amputated tongue next to her lips, licked it, and slid it in and out of her mouth. "Hey, Mooner, you like to French kiss? I bet you do. Hey Mooner, look at this!" And then she bit off the tip of the severed tongue, chewed on it and spit it out. "Oh dear! You have such a filthy mouth, Mister Mooner, offensive and vile. You're a bitter man, Mooner. You think you're funny, don't you? Well, I don't think you are, and I don't think you ever were. Just a second banana. That's all you ever been—a second banana. You shoulda stayed in Vaudeville where you belonged. *The king of pratfalls.* What was Arthur thinking, putting a no-talent piece of shit like you on a Broadway stage? On the same stage the one and only Mona LaBaron was on! *Remember her?* You're a stupid old fool. And guess what? C'mon, take a guess. I can't hear you. Cat got your tongue? Oh, dear. Did I really say that? Cheap humor. Your kind of humor. Simple-minded humor. Childish humor—if it can be called humor—and worst of all, derivative. Shame on you, Mooner. I may be picking up your bad habits. *Cat got your tongue?* Well, nobody's laughing. *Hmm.* I am genuinely sorry for that. I shouldn't want to demean myself with cliché...like you do every time you put your foot on the boards. So, can you guess? Still not talking, *huh?* Alright, so I shall make a guess for you. Ready? Here goes. I...think...you...need...to...be...*punished!* What have you got to say to that? *What?* I still can't hear you. Poor baby. Still can't talk, *huh?* Let's hear what our star witness has to say. But first, let me tear your ticket to Au Théâtre LaBaron." Mona raised the nine inch paring knife then, more swiftly than Zorro, carved an X across Reggie's belly. His screams sounded like laughter. The rattling of his chains sounded like applause.

"Reggie Mooner, it is my pleasure to introduce to you, the one, the only, Charon the ferryman! Charon the magnificent! Our star witness!"

Charon entered and took a bow. Earlier, Charon had severed Willy's head from its body, at the Adam's apple, where Mona had stabbed it with a boning knife, and then he sawed the head completely in half from ear to ear, scooped out the brain, and now he was wearing it as a mask. Charon chanted, *"Guilty! Guilty!"* while he danced and pranced from side to side in front of Reggie and continued to chant, *"Guilty! Guilty!"* over and over before he abruptly stopped directly in front of Reggie and pressed his lips against Reggie's lips, but they were not Charon's lips, they were Willy's lips. "A kiss from Willy. Did you come back to avenge Mister Willy's untimely death? Was that it, Mister Mooner? Yes? Of course it was. *Guilty as charged!* I sentence you to the most exquisite pain you have never known—until now. But first, I have two ladies to bring back to my workroom. Miss Mona will stay here and punish you."

"My pleasure, dear Charon." Mona made a sly smile, then winked.

"Good. I will not be gone long, Miss Mona." Charon said while he was already walking down the tunnel towards the ocean.

"Why are you walking. You can just…be there."

"I know. But this tunnel is filled with magic. Run your hands along its wall and you can feel it."

"Take your time then," Miss Mona shouted back. "I'll be here playing with the Mooner man and having fun," and then she began carving little Xs helter-skelter on the canvas that was Reggie's body.

Reggie moved his head from side to side as tears slid down his face and mixed with the blood that was drooling from the corners of his mouth.

Mona soon got bored with carving Xs into Reggie's flesh and tired of listening to him trying to scream, so she made one last X on Reggie's belly before she slowly pushed the boning knife into his guts, making sure to twist the knife as it sank into him. Then, with glee, she ripped his belly open, reached in, pulled out a handful gut and rubbed it on her face, licked them, and ate them. Fortunately, after that, it did not take Reggie long to die.

The moon, not quite full, was bright white. Shadows of the gnarled pines lay across one another in a queerly convoluted pattern. A web of asymmetrical design swayed on its own volition in the dead-still night, creating a spectral network of ashen shadows of the pines that crept along at a fixed distance, a relative and equal distance from one another, as the moon slowly slid away. At times, the trees and their shadows were indistinguishable, one from the other, as they moved to the beat of unheard music. They were awakening, yawning, humming, stretching, scheming. Their hum grew into, if not fevered, a close-to-it pitch in tiny increments that could easily go unnoticed, until it is suddenly there, loud and unexpected, even though it had been there all the while preparing the way to announce the birth of the dark souls that foretold another self-destructive, hundred-year epoch of turmoil, hatred and chaos: The Age of Greed and Hate.

In a world where uncontrolled greed is rampant, where the goal is to be number one above all else, everyone is in constant danger of being eaten by anyone at anytime, just for the hate of it, with neither notice nor provocation; thereby, causing a continuous state of suspicion, a state of flux where friends are friends until they are not. Hate rules. With that in mind, it would be a sure thing to bet on The Agency having something to do with it—everything to do with it, actually. Point being: The Agency's primary objective is to create a world at war with itself, a world of self-devouring, a world divided by hate. *For what reason?* Reason had nothing to do with it. It is the nature of each and every dark soul. It is simply the nature of the beast and there is no way of changing its nature—it just is.

Charon does not sleep—*death does not wait 'til morning.* Back in his ferryman days, Charon's nights were filled with souls in limbo, a place of nothingness, where they were unaware of their own existence. They waited for the ferryman to awaken them and escort them to their future, or to no future at all. Each soul had its own destination, created long before by its host; souls must always face-up to their responsibility for their accumulative misdeeds.

Then, long after his life as a ferryman, Charon's nights were spent in the bleak and poisonous atmosphere of the cave beneath the lighthouse, tending to the harvesting of the ambrosia for the dark spirits within the gnarled pines. Given the sterility of the island, decomposition to create the proper consistency relies on Charon's especial tenderizer. His responsibilities were many. Sometimes there was the after dark lurking on the mainland, the following of his next victim, the murdering by knife or by choking; choking was his favorite way to kill the ladies. It was the sensation of wrapping his hands around a long, slim and smooth neck, and the sound of the popping of tender bones, and the smothering and desperate gagging, that he enjoyed the most. With the men it was usually a vigorous stab in the back, or the quick, precise slitting of the throat. Sometimes, for a change of pace, he enjoyed garroting his victims, seeing how far into the flesh of the neck he could sink the wire. There were the bodies to be collected and hauled back to Gnarled Pines for dismembering, gutting, grinding for stewing and distribution around the base of the pines. Alas, there was the general maintenance and, of course, the running of the lighthouse. Together with doing all the same chores inter-dimensionally, Charon was purely and simply a force of nature.

Over time, Charon became lonely. Charon had never felt pain of any kind until he became aware of his own isolation, his unhappiness. He needed someone to share in his existence. Unrequited in every potential relationship of any kind, both real and imagined, Charon sought safety in detachment. Ultimately, it was with indifference he greeted every possibility.

Those who came to Gnarled Pines soon found themselves plotting their escape; it was not in anybody's nature not to plot, scheme, or do whatever it takes for their survival. Charon's line of work required him to thwart any attempt, by any means, until their death. The elixir of life the dead provided was, above all else, the most important order given by The Agency to guarantee their continued existence. One hundred years of feeding the trees in preparation for a rebirth of death and destruction, soon turned Charon's lassitude, his detachment from life itself, his indifference, into a passion for enjoying the kill. No longer did he do only The Agency's bidding, he went above and beyond; he had his own agenda. His apathy toward the horrors demanded by The Agency created his passion for disfiguring the dead in the most creative and arousing ways. The feel and the taste of their flesh was an exquisite experience. He hated his victims. They had bodies of flesh and blood, but his was made of mud. His emptiness became satiated with an erotic pleasure he had never gotten from any living human being, except Miss Mona LaBaron—her beauty was unlike any Charon had seen before—her sweet and palatable darkness was inborn.

TWELVE

It was midnight on the island of Gnarled Pines. Directly overhead a luscious moon threw a spotlight onto the stage below. Little goes unseen beneath a white moon's brilliance; prowlers and two-bit criminals who do night-work take a holiday. Those good folk, the vast majority who live with good spirits, who mean no harm, who embrace their lovers while strolling, who take their dogs for a walk, who take a circuitous route to avoid the insanity of chaos, who go about their business doing whatever it is they do, who simply walk to walk, who go undisturbed by the intensity of the limelight; marvel at the strength of the white moon that can raise the ocean's tide and mirror the omnipresence of the sun that shines half a world away.

On a flat tablet of rock thirty-plus feet above the ocean there is nowhere to stay out of sight; nowhere to exit. Any clandestine actions need to be performed in full-view of their assailant, and it is essential that the actors give a bravura performance; anything less is death. Arthur, Florence and Annabelle, all well-seasoned in the Art of Theatre; as well as Adam and Sam, psyched and ready in another dimension, must strut their hour upon the stage while acting casual, natural, and usual. The execution of their escape will be attended by the very real possibility of a heinous slaughter at any and every step of the way.

The ghosts—King, Ídolo, Willy, Hudson, and Reggie who had only recently appeared—were out on the front porch talking about possibilities.

Adam and Sam sat in front of the MacBook, taking turns typing. Adam would type notes relating to their plan for escape. Sam would read and respond. When they had nothing else to propose regarding their escape plans they spoke. Otherwise, they used the Mac because it was easier than scribbling in a composition book.

"I didn't set out to write the kind of novels I write, Sam."

"What kind did you set out to write?"

"I'm not quite sure. Something better than good. Something that'll last. Something great, I suppose."

"Great, *huh?* The kind of books you write aren't great?"

"No. Not at all."

"I don't believe the genre matters. Great just happens. I don't think you have a lot of control over it. Great happens or it doesn't."

"In part, one does have control over it. You gotta be prepared, right? You have to get ready for it to happen. I actually wanted to master the craft, to make literature, but I never did, of course, although I went as far as I could along that torturous, but often gratifying, road. I was young, so naturally I thought too grandly—not to be confused with pretentiously, I hope. Although, on second thought, I must confess to some outrageous pretensions that were anything but grand, or flattering. Once, when I was on the train going from Brooklyn Heights into the city, I was holding a copy of Sartre's *Being and Nothingness,* trying to impress my intellect upon strangers…I was eighteen, maybe nineteen at the time, and there I was, believing I was really and truly stupid, unprepared for anything, pretending to read while sitting in my seat posing. It wasn't until the train reached Times Square when I saw that I had been holding Sartre upside down; Sartre was on his head! I proved my intellect alright—I posed my ignorance for all the world to see."

They both burst-out laughing. "That's funny, Adam!"

"I've got more examples for you...lots of them."

"*Oh, no.* Let me savor this one for awhile. I have a question for you, Adam. This is part of the interview...assuming we'll make it home; how *have* your prepared yourself? What steps have you consciously taken to get where you are today?"

"Well...*umm*...I hadn't really prepared myself, unless a ferocious appetite for reading little other than the greats counts...or at least, *great* by reputation; Reputations are made by proclamation; proclamations by academia. I was taught who the great ones were...I had no way, other than my taste, to know who they were. So, I read the authors and the books I was told were great. I read them with the intent to learn from them. There were those with whom I strongly connected—whose voices were also my own voice, or similar to my own. I absorbed them into myself...so to speak...like being their host...they allowed me to express myself more fully, to write more intelligently. So, naturally, and assisted by my arrogance, I proclaimed them great based on the opinion that they spoke to me. That was my criteria; did they remind me of me. They were great because I said they were. Naturally, great writers all shared one thing in common: *me*. If I understood them, they were great. Simple as that. That's too funny. Maybe, I'm totally messed-up...just plain delusional."

"Does it matter?"

"*Wow. Does it matter?* Do you mean, does it matter if I'm delusional?"

"*Yeah.*"

"Well, I don't know, but I think it might matter...to me... but I can also see how it doesn't matter, to me or to anyone. But then, I'd be the last person to know if I were. I've made it this far. At my age, I'd hate to be shocked into a different reality, a different vision of myself; other than making friends with ghosts, and getting off this island...That's about all the new reality I can digest. That's an awfully big shock for me too, Sam, but real reality—one that would shock me into seeing myself, *really* seeing myself warts and all, if there's anymore *'all'* left—that's pretty scary. Seeing myself and actually liking myself; what a rare and wonderful event that would be. Then I wouldn't care how delusional I was. I've been there at times, but never long enough to be truly acquainted...with really liking myself, I mean. I want to know exactly where I stand; whether I'm bonkers or not, 'cause it would save me from a lot of wasted time. Although, I think I'd be terrified seeing myself, my soul. So, in the end, what does it matter? That's really a good question, Sam. I see that it might matter, that my knowing would matter if it led to a better me. In that case, yes. It certainly *does* matter; even though those goddamned warts might terrify me."

"I see you and I'm not terrified. No warts here."

"You only see what I want you to see, Sam. I think it's what we all do, to one degree or another. We let people in only so far because, rightly or wrongly, we believe too far, too close, can be fatal."

"And the problem is?"

"Nothing I've ever written rose anywhere near to the level of those great writers with whom I thought I shared a language. In the end, I realized I didn't. They had their own and it wasn't mine. I have never been able to transcribe their language, assimilate it into myself, into my work; at least not consciously. If I thought I had, if I believed it, I'd only be fooling myself. Well, there you go, kiddo. That's me in a nutshell. Stuck with a voice from Brooklyn; stuck with my own."

Sam thought a bit before asking, "How do you know that?"

"*Umm*...I know...I just know. You know how it is when you know a thing, when you just know it and that's that, you just know?"

"No. I don't."

"*Hmm,*"

"Okay, Adam, let's go back; it seems that your idea of a great writer are those whose level you believe you never reached? What do those whom you perceive as great share in common, other than yourself?"

"*Umm*...I suppose it's one who lasts...at least, beyond one generation."

"Is that something the writer controls?"

"Of course not, but that comes right back to preparation. You know, Sam, these conversations always seem to end by talking about myself...all vanity...fame for the sake of fame. *Mea culpa.* I'm too often self-conscious and vain."

"You're a riot, Adam! Of course it's about yourself. I am the one doing the interview, am I not?"

"Of course."

"Don't you think that just doing your best is the best any writer can do? Anyone, really. In any endeavor. You might be great, or you might not. Who's to say? I suspect the writer, the artist, or simply a plumber, can achieve greatness in their own field without being conscious of it. It's paying attention and doing the best you can. One never actually knows one way or another. It's a crap shoot."

"*Maybe*...for some. But '*purpose*,' comes to mind, Sam. I think 'purpose' is, or is at, the foundation of greatness. They all had '*purpose'* in common...they all wrote on purpose. I can't explain it,

Sam. I can only think of Mann, Proust, Hesse, C. S. Lewis, that Tolkien guy, even Gertrude Stein—they all wrote on purpose. I can't explain it better than that."

"A bunch of oldies."

"*Yeah*. I s'pose. Me, too."

"*Hmm*. You know, Adam, I'm not a stranger to writing either. It's how I pay the rent."

"I am so self-centered. Let's change the subject. Sam, I want to read everything you've ever written."

"I keep copies." Her laugh was infectious.

"*Clever you.*"

"What's your greatest fear, Adam? I mean, as a writer."

"This is still part of the interview, right?"

"*Yup*. So…tell me."

"*Oh, boy*. I need to think about that one." Adam thought a bit before answering, "I think my greatest fear is that I'll never be good enough. I keep coming back to that…once a day, I come back to that. I seem to be in my own world, self-applauding."

"Well then, none of us are alone, are we?"

"As clever as that sounds, it feels that way. Now here's something funny. I'm often conscious of trying to think about behaving as an adult, I'm never sure if I can…especially in the company of 'serious' adults. They scare me. You know the kind. *Nope,* I don't ever want to grow up!" He scoffed. She giggled.

"Then don't." Sam said firmly. "Most people are no fun when they grow up, anyway."

"Thank you, Sam. I suspect that if I had ever really wanted to, I would have made that choice, like all of us."

"That's right and look where you are: not stodgy and forever young. I wanted to go to MIT."

"What?"

"You sound surprised, Adam."

"Surprised that you didn't go, that's all."

"Money. And I couldn't get a scholarship."

"I'm sorry. Why did you want to go to MIT, Sam?"

"Or Caltech. Astrophysics. Anyway, there was another problem, Adam. At the time, I was undiagnosed for having a bipolar disorder. Just depressed from time to time and there was nothing to be done about it. That was a big problem. Now it's all good. I stay medicated—when I don't forget them—and I'm reasonably happy with what, and how, I'm doing."

"*Hmm*...I have a question for you, Sam. With time going faster on the mainland, or time on Gnarled Pines going more slowly—although, I don't think it really matters which is which—the result remains the same; still, I'd like to know if there would be anything to go back to...a place to go back to...a life to go back to?"

"I don't know, Adam. Assuming I believed that, I'd still have no way of knowing. I think that time happens all at once..." She stopped and whispered in his ear, *"I think that's how Charon is able to do what he does with time. He has the ability to navigate it."*

I've thought that, too, Sam—that time happens all at once. I don't know why. It's just a feeling, but a strong one."

"I'd trust my feelings. Well, anyway, let's get down into the world in which we all live. *Tea, darling?*" Sam plays it with pseudo-sophistication, "If I don't get my Earl Grey soon, darling, I'll die. I'll simply just die. I *wrally-wrally* will."

"If you're *wrally-wrally* going to die, I would be *wrally-wrally* happy to join you, madame...keep you company while we go into that good night...but, since you're not *wrally* going to die, my life is spared." Adam sighed a sigh of relief. "Besides, we only have instant coffee, m'dear. And a broken mug—my favorite."

"Truly and sincerely sorry about that. One more question, Adam, and the interview is over. Do you believe that a demon has influenced, or taken over some of your novel?"

"Don't be silly, Sam. That's absurd. I don't believe it for a second." Then Adam typed into the computer. *"Time to go."*

Then Sam typed: *"So soon?"*

Adam stuffed his pockets with flash drives. They hugged tentatively and nervously kissed. They had become friends; the kind of friends that are difficult to find. Together they left through the backdoor, from off the kitchen. The unexpected moonlight had been overlooked in their planning and its brightness assaulted them. It slapped them with the intensity that might accompany a spine-chilling epiphany, like the jolt from suddenly realizing that footsteps are following you, on a darkened street, in a dangerous neighborhood—that sensation, right there: the sensation of vulnerability. Adam and Sam had to act fast; every second might be their last. Though they had expected Charon would be sleeping by midnight, there was no way of telling, so they decided to act as if Charon were watching, and listening, or sniffing, or using whatever extra senses he had.

Adam and Sam began to execute their plan with care and nonchalance.

* * *

Arthur and the ladies hid among the rocks until midnight. The heat from the July sun that had penetrated the rocks and boulders cluttering the shoreline were still warm to the touch; although, they did cool sharply after sunset, but remained warm until sunrise. The breeze that glided in from off the ocean brought with it an invisible mist that helped to decrease the intensity of the tempestuous rocks. And rock was pretty much the entire surface of Gnarled Pines; the trees themselves were rooted in solid rock. The mist acted as a magnifying glass and enhanced the beauty of the tiny pulsating suns that reflected a single source—the moon—sprinkled upon the undulating pulse of the Atlantic. Dazzling sparks bobbed and buoyed like shattered crystal rainbows within the mist.

They readied themselves—the best they knew how—to be psychologically prepared for what may come; although they both knew that there was no way to be prepared for what may come; especially when what may come might be torture and death. Preparation was merely a matter of acceptance and trust: accepting the situation, and trusting oneself to take the helm; that was preparation enough.

Florence and Annabelle embraced. The embrace spoke for itself: *If we never meet again remember me. I will remember the comfort of being here together with you. The two of us. I am frightened, too. You are not alone.* That kind of embrace.

"Should anything happen..." Florence whispered, "...you know...if it should...happen...don't make a fuss, Annabelle. Please, just get on that boat and go home."

"You're talking nonsense, Flo."

"Just...."

"*Stop. Stop. Stop.*" Annabelle took her time to think, then quickly said, "Flo, do you know how to drive a boat?"

"*Nope.*"

"*Oh shit.*"

"Never been on many boats. Just the one that brought us to this goddamned island." Florence was visibly frightened, and Florence was angry with Mona for being Mona, and angry with herself for not killing the bitch when she had the chance—*the bride of Satan!*

"*There was something about Mona I liked…the audacity! Loads of it…but…I think I only wanted to be like some of her…not all of her, of course…but to have what she had, only not to use any of it to hurt others. Mona could be hurtful…surprisingly brutal… but…but…there goes those buts…but she made me feel good about myself, for a time…for a very short time. She was spontaneous and fun-loving. And the game…oh, yes…we played a game…a dangerous game…although we never spoke of it as a game…we never mentioned it…never talked about what we were doing or why…it just happened…we just did it. The game began with friendly sparring…and before I knew it, out came the sword…keen and dangerous…the edge carefully sharpened, taking pains to hone it razor thin…razor sharp. Why did I play? I wanted a friend…a goddamned friend! I wanted to share in her jollity, to be a part of it…but it didn't take long to discover that she hadn't a sincere bone in her body…or a kind one. No, no, no, no…that's not true, not entirely…at times, her kindnesses were overwhelming, but as the saying goes: too little, too late. I was never as quick as Mona…when the ball fell in my court, I wasn't keen enough at saying…responding…getting one in…biting…yes…the game was destructive. I was always second best. I got to thinking lately…at my age...my age...yeah...huh...well, I can't do anything about that...but my life...I could have done something about that...how I lived it...everything...all of it was a long string of choices...I made them, and look!...I'm what happened...everything...my life...my entire life...every bit of it I choose myself...I'm now the sum total of every single one of them...choices. I sure made some doozies...live and learn...we better...we gotta...learn...to live. Too bad we can't go back and do it all differently. But the thing is...what's important is the final choice: own it and love it, or not. Flo? She called me Flo. She never called me Flo before. What happened to calling me Florence? Ahh...the familiarity of near-death!..the letting go... good kid...Annabelle...well, not exactly a kid...genuine, I think... and...life...it's all gonna end now or later...looks like sooner than later. What kind of shit would Mona do to me?...pain...who doesn't hate pain...those bondage people...they like pain...well...you know, I don't give a shit! What do I care? We all rot...tiny pieces... bigger pieces...and finally chunks. Jesus Christ! Like poor Arthur...rotting waits for all of us. We melt in plain sight. Gnarled fingers like gnarled pines. Arthritis. Goddamn knee...I don't think I can walk...stop counting the negatives. I'll try. Good. I was Mona's only friend...for awhile. It was fun...sparring...for awhile...but when it got serious...it hurt...barbs that dug in...got under my skin...so goddamned painful...and worse, she enjoyed it. Why? What did I do? She just got tired of me, I suppose...threw me away like she did everybody else. I was tired of the stings...the disparagement...but...but, I really was her friend...true to her...for awhile...and I sure as hell wanna know why she thought so little of me...she played the queen...I played the jester. I gave her my trust...so much for trust. Wait! I think it was me...yes, it might have* been me. I remember now...I'm sure it was me...I'm the one who got tired of her...sick of the bitch! Sparring with a friend is a dangerous game...I had to get away. There it is. Is it? Yes, that's it. There ain't no more. Think. I'm thinking...it was definitely me who up and left. I think I'm just the same...I'm no better...oh, God, help me. Am I better? Of course, you are better. I knew her and she knew me...we were friends...for a time...Mona and me...and it's all gonna end anyway...isn't it? So why should it matter?...but it feels like it matters...like it matters more than anything. That's it. Do you hear me, God? That's all I have to say for myself. Well, there's that...and maybe a little more. That's my confession, God. Thank you for your time, God. I pray I used it well."

"I have been on boats. Lots of times," Annabelle said."Many a Monday, a bunch of us girls in the *Follies* would take a day trip up the Hudson. It was loads of fun."

Annabelle, with all her talent, was a calming force in the cast; she did not compete, nor upstage. She was the perfect supporting actor. Unlike many, she actually supported the other actors. She was popular, enjoyed a compliment, but never sought them out, never fished for them. *"No river trips in Albuquerque... not much of anything really...but New York...it can be an awful tough place, ya know?...rough place...cutthroat...a terrible test of character. I was a whore...once....Jesus!...on Broadway...steady work...sure ain't Albuquerque. I can spread my wings in New York...better than spreading my legs. I've worked with everyone who came to Manhattan...this godforsaken island...God bless their souls...I enjoyed the company of every one of them...worked with every one of them...King... Ídolo...Willy...Hudson...oh my God!... what they did to Hudson...I'm sure they got Reggie...Jesus...the loss...I can't cry...I can't think about it...won't...will not...not now...cannot...period. I'm dried out. I'm not acting myself...I need to...keep a stiff upper lip...it's an English saying. I had to say it in a play once...I don't want to die...be strong...strong for Flo...we're going to do this together...a stiff upper lip, old chap...get to the boat and go...Arthur!...what the...I mean, really, he's a zombie...a real zombie...he's dead yet he's still Arthur...I've always liked Arthur. I never smelled anything so repulsive in my life! I didn't want to say anything...I mean, it was Arthur. He was the producer...the one who has a 'Mister" before his name. We all knew him well enough...out of respect...to call him Mister Baumgarten around newbies; otherwise, we called him Arthur. Christ! I never tell anyone when they have bad breath...maybe I should...I mean, it's not like telling somebody their shoes are untied...but maybe I should, for their own good...good gravy!..they could fall and kill themselves. But Jeez...it's not Arthur's fault...no, I guess not...what happened to him? He's dead and decomposing... I mean, he stinks...walking and rotting...he doesn't seem concerned about it. I would be...you bet. He knows Charon. I mean, he actually knows the creature...Arthur's owned this island a long time, I believe. Maybe he could talk some sense into him... Charon. Guess not. I don't understand any of this...who could?... it's not happening...is this happening? No...I don't believe it... Yes...this really is happening...stop telling me that! I don't want to hear it. I'm trapped in here. I know every inch of this boulder that I am hiding behind...hello, rock...I can feel your heart beat...I'll keep that to myself...I'll share it with you, of course, God...but anybody else would think I'm crazy...but I hear its heart beat...I hear you rock...can't fool me...I gotta get my mind off all this... I'm...I don't know. I wish I could...would...stop talking about something happening to me…depresses me…gives me the willies… don't show it…stay calm…a rock doesn't have a heart…oh, yes…it does. I can't show it…the willies…it will only make Flo feel bad. This rock is breathing. Tell me. Please tell me, God. Can a rock have a life of its own?"*

"When we get home, Flo, you and I are going to take one of those day trips up the Hudson. You'll love it. I promise."

"*Shh*…It's time," Arthur whispered.

The ladies gulped. They were paralyzed. Nothing moved, neither legs nor arms. "Okay, ladies. The boat is there and ready to go."

"Arthur?" Florence raised her hand like a schoolgirl.

"Yes, Florence?"

"Neither one of us know how to drive a boat."

"It's a cinch. It's not all that big, so you shouldn't have too much trouble maneuvering it. You have a cord attached to the outboard motor and…*shoot*…I'll get the thing going for you. And once you get going, just keep your eyes on where you want to go… and go."

"Why don't you come with us? You could get killed staying here," Annabelle said with sympathy and caution. Florence gave Annabelle a little-more-than-gentle kick. "Oh…I'm sorry…I guess that doesn't matter. I mean…you know what I mean. I'm really sorry that you're dead. I really am."

"Me, too. I have always liked you, Annabelle," Arthur said with a jovial smile. "You're one of the nicest people I know and you're one of the best talents to grace a Broadway stage. And you, Florence, you changed the whole direction of modern Theatre. Your style of acting, brave and original. You brought a raw grittiness never before seen by a Broadway audience. *So-o-o...I want to say goodbye and thank you."

"Thank you," the ladies said in unison.

"Florence, do you think you can make it to the boat. I'd be glad to carry you, if you just hold your nose."

* * *

Meanwhile, Charon and Mona were playing in the workroom. Charon was given no sense of fear. Although, after many centuries of isolation he found, by watching endless nothingness, that he actually had a self he could talk to, one that would talk back, that would answer him, so he asked himself if his life of nothingness would persist for all time. Had it any meaning? His answer was, *there is no way of telling*—and right then and there, Charon learned fear: He was conscious of his entombment, and damned by the knowledge of *there is no way of telling.*

Miss Mona feared nothing either; she was dead and gone to where there is no way of telling; it was a dark spirit in control of Mona LaBaron, playing the role of Mona LaBaron, the role of her lifetime and having fun, practicing physical pleasure, experiencing the thrill of being a woman.

"Who is next, Annabelle or Florence?" Mona asked.

"Why not both at the same time?"

GNARLED PINES

Edward Crosby Wells

THIRTEEN

One day the moon will grow tired of suspending itself over Earth and fall, or perhaps it will float away to somewhere else, if somewhere else has not yet come to an end. One day there will be only one last possibility, only one last choice before there is no more. One day all will rust, rot, and disappear; that will be the day when time itself comes to an end; when existence ceases to exist.

Somewhere on Earth, or in the ether, hidden from view, or in plain sight…there is no telling…there may remain a single esoteric dimension, a secret dimension: the dimension of the eternal and of gods. But for now, nineteen twenty-nine and the present are a single event at a point of alignment; a point where time and space are one. Adam and Sam, along with Arthur, Annabelle, Florence, Mona and Charon (there always was, and is, but one Charon) are all together in a single dimension made of two: the dimension of the neo-present.

"Got the matches?" Sam asked.

"*Crap!* I'll go get 'em," Adam ran back into the kitchen and grabbed the box of wooden matches next to the stove. He began to walk away, but he thought of something, something he had not thought of before. *"Yes!"* Adam announced to himself. *"Yes!"* So, he stopped, turned around, walked back to the stove and opened every gas jet as high as it would go. Adam walked to the backdoor accompanied by the hissing of escaping propane beginning to fill the kitchen.

Sam had already begun pumping gasoline into one of the gas cans; she saw no way to pump gasoline while remaining nonchalant about it. With their charade most likely exposed anyway, they decided just to do what they came out to do, and do it *quickly!*

"I've got the matches."

"*C'mon,* Adam. Let's get this show on the road."

* * *

Mona busied herself by playing with the dead body of Reggie Mooner—poking her fingers in all the little Xs she had carved into his body, including one at the end of his penis, which she ultimately ate. But, since that abomination was no longer Mona LaBaron—Mona was therefore blameless. Her original human spirit did not go to future-time where the murdered victims, for which she was responsible, had gone. Mona's badly damaged spirit was transported to a place of dire consequence. It was a dark and nameless spirit that now possessed and animated her body, that delighted in the most repulsive of acts, and that was the same spirit that once possessed many other bodies throughout history, including those of Adolph Hitler and Joseph Stalin.

Charon treaded quietly through the cave's tunnel toward his next victims. And, though the trees could survive without further human nourishment—they were laboring to give birth—still, the capture and the kill remained Charon's greatest thrill. Even with Arthur helping the ladies by orchestrating their escape, Charon was certain Florence and Annabelle were easy pickings.

* * *

The ghosts were gathered on the front porch of the lodge.

"He is wearing my trousers."

"Who is? Who is wearing your trousers, Reggie?" Willy asked.

"Arthur! The goddamned zombie is wearing my trousers."

"That's funny," Hudson said with a great big smile that drew attention to his bright white teeth; a ghost, and still arousing.

"I suppose, my dear boy. It's all in the way you look at it. Even without your body, you are as engaging as ever. God endows the most trivial! I mean that in a good way, Hudson...a loving way. *Oh-h-h*, dear boy, how you are envied."

"Thank you. That's a good thing, right?"

"Yes, Hudson. That's a very good thing. It saddens me that no one will ever touch or comfort you again."

"Why not?"

"Because you're dead, Hudson, *dead*." Willy informed.

"*Oh, yeah.* That's right. I forgot."

"But, dear boy, you might find a willing host where you can stay and be for another lifetime. There's hope for you yet, kiddo. There's hope for all of us."

Sam and Adam were behind the lodge, going about their business as though Charon was watching, but he wasn't. Charon's mind was on Florence and Annabelle, while anticipating the moment when he would surprise them and drag them both back to his workroom. Sam and Adam threw caution to the wind. They didn't care if he saw them or not. They had a mission and nothing, they thought, would stop them.

"If Charon comes, we're ready."

"*Pump*...Adam...I don't think we could ever be ready for him...*pump the goddamned gasoline*."

"We will be ready, Sam. When people do bad things to me, they pay for it."

"Huh?"

"I don't know how to explain it, Sam. It's just something that happens. Magical thinking, I suppose. It's like I have a secret power."

"Yeah, right."

Adam filled his gas can to the brim, then walked over to the large tank of propane gas; a tank large enough to fuel the stove in a busy restaurant for weeks, maybe a month. The tank was painted white and propped up by a maze of pine logs under the kitchen window. Adam emptied the can of gasoline on the logs beneath the tank, while Sam was busy throwing gasoline on the walls of the lodge. They refilled their cans of gasoline and went around to the front of the building.

Willy called out in a loud whisper,"Can we go with you?"

"I don't see why not. I am your host, after all." Adam was cheerful.

"Why not?" Sam asked rhetorically, under her breath.

"Don't worry about us, Adam. Nothin' can hurt us. We won't get in your way. Besides, we could go ahead and keep a look out." Reggie offered. "Charon won't be able to see us if we don't want him to, and there ain't no reason we would ever want him to."

"Good to see you, Reggie." Adam said, then continued quickly, "I mean...*um*...I'm so sorry you're here...but since you are here, that's good...I mean, if you had to go anywhere, I'm glad it's here."

"Adam! We gotta go." Sam reminded.

"*Yup*. Let's do this."

The ghosts came down from the porch and joined them.

"Sam, I'll take this row of trees. Why don't you take the row over there. We don't need to do them all."

"Sure thing, boss."

Sam and Adam separated, and then they began pouring gasoline around the tree trunks.

"We gotta do this fast, Sam."

"What about if we did every other tree? Don'tcha think that would work?"

"Maybe, Sam. But let's not chance it. We gotta do however many we can. I wanna see this whole placed go up in flames. I don't want to see a single pine standing."

They moved through the woods, pouring the gasoline along their way. However, it took little time to empty their cans.

"I'm goin' back for more," Sam said.

"I'll go with you." And that's exactly what they did.

* * *

The creature that calls itself Mona LaBaron came running down the tunnel until she reached Charon mid-way. She was out of breath when she said, urgently, "Come! Come! *Quickly!*" She grabbed his arm and pulled him.

"I am busy, Miss Mona."

"No. *Now.* It's about that Goodblood fellow. He and his woman are up to something…something terrible. We have no time to waste."

"I am doing my duty…for The Agency. Remember I work for The Agency. That is what I do, and The Agency is very precise in their demands, Miss Mona."

"This *is* about The Agency! If you do not come now, ferryman, I will make your life so-o-o miserable. You'll wish you were back in Babylon—without your prick! Sorry about using the old LaBaron attitude. *Let's go! Chop, chop."*

"It had better be important." Charon reluctantly followed Mona through the tunnel and up into the lighthouse.

Charon questioned himself about whether or not he really wanted to share a lifetime, however long, or short it might be, with Miss Mona. Charon was well-aware, of course, that it was not *his* Miss Mona's spirit in her body, he only wanted her body anyway, so it didn't matter, he didn't care—*until now*. Now, it occurred to him that he ought to rethink his presumption that the body is the same person regardless to whatever soul inhabited it. Now, he thought that he might care about the original human soul that used to be in Mona's body, more than the body itself; no other consciousness but hers would make her Miss Mona, he concluded. Charon had, with the benefit of latent enlightenment—somewhat badly lit by human standards—learned that there is more to a body than just a body. For a creature cobbled together with mostly mud, near the beginning of time, it was a giant step in his evolution. It was the uniqueness of Mona's human soul that made her body behave in the way it did. It was the spirit of Mona that made her spontaneous and unpredictable. It was a concept The Agency thought would not be beneficial to Charon, that it would get in the way of his employment. Now, it has. Charon was troubled. It was not a sensation he had experienced before. *"How is that so? How is it that she is Miss Mona and yet she is not? Her new foul spirit, though we share a common interest, is not my Miss Mona. I do not understand."* That dilemma will continue to haunt him until existence stops.

When Charon and Mona reached the catwalk of the lighthouse, Charon and the body impersonating Mona, observed the human activities that were taking place on Gnarled Pines. Charon had little concern for what any of the players were doing since, having the benefit of time-manipulation, he could turn time around before any of them could create an unwelcome occurrence. Consequently, as the audience, Charon and Mona were free to watch and enjoy the show below as it played out under the spotlight of a white moon.

"What fun!" Mona who was not Mona exclaimed.

* * *

Adam and Sam hurried back and forth to refill their gas cans. They decided that they would pour the gasoline helter skelter, counting on each flaming tree to ignite the next one, then the next one, and so on. They were too far into the woods to continue running back and forth, refilling and pouring. Certainly, the entire woods would go ablaze in short time.

Gasoline fumes rose into the gnarled branches that had begun to hum louder to an ear-piercing pitch. When Adam threw lit matches, the banshee-like shrieking of the dark spirits aborting, fighting for their lives, with their branches disfigured and swaying, swinging, and burning the sky, illuminated the woods. Towering tree limbs scraped the clouds and reached for the moon; shrieking against their doom. Flames sweep across Gnarled Pines faster than Adam had anticipated, and then—WA-A-U-UMP! The lodge exploded and it was brighter than the moon. Sparks and burning wood flew into the sky and rained down on the pines, igniting those that had not yet caught fire.

From the mainland, the glow of the island blotted out the starlight. Trees scattered sparks like fireworks.

* * *

"What's wrong, Charon? You are letting The Agency burn!"

"Hold on, Miss Mona. It is under control. Let me show you my favorite power. Ready?"

"What is it?"

"Time, Miss Mona. Time. I will stop it and then I will reverse it."

"You better hurry, Charon!"

"I am…I am…." But is wasn't long before Charon said with genuine distress, "It is not working, Miss Mona. I cannot move time back again."

Mona panicked. "What are you talking about? Of course you can."

"No. The Agency is losing too much of its power, and because of that, I have lost mine."

"How?"

"*Look!* Look for yourself. The Agency is dying! Get to the tunnel!" Charon yelled, while running down the the stairs. "We will take the boat to the mainland, but first…."

"Where are you going?" Mona asked.

"To kill Goodblood and that woman!"

"I will meet you at the boat," Mona yelled back. "Although, I don't need to take the boat. I can leave this body any time I want."

"You can, but I prefer you stay in it." Charon's voice echoed through the tunnel and back to Mona.

Charon spotted Adam and Sam on their way to the lighthouse. Fortunately, for them, the entire burning woods separated them from Charon. Charon could take the long way around in a nano-second, but when he tried to use that power, it too was gone, gone with the burning pines, gone with the last of The Agency. Although, The Agency had thousands of nests around the world, Gnarled Pines was the ideal nesting ground for the darkest of the dark spirits. The other nests never created spirits as dark as those on Gnarled Pines; they were the spirits that were to inhabit the movers and shakers of the world. Running without his power was stressful for Charon. His ability to run on his own was rarely exercised and so he was ill-prepared for the chase. For the first time in his so-called life, Charon was vulnerable to the humans.

Adam and Sam darted for the lighthouse. Tentacles of burning pine stirred the air.

Mona reached the bottom of the spiraling staircase and then she made her way down into the cave.

Arthur called to Annabelle and Florence, "*C'mon,* it's safe."

Annabelle held Florence firmly and helped her maneuver the rocks. When the women reached the boat, they saw that it was not the boat they had expected. In fact, it was nothing like what they had ever seen before. Even Florence, whose knowledge of boats was severely limited, knew that this boat was something from the future. Arthur's uncertainty about the boat from the future vanished when he saw the key hanging from the dashboard.

"Step down, ladies."

When Florence and Annabelle were in the boat, Arthur turned the key. *"Bingo!"* he happily said, and the boat was ready to go. As Arthur was stepping back out of the boat, Mona came barreling through the tunnel and ran into him. He pushed her against the stone wall, she staggered and slipped on some rocks, slid under the boat head first, and landed on the propeller blades. Chunks of her head splattered into the air and most of them landed in the boat. The hull of the boat was a stomach-churning mess. Florence was hit in the face by slices of brain matter and swatches of Mona's hair still attached to fragments of her skull. If that were not enough, Florence was blinded by the blood that sprayed into her eyes. Mona's lips were still intact as they hit Arthur in the mouth. Mona's lips on his lips went beyond irony—it was a mockery of their relationship.

Sam reached the tunnel and ran toward the boat. She and Arthur passed each other, nodded to the other and continued on their way—he to the lighthouse, she to the boat. When Sam reached the boat, Arthur reached the lighthouse. He was hell-bent on killing Charon.

Sam was out of breath when she finally reached the boat. *"Oh, my God!"* Sam muffled a scream. "This is sickening! What happened?"

"Mona LaBaron's head was caught in the propeller," Annabelle said while wiping her eyes with the back of her hand.

"On purpose?" Sam asked.

"Kinda," Florence turned to Sam and smiled, briefly. "It was self-defense."

"Yuk...if you've got a rag, I'll help clean this shit up? My name is Samantha, by the way."

"I'm Florence. This is Annabelle." Florence continued to rub her eyes.

"You're alive, right?" Sam asked, uneasily.

"Of course," Florence chuckled while wiping her eye with the hem of her skirt.

"Good. I thought you might be ghosts."

"Ghosts?" Annabelle quizzed.

Florence scoffed. "I don't believe in ghosts."

Sam said, "There must be something to clean up this mess." Then Sam saw the headless body of Mona bobbing in the water. *"Holy shit!"*

"If you knew her," Florence said, "you wouldn't feel one bit of sorrow. She was a bitch! Besides, that's just her body. Mona died a long time ago."

Sam could not believe what she was hearing. "*Wow.* The price for being a bitch. Goes to show."

"How is this going to work? I mean, you guys are from a hundred years in the past and I'm a hundred years in your future, and we're all going together in the same boat, to the same place, to a different time for all of us. At least, Adam thinks so. It boggles the mind," Sam said while scrubbing the vinyl covered seats.

"*Hmm.* I never would have thought of that," Annabelle said. "That's certainly interesting, isn't it, Flo? It's going to be a surprise."

While massaging her knee, Florence said, "A body could go crazy thinking about that."

Charon was only a few feet behind Adam when they entered the lighthouse. Charon shoved Adam against the bottom of the spiral staircase, blocking him from going down into the cave. Adam was not going to win a fight with Charon and he knew it. He maneuvered himself out of Charon's reach and ran as fast as he could up the spiral staircase. Charon was exhausted and he couldn't keep up with him. The ghosts cheered Adam on.

Arthur came up from the tunnel and saw Charon chasing Adam. Arthur took up the chase and followed after Charon. By the time they reached the catwalk the five souls from Broadway were there waiting.

"Are you sure about being our host, Mister Goodblood? No second thoughts?" King asked.

"Of course I'm sure. No second thoughts," Adam answered.

"You will be our ferryman," Ídolo said.

"Yeah, I suppose you're right. I am the ferryman!"

"Are you ready?" Willy asked.

"Yup."

Instantaneously, Reggie, Willy, King, and Ídolo were looking out through Adam's eyes.

"I don't know what to do," Hudson was worried.

Ídolo appeared beside Hudson and held his hand, "All you have to do is walk into Mister Goodblood, Hudson. Like this—" Ídolo and Hudson disappeared into their host; their ferryman. It was King who first saw that there was another soul who did not belong there, another soul was using Adam as its host.

"Who are you?" King asked.

"No worries. I shall leave now."

"What are you doing in here? You don't belong here."

"Just helping Goodblood with a few suggestions for his book."

"You're a dark one!?

"I am just a humble scrivener." The scrivener laughed and in a blink, was gone.

The island began to shake and tremble. Waves splashed against the rocks and boulders. The three ladies in the boat began to panic.

"What will we do?" Annabelle asked.

"We need to go," Florence said urgently.

"We're not going anywhere until Adam gets here."

Just then a wave came in and nearly knocked over the boat. They were in danger of being thrown against the rocks and boulders. Sam and Annabelle managed, after a bit of a struggle, to unmoor the boat.

"We can't wait!" Annabelle yelled.

"Who's going to drive this thing?"

Sam, who was already in the driver's seat, re-started the boat. Small pieces of Mona's head flew up, but landed away from the boat.

Sam could wait no longer for Adam. The waves were building. The side of the island was crumbling, rocks and boulders were falling away from Gnarled Pines. The island shook. It was an earthquake! They had to go, and they had to go now! There was no longer any choice but one. Sam was visibly crying as she took the boat out to where the water was calm. She looked back and saw that the entrance to the cave was blocked by falling chunks of the island of Gnarled Pines. With a rush of tears, Sam turned her attention back to the mainland. She wiped her tears, turned and looked straight ahead, "He we go, ladies…to a new future," and the ladies were on their way to Turtle Run.

Burning pines raised from the floor of the island and once again stood tall. The flames grew and flickered over the tops of the trees and, like fire-breathing dragons, they threw themselves against the lighthouse, and the lighthouse began the break apart. As Charon was about to grab Adam, a branch grabbed Charon, and then another and another, and they ripped him apart into burning pieces that they threw into the Atlantic. Another branch lifted Arthur and dropped him into the flames. Were Arthur still conscious, he would be grateful for the quick death from death that freed him from the alternative—slowly rotting away.

* * *

The ocean's waves crashed across the island with tsunami force, knocking over every last tree, and sweeping the surface of the island clean. Nothing was left but solid rock and the lighthouse with the beam of the lantern still warning sailors away began to break apart.

The lighthouse shook and leaned toward the ocean. As stone and concrete fell away, the ferryman stepped to the edge of the catwalk and together with five Broadway souls, A. J. Goodblood dove into eternity.

The ocean. The moon. Then…nothing until his eyes opened over the ripples of water below him. *Follow the water. We're going to leave you now, Adam. The island no longer has any pull on us. Where are you going? Back to Broadway, of course! Thank you. You're a good man, Adam. And then they were gone. The Pequod set sail with the young Captain Ahab at the helm. I warned you about that island, Mister Goodblood. I know. I should have listened. Addy, I'm sorry about your mother, may she rest in peace. Her coffin slowly sank into the ground. Will you be selling the building? I have no choice. Choices are endless, Addy. The frozen trees. The snow is knee high in the Colorado Rockies. Where is Colorado? I've got to get back. No. You need to go back to Brooklyn, Addy. Your mother is dead. Go back to Brooklyn Heights. Will I remember the island, the people, the thrill of it all? Sorry, Addy. You will not remember any of it. Hey, Addy. Wanna come over here and sit on my lap? Come back to Brooklyn Heights. C'mon. Come play Canasta with us. Stop touching me. Such a sweet little boy. There! See the river. I see it. Listen to the screams. Screams like the pines. Loud and terrified. Louder. Louder. Screams of anguish. Screams of desperation. Agonizing screams. The siren wails, Addy. Addy! Come back! She wails to the heavens. Her cries grow louder and louder as she begs the universe from an open window. Almost. There. Feel her warmth.*

Smell her scent. Yes! Then Addy flew back into his mother's waiting arms.

END

Edward Crosby Wells
Denver, Colorado
(2020)

Printed in Great Britain
by Amazon